THE AGREEMENT

JACQUELINE WARD

For Sarah Cassidy

CHAPTER ONE

The door clicks shut behind me as I leave the office for the evening, and I smile. I peer into the shopping bags I am clutching. I couldn't decide which dress looked best, so I bought them both. They were expensive, but it's not every day you get to go to a posh party.

Everyone will be there. All the juniors and each department have been invited. Even the directors are going. On the downside, my boss will be there, alone. It's a plus-one occasion – that was clear on the invite – but he never brings anyone. On Fridays at the pub after work he attaches himself to whoever's husband hasn't turned up. But it's fine. Because Jake is coming with me.

I feel a shiver of excitement. He even bought a new shirt. Going out isn't really his thing, but I told him how much this means. He'd laughed.

'It's taken over though, hasn't it? You're not usually a dress, shoes and matching bag person.'

He's right. I'm not. I'm usually practical and reliable. Black jeans, white T-shirt. Little black dress at a push when the occasion calls for it. But as I sit in my car in the multi-storey and peep into the bag, I see a riot of black and orange. Gold edging and a lace underskirt. And the little bag I bought, encrusted with crystals. A designer brand. I feel a prick of anxiety when I think about the cost and my credit card, but it will be worth it.

I turn the radio on and shoulder dance to a Katy Perry song. I know there will be dancing tonight, and I'm undecided between very high heels or something a bit more comfortable. Both match the bag and I decide to have a full try-on when I get home.

I am at the last set of traffic lights before the turn-off to our estate when the message comes through. I glance at my phone as it pings, and I already know. But I read it anyway.

> Babe. I'm so sorry. I'm going to be late. This project – well, you know, don't you? But I will be there. You go and I'll join you later. I love you. xxx

The lights turn to green, but I don't move for a long time. A surge of upset rises, but I push it down. No pressure. No possessiveness. Goodness knows we'd both had enough of that in the past. This is what we agreed. That we'd give each other space.

The driver behind me sounds his horn, and I put my foot down. I speed up the road and screech around the corner onto the estate. Avenues of well-appointed town houses turning to semi-detached. Then at our end of the cherry-tree-lined lane, detached properties. Not huge. Just right. For us.

The day we moved in three years ago, I thought it was perfect. It was what I had dreamed about. Three bedrooms and a loft. Patio doors and a conservatory. Jake and I had been married six months by then, but while we'd viewed dozens of houses, we couldn't find one that we agreed was perfect for us. But this house on Lynton Grove was just the right distance from our offices and, at the same time, secluded enough for us to have our privacy.

I pull up into the double driveway. The shopping has lost its shine a little now Jake won't be there to help me choose which dress I should wear. I carry it in anyway. I unlock the door and glance at the wall. There hangs the agreement. Our agreement.

We'd had it framed. Both of us had just come out of difficult marriages and neither of us were looking for anyone else when we met while out with friends at places that we rarely went. We hit it off straight away, me entranced by his green eyes and beautiful skin. The curl of his hair.

We went on a couple of dates, and we had so much in common it was scary. We were the same age. Our past romantic entanglements hadn't ended well, both of us leaving. He'd shook his head when I'd asked why.

'She held on too tight. There was no space to breathe. She got pregnant and, don't get me wrong, I love my daughter, but I wasn't ready. I want a life.'

I'd gone away that night and wondered if it was possible. Could you be in a relationship and give each other space? My past certainly did not confirm this arrangement. Ian had been jealous and possessive. He'd adopted the 'family is everything' line to keep me with his sisters and his mother, who are all lovely, but I wanted a job and I wanted to go out with my own friends.

When I did, he followed me, and we would argue. In the end, it got too much. I found out he'd been tracking my phone and monitoring my calls, and I left. He didn't contest the divorce and I haven't seen him since. We sold the house, and I put my equity into mine and Jake's love fund.

We made our agreement. That we would never hold each other so tightly that we had no freedom. That there were no rules except fidelity. That we would honour each other's lives and support each other.

Jake had it printed out and hung it in a black-edged frame on the wall so we would see it as soon as we entered the house. It seemed so right, and I was convinced it would make us stronger. I was sure I could honour our agreement. It was what I wanted. I would rather have been alone than be with someone like Ian. But Jake was different.

Once in the house, I go through my usual routine. I pick up the mail and open it. In some random hangover from my past, I open the bills first, expecting red letters. My heart momentarily skips a beat but there is nothing to worry about these days. I go to the kitchen and feel the kettle. Still warm. He's been here. His cup is on the coffee table in the lounge.

I take my shopping upstairs and hang the dresses on the front of the wardrobe. I know that there are two dresses in there I have never worn. I never took them back because I don't like a fuss. I don't like confrontation. I pull out shoe boxes and locate the objects of my desire. But I've made a decision. I'm wearing the fuck-me heels. I laugh to myself. Not like me to be so reckless. A tiny voice in my head whispers, *and that's why he can do this to you.*

I bat it away. Do what? Work late? Admittedly, he had been working late a lot in the past few months. I'd started to see a pattern to it. Three weekdays a week. He'd mentioned that someone had left, and he was covering that job. I'd initially felt sorry for him and would leave him little messages and a sandwich for when he came in later. But little concerns had started to bite at me. I'd eaten dinner alone three nights out of seven. I'd even started to plan meals for one, as he refused to let me cook for him if he was going to be late.

'Oh God, no, don't go to any trouble. I'll get a sandwich or something. Some of the guys order in. Honestly, Kate, it's fine.'

He'd touched my face. He always did that. I feel a surge of love for him and a stab of annoyance at myself. I flick on the TV in the bedroom and try on the dresses with different bras. Bare legs or tights? Hair up or down? Jake always chooses down. He told me he likes women with long hair, so I let mine grow, just having the ends trimmed. I'd forgotten the thrill of getting ready to go out and I feel the butterflies in my stomach. I take photographs in the full-length mirror and message them to Jake.

> Which one?

He replies almost immediately.

> The gold one, definitely. Hot. See you later x

We have an en suite. The day we came to see this house, the estate agent made a big deal of it.

'There's an en suite just off the master bedroom.' He was conspiratorial. 'With a shower.'

I'd pretended I was unimpressed, but this was just another piece in the jigsaw puzzle of my perfect life. After the shock of my childhood, I take nothing for granted. But I am getting to where I want to be, and this is not the right time to rock the boat. I'd grown up with my three brothers in a tiny high rise in Manchester. Mum and Dad had moved from place to place with ever-mounting rent arrears, and it was the only place available. They were both heavy drinkers and, in many ways, a lesson in how not to be. No, I would not be irresponsible.

When I left home, I moved to the other side of the city. I could only afford a place five miles out of town and would commute in every day to my accounts job. I was never absent. I knew, even then, that to rise up from where I came from took commitment and persistence. I saved and saved and eventually had a deposit for a small house. Then I met Ian.

Later, I moved into advertising. Just a small agency, but I fell in love with it. I write the copy. I come up with ideas. I manage a small department and I hope that one day, maybe soon, I will be promoted. I guess you could say I am creative, but Ian didn't see it that way. He sneered at my new job, telling me I couldn't succeed and asking when was I going to have a baby like Denise and Carol?

It never happened. I never got pregnant. Not because I tried to stop it. It was just another confirmation that Ian was not the right person for me. When I met Jake and he told me he had a daughter called Polly, I almost collapsed with relief. I didn't want children immediately. I needed everything to be perfect before I could bring a child into this world. I would not repeat my parents' mistakes.

I take a shower. Once the room steams up, I see the usual message Jake has left on the mirror.

Wish I could see you now... mmm... x

Looking down at my nakedness, I laugh. I apply some moisturiser and towel-dry my hair. I consider myself in the mirror. Not bad for thirty-four. My hand runs over my tummy, and I stick it out and turn sideways. Still time for a baby.

The steam clears and I am about to get dressed when I see the sink has tiny hairs in it and a tide mark of shaving foam. The anger rises again. That glint of a flame that I know only too well could burn out of control if I let it. He's been home, had a shave and had time for a coffee. If he's so busy, what is he doing here in the middle of the day?

My rational mind tells me he has come home before his meeting to get changed for the party tonight. But I'm less rational these days. More than once I've sat in my car, white knuckles on the steering wheel, after one of the *sorry, babes, I'm going to be late* messages that always arrive just after I leave work but before I arrive home. Each time I have an ever-increasing feeling that I will do something rash. That I won't be able to do what I agreed. That one day I'll wake up and no longer be calm, cool Kate, and more someone I have avoided for the longest time.

I look in the washer. His blue shirt with the bluebird cuffs is in there. I sniff it.

What the hell am I doing? I have no reason not to trust him. I snort to myself. I've been watching too many soap operas. Too many mini-series. He's just working late. I lean on the pristine white worktop and remember how I felt when Ian snooped on me. When he brought things up that confirmed what I'd suspected – he was monitoring me. And now I'm monitoring Jake.

CHAPTER TWO

Once I have zipped up the gold dress and put on my shoes, I stand back and appraise myself. The little hook at the back is hard to reach, and it pinches at me that Jake is not here to help. But I love the dress and I love the look. I take another picture of myself and send it to Paula. I've known Paula for years. We've worked at the same places; we'd hurriedly send job vacancies to each other so we could work and lunch together.

We could not be more different. She comes from old money; generations of family business in Cheshire. I don't. But we love the same things and laugh until we cry. Over the years, as we have dated and married, we have gone through long periods of not seeing each other, but as soon as we do, it's exactly the same as it always was.

And she is always there for me at the end of the phone. As I am for her. Synchronised complaining, then roaring with laughter. Instead of replying to the message, she rings me. I smile as I answer. She jumps straight in.

'Wow, you look amazing!'

She is outside. I can hear traffic and voices. On her way to the party, I expect. She works in a different building than me, but everyone was invited.

'Thanks, mate. I wasn't sure, so I bought two dresses.'

She laughs. 'Bought two of them, did you?' There's a pause and I hear the chink of glasses in the background. 'Listen, I'm not coming tonight. John's asked me to meet up to talk about things.'

I sigh. John. Her long-time ex. John likes to meet up and talk, lure her into bed, then change his mind or find some problem with why they can't get back together immediately.

'Bloody hell. I'll be there on my own. Katy-no-mates. Jake's working late.' She tuts. She's heard a lot of 'working late' complaints lately, but that doesn't stop me from spilling. 'Honestly, he's always doing it. I'm starting to wonder what he's up to.'

I surprise myself. I'm not the kind of person who easily shares my feelings. It comes with being independent; I don't want to bother anyone with my wonderings about my relationship. But she is right on it.

'Jake? Don't you trust him?'

She sounds surprised. And I know why. He comes across as Mr Dependable. When we are out, he is attentive and funny. I've seen her side eye him, studying him as he looks at me and fetches me a drink. I blink into the full-length mirror. Do I? Do I trust him? I have no reason not to believe what he says. I could drive over to his office anytime and see if he is there when he says he is.

But I don't want to. I want to stay true to what we promised each other. I'd have to snoop around, because he'd know immediately that I was checking up on him. There would be no suitable excuses or mistakes. He would know I was monitoring him. When I don't answer straight away, she carries on.

'Because there's no love without trust, is there? And love's not hearts and flowers, is it? It's how you gel. What you agree. It's commitment.'

I feel my stomach sink. 'I am committed but... I don't know if he is. He keeps...'

She sighs. Well, like we've said before, if it isn't right, it's wrong. Don't waste your time on–'

I interrupt. 'Hang on a minute. I wasn't saying I was going to leave or anything. I just want to know what's going on. Let's not alert the divorce court just yet.'

She pauses. In my mind's eye, I can see her pondering what I said. Playing devil's advocate. Her dark hair flicked over her shoulders.

'But if you don't know what's going on, you have to ask yourself why.' Her voice has dropped to a whisper.

Laughing, I ask, 'Where are you? Why are you so quiet?'

'I'm in a bar. Waiting for someone.'

'Someone being John?'

She giggles. 'Got to go. Have a great time. And watch out for Clint's hands.' She ends the call.

I know Paula is right about Jake. Why don't I know what's going on? Is it because he's deliberately held something back? Not told me what he's up to? Or is it simply because he is actually at work and there is nothing more to explain?

It's hard to admit to myself that I'm annoyed with Jake because I want to come before his job. Before anything. I'm not worried there's another woman. Not really. Maybe a little bit. But I'm jealous of whatever is keeping him away from the intricate meals I cook for him, our box sets and this party.

I call an Uber. As I wait for it to arrive, I go over what is bothering me and it's two things. The first one is my neediness. I'm not usually insecure. The second is something I couldn't put my finger on until tonight. Jake is distracted. He's a little distant, and he blames that on his job, too.

I like everything on an even keel. Good old dependable Kate. And this keel is not even. Jake has changed somehow. He is constantly checking his phone and never hears what I say the first time. Yet he isn't unkind and doesn't appear unhappy. Our love life is the same and Paula and I always say that is the first thing to go. Especially if your partner has someone else.

I push all thoughts of trouble away as the taxi arrives. I know the party will be sumptuous and, if I am going to stand a chance of promotion, I need to schmooze for all I am worth. I take one last look in the mirror. The shoes make my legs look long, and I smile. Jake will have a big surprise when he arrives. He hasn't seen me this dressed up for ages.

Ten minutes later, I am taking a glass of bubbly from a server's tray. He offers me a prawn skewer, but I decline. I spot Pamela Corn by a huge chocolate fountain and saunter over. Pam was my first colleague at Resner Platt, and she smiles as I approach.

'No Peter?'

She laughs. 'Oh my God. I'd have to drag him here by the hair. No, he's probably in his pants making himself a bacon sandwich and watching the footy.'

I relax. Of course. Of course, men complain about coming to their partner's work dos. My brain shuffles Jake into a category with other men who would rather walk over hot coals than attend something like this.

'Yeah, Jake too. Although he said he would pop in later.'

'Lucky you! Chauffeur home on tap.' She fixes her eyes on Clint who is on the dance floor with the junior from accounts. 'Four more hours to go and it looks like he's half-cut already.'

I scan the room for confirmation that most of my colleagues are partnerless. Before I know it, Pam grabs my hand and pulls me onto the dance floor. Everyone joins in, probably in an effort to avoid being cornered by Clint, and we laugh and dance the evening away.

The next time I check my phone, it's ten o'clock. My heart sinks. I check again. It doesn't seem long since I got here, but champagne has that effect on me. It makes time and motion elastic in my usually precisely ordered world. I check again for a message or call from Jake.

I scan the room to check if he arrived and saw I was having such a good time he didn't want to interrupt me. But he isn't here. I call him. It rings and rings and then it goes to the answerphone.

'Where are you? You're missing a good party. Call me. I'm heading home in about half an hour, so pick me up if you can.'

I hear my voice, chirpy and positive. It isn't how I feel inside. No, I feel like he's let me down. There were no promises, but he did say he would turn up later. I check the message again to make sure I hadn't read it wrong. No. I haven't.

> But I will be there. You go and I'll join you later.
> And see you later x

I feel a shiver run through me. What if something has happened to him? My mind whirrs through all the possibilities and I'm almost dialling the hospital when Pam drags me out of the way.

'Clint incoming.'

We hurry over to the bar, grab some leftover bubbly and watch as Clint suctions onto one of the newer women from the production room. She seems up for it, and I turn back to my dilemma. I am just worried, I tell myself. This has nothing to do with jealousy. If I were, the natural target for anything suspicious would be Jake's ex-wife, Veronica.

They were together for seven years, split four years ago and have an eight-year-old daughter, Polly. Although I have never met Veronica, I have seen pictures of her. Jake is adamant that he wants to keep his old life, as he calls it, completely separate from his life with me. I've looked briefly at her Facebook page, just to see what she is like. I didn't linger, and I felt guilty afterwards because it was like a betrayal of mine and Jake's relationship.

Don't look back. That's another thing we agreed. And I haven't, really. I've never had a reason to until recently.

I don't think I have much reason to worry about Veronica. According to Jake, she is the worst person he has ever met. He told me he only stayed with her because she got pregnant with Polly. I know there are two sides to every story and inevitably Jake wanted to paint himself in a good light, but what he told me about Veronica did not sound good.

He told me she was lazy. She wouldn't work and she always wanted money. In the end she ran up so many debts that she nearly bankrupted him. He didn't really complain about her; in fact, he defended her. He told me she was Polly's mum, and he respected her for that – and the implication was that I needed to.

Polly stays the weekend every three weeks. In between, Jake takes her out to McDonald's or to Blackpool for the day, work allowing. When she stays, she is polite and quiet and never talks about her mum. I tried asking once, mainly because I wanted her to feel comfortable with me. She told me her mum was lovely, and that she said nice things about Daddy and Kate.

It might be the champagne, or it might be the fact that I am a little upset, but I feel doubts snake through me. He has mentioned Veronica a lot. And he has been out a lot. I shake it away. I'm being silly. I drain my glass and look at my phone for the millionth time. The battery is on fifteen per cent, and I need to get an Uber before it runs out completely. I hug Pam and thank her for a brilliant time, then I go and wait outside the hotel.

The niggle from earlier has turned to concern. Something is wrong. He has never worked this late before. He's a software engineer and anything that needed late hours would be done in his home office. It's kitted out with the most up-to-date, expensive equipment and, from what he told me, is a mirror image of his office at work.

I remember the day he installed it. He'd reserved the loft the day we viewed 17 Lynton Grove. While I was thinking about curtains and flooring, he was climbing the loft ladder and surveying what would become his domain. I'd touched his arm gently as he climbed down.

'You could have that third bedroom.'

We'd never really spoken about having children. Not with Polly and my not getting pregnant with Ian. I'd just assumed he didn't want any more.

'But we might need both. In time.'

He'd looked deep into my eyes, and I was more in love with him than ever. No pressure. That's what we agreed. And it seemed to work perfectly. No pressure, and things happen in their own time.

When we'd moved into the house, Jake had bought some very expensive flooring for the loft. I'd seen the cost on an invoice and wondered how he'd paid for it. I found out when his credit card statement went out of our joint account. He'd explained that the floor needed to be strengthened for 'what was to come'. He was like a little boy at Christmas as the equipment was delivered. And in no time, his home office was operational.

It turned out to be invaluable during lockdown. We worked from home but had our own space.

So, none of this makes sense now. He could work late from home. Unless he didn't want to. But that was nonsense. If he didn't want to be at home with me, why leave steamy words on the bathroom mirror? Why tell me he loves me in a message?

No, none of this makes sense. The Uber turns the corner into Lynton Grove. I expect to see Jake's bronze BMW next to my blue one, but it isn't there. He isn't there. My heart sinks.

Where are you, Jake? What's going on?

CHAPTER THREE

The house is in darkness. As I enter, I flick the light switch and scan the room quickly for any sign of him. Nothing. Nothing at all. I hurry to our bedroom and pull off the heels. I grab my phone from my bag. No messages. No calls. I quickly dial his number.

It rings out and then goes to answerphone. I whisper into it.

'Jake, I'm worried now. Please call me.'

It's later than I thought. Almost midnight. I take off the dress and hang it in my wardrobe. I empty the bag onto my bed. I will take them back to the shop. I feel my skin prickle. It's all been an expensive waste of time. The fact that normally frugal me spent so much on dresses – two dresses – and a bag underlines how much I want to impress Jake. And how things have got between us.

I fume as I get under the duvet. I will take them all back. Even the dress I wore. This is not something I would usually do but, if I am honest, those clothes are not me. I will never wear them again. I wanted to appear enticing, exciting. Different. So different that Jake would notice. But he isn't here to notice.

The mix of alcohol and annoyance makes my heart race. I am

tired. He will arrive home at some point – he has to. There will be some excuse and I will have to accept it. I check myself. Just because he isn't doing what I want him to doesn't mean he is doing something wrong, does it? I need to find my level-headed calmness, but somewhere deep inside, I feel like I am on the edge.

It's crept up on me. The unsettling feeling of never knowing if Jake will be home after work. The mist of sadness that rests on top of everything I do. The realisation suddenly hits me. Are we drifting apart? Are we?

It took me a while to realise what was happening between me and Ian. I had been so wrapped up in my job that I just kept meeting his ever-increasing demands. My mental list of what he needed me to do was eventually so long I had to write it down. It wasn't until he downright refused to 'allow' me to go to a hen party that I realised how far it had gone. Was this the same?

I mentally calculate how much I have had to eat and drink. Probably three flutes of champagne over five hours, and a load of canapés. I get out of bed and in the darkness of the bedroom, I pull on a pair of black leggings and a long hoodie. I stop at the bedroom door. I am a rule keeper. I would never usually consider driving after drinking. Never. But I need to find out where Jake is. I need to settle this once and for all.

I hurry downstairs, my heart thumping. I get into the car, and I drive slowly to Jake's office. He works at a business hub that has twenty-four-hour access, and he has his own designated parking space. I can see as soon as I turn the corner that his space is empty. All the spaces are empty.

I park outside the gates and look up at the corner office Jenkins Stewart Services occupy. The offices are in a neat row from the corner to halfway across the complex. I've been inside a few times when Jake's car has been in the garage. I count across to his office. It is in darkness, with only the low lights of the alarms glowing. My heart sinks. No one is there. No one works late until one in the morning.

I am suddenly aware of what I am doing. I am full of champagne, driving around to spy on my husband. I am actually dressed in black, like some super-snooper. Checking clothes and feeling how warm the kettle is. How have things got so bad? We always said we would talk honestly about any doubts we had.

I sit in the darkness and think about my mum and dad. Their roller-coaster relationship was punctuated with vodka and takeaways and, I grudgingly admit, sometimes laughter. They loved each other and then they hated each other.

The loving bits were all giggles and days out at the zoo with us kids. Picnics and singing in the car. 'Ten green bottles'. I can see her now, conducting us like we were an orchestra and then collapsing into uncontrollable laugher. Dad's hand on her knee and the loving looks. Her arms around his neck as he did his Elvis impression.

Every year they would drive down south to Cornwall. Haven Holidays was the destination; camp hell for me as it meant swimming costumes and singing contests. It meant I was required to take part and, for them to be happy, win. I never won, because my heart wasn't in it, and as soon as I didn't win their attention was on something else.

They collectively loved those fairground stalls where you throw a hoop to win a big, big prize. Their whole lives were a continuous race for the prize, a sprint to that endorphin rush of this or that, inevitably followed by the tumble of disappointment. I tried to join in, I really did, but right from the off I could see that the chances of the hoop going over the pole was slim; the hoop was small, and the pole was thick. I couldn't buy into the excitement.

There was a particular moment when I realised I could never be like my mother. On one trip, she dragged us to a remote beach on the edge of the holiday park to watch the sunset. I was fourteen. I tried to stay behind in the chalet. I pleaded with them to let me, because by then I instinctively knew it wouldn't end well.

They pulled me up and marched me across the hot grass and up the coastal path, laughing and whooping with my brothers. In those moments it seemed like the adult and child separation between us all had disappeared. I never saw it happen with my friends' parents. It was fun, to them. But to me it was a temporary annoyance that ate into my teenage angst.

We reached our destination, a steep set of steps down to the beach that cut in between two cliffs. Dad went to descend the steps, but she swerved to the side. She hurried towards the cliff and stood on the edge, laughing. Then she held out her arms and leaned backwards. Her face was manic with excitement.

Dad stepped forwards, but she laughed louder. I felt the scream form in my throat. It came out as her name, thrown at her across the chasm that was opening between us. She steadied herself, still laughing.

'Come on, Kate, I dare you. Come on. Over here.'

I stepped backwards. She carried on, arms outstretched again.

'Where's your passion, Kate? Where is it?'

I ran back to the chalet and sat on the bed worrying if she had fallen or if she would walk through the door still berating me about being too sensible. I knew where my passion was. I had a boyfriend. I felt that passion, but it was under control. I didn't have that wildness she had, that crazy look in my eyes. I worried I was missing something, but I found out later that I wasn't. It was her loss. Loss of control and, eventually, loss of everything.

Of course, she did come back that night. She always did, except for that one time.

Over the years I learned that times were only happy if there was a night out or a bottle of vodka in the cross-wires of the day. I gasp. Is that what I was doing? Trying to create happiness? Is that what the clothes and the bag and the party was about?

When there was no alcohol or dancing, when normal tasks of

the day had to be carried out, the holes began to show. No-shows at parents' evening by one or the other, leaving the fuming focus on their damaged relationship rather than celebrating my achievements. The Friday night twitching of curtains as Mum waited for him to appear in the early hours.

They didn't talk about things. They screamed and shouted. We knew, when the air went thick with resentment, what was coming. One of my brothers would hide in the cupboard under the stairs. I would lie in bed, staring at the woodchip ceiling in my tiny bedroom, waiting for the noise to stop.

Because that's what it was. Just noise. Followed by days of stand-offs and banging doors. I swore that I would have a quiet life. There would be no angry confrontation. No, I would be upfront about what I wanted. People argue, but I would never hold grudges and resentments.

I tap my fingers on the steering wheel. It's an ideal I hold myself to, like not driving when I am drunk. But the way I feel now, if I saw Jake, I would let him know. I glance back at the car park and the empty space. This is a red flag. Not the fact that he was not here, the fact that I was in danger of compromising myself twice in one night. Three times if you count the peacock display of out-of-character outfits.

No doubt he will turn up with a suitable excuse and I will talk to him then. But I am starting to feel like I did that day on the cliff. Out of my depth. Uncomfortable. It would be so easy to blame all this on my upbringing, but I consciously built a life that was not like theirs. And this is how I recognise where I am now.

I drive home and park up. He still isn't here, and I check my phone again. He hasn't called, and he hasn't messaged. It's very late and I have to be in work for nine. Tomorrow is reporting day and the day after the party – no excuse is going to cut it and any absence will look like a hangover.

I creep in even though there is no one home, and get into bed. My mind races over what could have happened, why he would send me those messages then disappear. If he'd had an accident I would know by now. Someone would have found his phone or his wallet. Someone would have contacted me.

I turn my phone volume on just in case, but right now I need to sleep. Whatever this is, I need to stay calm and carry on with my own life. We made an agreement. He will explain when he turns up.

But as I drift off, I know this isn't right. I feel like we are entering the territory of my parents' relationship, where no matter how much calmness I promise myself, there is a spark inside me that could ignite into accusation at any moment. It feels like fire, hot and contagious. I can't let it get the better of me. There is bound to be some reasonable explanation for this.

It's just that at the moment I cannot for the life of me see what it is.

CHAPTER FOUR

I'm up on my alarm and I head into the kitchen, trying to ignore the fact that Jake's car still isn't there. I've got a deep sense of doom, and I'm tired and hungover. But I have to go to work. It's my turn to present the figures. Figures for the advertising campaign I have worked on for a year. Half of me wants to go back to bed, but the other half wants the glory.

Clint usually takes all of it. Every single drop. But his line manager, Jerry Long, personally asked me to present just after lunch and I am not going to miss it. I tell myself I will come straight home afterwards. No doubt Jake will be back by then and we can talk. My stomach turns over at the thought, but it's the only way to get this sorted out.

I check my phone diary to see what I have on today. I zoom in on lunch with Paula. Good. It will give me a chance to find out what she thinks. I can lose myself for the rest of the day in departmental presentations.

Fifteen minutes later I am at work. I had to force myself to not drive by Jake's office to see if his car was there. I need to focus on work. I just need to get today and tomorrow over with then it's the weekend and I can sort my life out. I snort to myself

21

at the thought of me managing to sort my life out over the weekend. Very me.

The office is quiet. As far as I can see, there are no casualties from last night. Today is important. This is the last presentation session before the year-end bonus decision. We all know there is a direct correlation between our performance at this seminar and how much bonus we get. My competitive nature means I am going to go in there and do everything I can to make sure I and the others get the reward we deserve for working on this account. It hasn't been easy.

I see Pam at the water cooler, and I go over.

'Fun last night, wasn't it?'

She laughs and holds her forehead. 'A bit too much fun. Did you get your lift home?'

'Oh, yes. He was just at work.'

This is how it begins. Trying to save face. This is how lies turn you into someone else. I know that but I can't help myself. I can't admit my husband didn't come home. It's like some fucked-up mechanism to filling the cracks of a temporary weakness to make it stronger than ever. She nods.

'Yeah, that's what I thought. Mine would do anything not to have to come along.'

I change the subject. 'Ready for the presentation?'

She half turns and raises her eyebrows at Clint. 'Still leathered. I don't think he's even been home.'

She's right. He's still got the same shirt on. He's talking loudly on the phone. I fast forward in my mind to my presentation this afternoon. He should be sober by then. Unless he goes out at lunchtime. Clint is my presentation partner. He insisted. He'll be doing the intro and outro. I agreed to this as it would make me look good – an introduction from the department head. He would inevitably say nice things about me. If he was sober, which he isn't.

I run through all the possibilities. Sober Clint is a car crash when it comes to our equality and diversity policy. But drunk Clint? I shudder. Pam sees my despair.

'Don't worry. He might pass out before then.'

She pats my shoulder and walks away.

The presentations start at ten. Clint sits through them tutting loudly and checking his phone. He's sipping from a bottle, and I wonder if it's water or vodka or gin. At the end of every presentation he stands, claps loudly and shouts, 'Yes, come on.' He does his trademark hand roll and walks the presenter back to their seat.

I know the content of most of the presentations, as I have reviewed them. My mind wanders to Jake, and I click onto our mobile phone account. I've always known that I can track his phone. It would be easy. I could have done it last night, but I didn't. I wanted to, but I didn't. My thumb hovers about his phone. Jake's phone.

I think about the moment I found out Ian had been tracking me. The moment he presented me with a buff folder with printouts of all my movements for the past month. How he had carefully drawn a red line along the route I would take every day on my way to work. The time I spent at an address just off Lowther Crescent before work. Forty-three minutes and twenty seconds. The times I had gone to the same address after work. How he had built a case against me.

'I knocked on the door, but no one was in.' His red face and the throbbing vein in his forehead. The receipts he had found for clothes I had bought. The colour-coded matches to visits to the address. 'I didn't want to follow you, Kate, because, to be honest, I was afraid of what I might find.'

And all he would have found was me with a large coffee and muffin. Or a doughnut. Me going over the figures before work or occasionally afterwards. Me eating the illicit fast food that Ian insisted was the root of my weight gain. At the McDonald's on the corner of Lowther Crescent.

I don't click on Jake's phone. No. It's opening a can of worms. I'll hear him out first. Ask for the truth. I could easily follow him or track him, but that goes against everything I stand for and the agreement we share.

By half twelve I've had enough. I'm meeting Paula at one in the pizza place on the high street. I need a drink. I shouldn't, really. I need to be absolutely on the ball for my talk. But it will be fine. I will have eaten, and one drink won't make me forget the last three months of work I have put in.

My mind flits back to Jake. I check my phone and there are still no messages. No calls. I am just about to try ringing him when I see Paula. She isn't in our usual place in the restaurant; she's across the road in the Planter Bar. I duck behind a tree and watch her for a second. She looks sad. I rarely see her outside our scheduled lunch dates these days.

She is alone and nursing a bottle of red wine. And the bottle is nearly empty. She is checking her phone and looking around. My heart sinks. She's drinking again. I wonder what's going on in her life. It doesn't take much to tip her one way or the other. But I already know the answer. It's John. He's messed her about for almost a year now, breaking up with her then messaging her when he gets bored. She told me it's the thrill of the chase. She also told me she wants to meet someone and have a baby, which is a far cry from the Paula I first knew.

Ironically, we first met in a nightclub. She was there with Stella Jackson, one of my friends from school, and I hit it off with Paula straight away. She is blonde and pretty and very, very paranoid about her build. She has three sporty sisters and all of them are tall and muscular. Paula played her best assets down with flat shoes and long-sleeved dresses. She could, and still can, eat anything she wants to without putting weight on.

We went to Ibiza together and after that we were inseparable. Then she invited me on a family holiday to France. I don't see my own family, so I declined at first. But she cajoled me and insisted and even bought the flights. So I went. It was there I discovered other families were dysfunctional too, just in a different way to my own.

They were all there. Paula and her sisters and her parents. She is the youngest and her sisters are all married with kids. Paula's dad, Henry, had rented a huge, sprawling farmhouse and it all seemed perfect. Until dinner. I hadn't understood that we would be required to dress for dinner. I had taken holiday clothes and nothing remotely resembling the high standards expected by the Smithies family.

Paula came to my rescue with a black evening dress. It didn't fit – I am the opposite of her in appearance as well as nature. Not as tall and curvier. But she tied up the shoulder straps and tied a ribbon around to hide the tightness. I wore it every night for a week with a different coloured ribbon. The days were spent walking country lanes and lazing on a nearby beach. We read novels and talked about the future, but all of it was laced with a generous splash of whichever alcoholic drink came to hand.

Dinner was served with crates of red wine. Even after my childhood experience of parents bordering on alcoholism, I love a good glass of red. But I noted glasses were always fully refilled and pushed to finish whereas the over-laden food trays were not. Paula lapped it up and things fell into place. She sometimes disappeared for weeks on end. No contact. And it was usually after a spectacularly badly behaved episode at a party or after a club night.

When I broached it with her, she would be vague and claim not to remember. During the holiday she argued with everyone and had a physical fight with one of her sisters. All after copious amounts of alcohol.

We had a talked about it, but she never admitted she had a problem until Mark Platt. Mark was a predator. We all knew it and we all avoided him. But I watched as, week after week on a Friday night, Paula would drink a river then make a play for him.

He ignored her at first. Then he jumped in. She ended up pregnant. I knew she was on the pill. We both were. It didn't make sense. Until she told me she had been throwing up most weekends and often didn't eat from Saturday to Tuesday.

She lost the baby, and she almost had a breakdown. Like some mad version of *St Elmo's Fire*, I found her barricaded into her flat off her face on booze and painkillers. Her parents didn't understand what all the fuss was about and blamed me for over-dramatising. But they did pay for rehab. It turned out they had paid for their daughter's rehab, sometimes multiple times. They were detached from reality, and nothing would change until Paula stopped doing exactly the same as they did.

Surprisingly, she did. She went on an accounting course and got herself a job. By then I'd met Ian and she'd met sensible Stefan. Stefan was good for her. He cooked and cleaned, and she worked hard to match his household prowess. She didn't love him though. I thought she would have drowned her sorrows when he finally left her, but she didn't. She became one of those people who criticised heavy drinkers. She was proud of what she had achieved.

I peer at her through the bar window. Still staring at her phone. Absently swirling the wine in her glass like she used to. She looks very serious and a little flushed. I walk past the window like I haven't seen her and into the pizza place. I sit in the window and order a bottle of fizzy water. I suddenly feel like the most boring person in the world. Everyone else having fun with their drinking and secrets and me, well, sitting here with my water.

I suddenly feel angry. Is that how it is? Jake staying out all night. Paula enjoying her wine. Clint turning up at work drunk. And me? I'm just as dependable as ever, aren't I?

CHAPTER FIVE

She is suddenly standing in front of me. She holds her arms out.

'Kate. Hi!'

This is Paula's 'I'm ready for a party' voice. Long vowels merged with her slight Manchester accent. I hug her and she feels very warm.

'Hello, you. What a morning, eh? How did your department presentations go?'

She laughs. 'Oh, I only stayed until about an hour ago. Got pretty boring fast so I snuck out.' She glares at the water. 'Oh, don't you want a bottle? To celebrate?'

I stare at her. She clearly hadn't listened to me last week when I told her about my presentation.

'Nothing to celebrate yet. I'm up next.'

She nods and waves at the waiter. We order and she smiles at me. 'How was last night?'

My mind defaults to my panic and driving through the darkness, but I pull up short.

'It was fun. Nice food and lots of champagne.'

She is looking past me trying to get the waiter's attention. He comes over. 'Oh, can I get a bottle, please? Not a glass, a bottle.'

I shake my head and cover my glass. 'No, I'm not drinking.'

She laughs loudly. 'No? And I'm not going back to work. I'm meeting Carole here at two. Aren't you going to ask me how it went with John?'

I smile at her. 'How did it go then?'

'It went okay. He's wanting to get back together, but I'm not sure, really. He's got issues.' The bottle arrives, and she pours herself a large glass. 'I'm not sure I'm ready for a serious relationship.' I shake my head and roll my eyes. 'So, what about you?' She sips her drink and looks around. 'Did you sort it out with Jake?'

I look at her. I don't think she's really interested. I've known her long enough to know that this lunch is about her showing me where she is in her life. And by the looks of it, she's heading towards another crash. We've always supported each other but more recently it seems like I'm doing all the holding up.

'No. He didn't come home.'

I've got her attention now.

'Bloody hell. Have you heard from him?'

I shake my head. I know my pasty, tired face will tell the story but I fill her in anyway.

'No. I need to get today over with then I'll...' I feel tears threaten. A warm feeling spreads up my chest and my cheeks redden. 'He's not dead in a ditch or in hospital. I'd have heard by now. So...'

She leans in and her eyes narrow. 'So, what? Where do you think he is?'

It a rhetorical question, but I answer anyway.

'Probably pissed at someone's house. Or, well, worse.'

Her lips narrow. 'I have to be honest, this doesn't sound good. I mean, not after what you told me before about working late and that. It seems like... well it's not my place.'

But I know what it sounds like. I know exactly what this looks like. I feel my temper rise and I pick my phone up again. It's becoming a habit. Still no call or message.

'I know, but I need to hear him say it. I need to hear it out of his own mouth.'

She sips the wine. It occurs to me that this is so similar to other conversations we have had about other men over the years. All that's missing is the thick black eyeliner and cigarettes and we could be back at the beginning of our friendship, moaning about men over lunch.

'And then what?'

I stop in my tracks. 'What do you mean?'

'Well, you wouldn't stay with him, would you? If he'd—'

I interrupt. 'I don't know what's happened yet, so let's not jump to conclusions. Not yet.'

Tears form and I try to compose myself. She brushes her hair back and takes my hand, leaning in close. I can smell her perfume. Still Poison, as always.

'Well, don't let him take the piss. Don't let him use you. Cut your losses.'

I nod but feel like she is getting ahead of the situation. Then I remember she is a bottle into a two-bottle day where she's skipped most of the workday, and she can't sort out her own love life. The red flags are raised, but I have a lot going on and I just can't take on Paula's bad habits at the moment.

We eat our pizza, and she is telling me about her sister's teenage daughter and what she is getting up to. As usual when she is like this, she is looking past me to see the next thing. Looking for fun. Looking for excitement. I'm relieved when the plates are cleared. I put down my credit card and expect her to do the same. But she doesn't. She leans over the table and tries to hug me.

'Aw, thanks, next one's on me!'

I am irked. More than usual, because this is expected

behaviour. However, she's made me focus on what could happen next. How my whole world could fall down around me, and I know the pressure is piling on.

We say our goodbyes and she waits for Carole as I walk back to work. All I need to do is get through the next hour and then I can concentrate on my marriage. I sign back in to the office and go up to the presentation room. My slides are already loaded, and people are starting to file in. I spot Clint talking to Neil Jones in an adjacent office. His gestures are even more exaggerated than normal, and I take a deep breath.

I take a drink from the water in front of me and smile at Pam, who is sitting front and centre. She gives me a thumbs up and I nod at her. I am so proud of myself and my team for this campaign. We've worked with the most difficult people and gone the extra mile to produce something really eye-catching.

I spent hours and hours visualising and interpreting the ideas sent to us by people who don't understand advertising at all. They wanted online, I thought it should be external and online. They didn't want to pay the extra, so I designed the entire package. I hadn't envisaged how good the work was until I stood underneath a huge billboard in Manchester city centre. The visual effects plus the client growth report underlined just how pioneering our work had been.

The client was happy, but it all comes down to this moment. I watch as Clint walks towards me. His face is red, and I am horrified. He is really, really out of it. He sidles up to me and his arms encircle my waist. I move away quickly. His breath smells of cigarettes and booze and I turn away. He laughs.

'Okay, bit of a hangover. So, you can do this on your own, Katy. I'll give you marks out of ten.'

I nod my relief. Thank goodness. I can read the intro from the slides then move on to the data. He wanders over to a seat on the front row, to the right of me. All eyes are on me, and I begin.

I introduce the team one by one then show a video of the

billboard before displaying the slides of the digital adverts. People actually clap at the end of the video presentation, and I feel my heart lift a little. I begin on the sales figures. Then, all of a sudden, Clint holds up a hand.

'Can you just make it a bit more upbeat, Kate? Only I'm not getting the feeling of success.'

I nod at him and go back a slide. I fix a smile and read through the figures. But he's not happy. He stands now.

'No, no, no.' He makes a beckoning motion with his hands. I look at Pam and she shrugs her shoulders. I see Jamie from Sam's team make the international signal for drink and his row laughs. I stand stock-still as he approaches. Everything goes into slow motion as he takes the PowerPoint pointer from my hand and pushes me to the side. 'Let me show you how it's done.'

I need to remain professional. I need to make sure this is finished, and my team get their bonus. I smile at him.

'Thanks, Clint, but I can manage.'

He blinks at me for a long moment, and I think he is going to push me again, but he doesn't. He holds his hands up and goes back to his seat. I watch as he plops down and looks left and right, shrugging his shoulders.

I continue. I get through another slide, and he shouts out. 'Put some life into it.'

Then another slide, and he shouts out again. 'Boring. Boring. Boring.'

He is laughing, but everyone else looks embarrassed. I look at my shoes. I can feel anger and a strange sickness rise. I look at my team. Janet Price has twins and she needs this money for Christmas. Tom Hawkins has just moved house. Laurie Percival is a huge talent and will go to a rival company if she doesn't get this bonus.

They have all worked so hard on this account. So hard. They are credited at the end of the presentation and that is where I must get to. The pressure is overwhelming, but I continue. It's embarrassing and I feel like I am on the edge of telling Clint to sober up.

I can feel my phone buzzing in my suit pocket, and I need to answer it. But I can't. I will get through all this in order and then...

He's up again, doing a dance reminiscent of Homer Simpson and I know that whatever happens now, I can't be blamed. That I will be able to appeal his decision if he denies the bonus and it will most likely be granted. Everyone has seen him.

I carry on. I talk over his heckling, and I ignore his requests to 'liven it up' and 'show a bit of leg'. I get to the final presentation slide and it's a video of the team saying thank you. I turn up the volume and it drowns him out. He sinks back into his chair, laughing and slouching.

Finally, we are nearing the end. My final words are supposed to be to thank Clint and the management team, but I just flick the slide on. However, he stands and holds his hands up again.

'Whoa, whoa whoa. Haven't you forgotten something?'

I stare at him. 'No. I don't think so.'

He shakes his head. 'Say it. Go on say it. Say "thank you, Clinton". Go on.' I point at the slide and I run the red dot over the part where I thank him, but he's looking around. 'You see, that's what her problem is. She's just, I don't know. Nondescript. Not really anything. Just nah-nah-nah. Monotone.'

The room is silent. I feel the tears again, threatening to escape, but I won't let them. Not here. He's still speaking and now he's pointing at me.

'I've carried you. You and them. None of that would have happened if it wasn't for me.' He walks unsteadily towards me. 'You bored them to death, Kate. You're bland. Yeah, that's it, bland.' He leans forward, his beer breath in my face. 'Where's your passion, Kate? Where's your passion?'

Everything stops and I am back on the cliff edge with my mother. Her mocking and accusing as she balances on a narrow precipice in front of us. I am an awkward teenager again, just fourteen, blinking at her as she laughs and taunts Me shouting her name. Or is it my father?

'Collette! Collette!'

Clint could not possibly know the power of his words, but he has triggered something inside me.

I grab my bag and run for the exit. I hurry through the building and out of the reception doors. It's only when I am outside that I stop running. *Where is my passion?* It's in my work and in the way I support my team and Clint. I've covered for his sexist behaviour more than once, his invasion of people's personal space. But I know only too well what he means.

I know full well that anyone who witnessed what just happened could never blame me. He was obviously inebriated. But it's dialled up the pressure that has been building inside me these past twenty-four hours and I have to get out of here.

CHAPTER SIX

She told us all she was Irish. I think it was the name. Collette. All the tea towels in our kitchen had four-leaf clovers on them, she dressed in green on purpose, and there were rumours she had land in Galway. Of course, we celebrated St Patrick's Day down the local pub.

She carried herself with an air of confidence. When she danced, she spun, taking everyone with her. The only problem was she enjoyed spinning too much. Or too much in my opinion, I check myself. For who was I to judge? Everyone else in our lives seemed to think it was okay that I was left in charge of my little brothers as soon as I turned thirteen so she could go to the pub.

I was left in charge of three younger boys and, more often than not, of the cooking. Dad worked on a building site. She worked, but none of us were sure where. She seemed to come and go at different hours, which was not how I understood work. Now, with the benefit of a nine-to-five, I know she was in the pub. I know that her love of what she called fun was really getting as blitzed as possible, and it colours what I think of others. And myself. And it's no coincidence that a lot of people in my life need rescuing.

She would come back and demand that I flip some burgers or make beans on toast. On Thursdays she would send me to the chippy, and we would split three portions of pie and chips between six of us. As a result, we all loved school dinners. And school. I was studious. She told me that was boring too. But I didn't think I was boring. I thought I was trying to help. It's pretty much the same now. I feel like I am trying to hold it all up. Spin the plates while everyone else just spins.

I sit in my car and look at my phone. The call was from Jake. No message. I almost cry with relief. At least I know he is okay. I feel a burning inside me. The same burning that I felt when I walked away from our family home. As if something inside me was trying to break out. Yet I press it back every time. I keep it in until the flame extinguishes.

Because what if it's her? What if that flame is Collette?

I drive home. My phone is ringing all the way. First Clint's number and then Pam. Then Suzie from my team. I turn it off. It's almost five now and I will address what just happened tomorrow. As I turn the corner, I see Jake's car.

I park up and go inside. He is sitting on the sofa with a cup of coffee. His dark hair looks tousled, and he smiles at me. Like nothing has happened.

'Hi, babe. How did it go?'

I stand and look at him. He's wearing lounge pants and a grey T-shirt. I can feel the heating blasting out. I put my keys down and speak quietly. 'Where were you?'

He frowns. 'What do you mean?'

I blink at him. Of course he knows what I fucking mean.

'Last night.' The words stick in my throat.

He laughs. 'In the spare room. Didn't you read your messages?'

I pull my phone from my pocket. 'Yes. Yes, I did. There were no messages, Jake. I was worried sick.'

He stands and I see his day-old stubble.

'Look, I'm sorry, okay? I got a bit pissed. We all went out for a pizza, and I got wasted. I had to leave my car outside the restaurant. Billy brought me home.' He holds out his phone. 'I can't believe I'm saying this, but if you don't believe me, call him.'

I switch my phone back on. I find his profile and click on the messages. The same messages I have clicked on so many times over the past twenty-four hours. My heart skips a beat and I feel like I am going to faint. There are three messages. Three messages that I swear were not there before. The first one telling me he couldn't pick me up. The second saying he was on his way home and not to worry. How sorry he was. The third telling me he was in the spare room because he felt sick.

I look at the times. All before eleven last night.

'I... I... didn't see the messages. They weren't there...'

And I know I would have felt it if he was in the house. Surely he would have taken his shoes off down here? Hung up his coat? Unless he was really too smashed to even do that. I have to admit he does look a bit rough. His head is in his hands.

'The network. It must have been the network. Bloody hell, love, I'm so sorry. I didn't even hear you come in.'

'Or go out,' I murmur. Because I had been in and out twice since then. But I keep it to myself. I quickly decide to see how this plays out, because I could be wrong. I could be oversuspicious. If that is the case, I need to have a close look at what the hell is going on in my mind. I'm already reassuring myself that I am overworked, and Clint is a nightmare and Paula is back on the booze. He is beside me now, his arms around me. He smells fresh and clean, and I feel a surge of love for him.

I am an idiot. I bet if I go upstairs the spare room will smell of stale beer and his socks. The washing machine will be full of his clothes from last night. I kiss him and pull away.

'Sorry, sorry, I've just been a bit preoccupied. And now Clint's been... Look, I'll cook some dinner and I'll tell you later.'

He follows me into the kitchen. 'To make up for it, can you take the day off tomorrow? So we can do something?'

I nod. It will seem more convincing if I ring in sick. Less like I stormed off. Even though it wasn't my fault.

'Yeah, sure. The presentation's over with now.'

'And did you get the bonus?' He's looking at his phone as he asks. Clicking away and typing with his thumb.

'I don't know. I left before the end. I wasn't feeling too good.'

He looks up suddenly. 'Oh. I hope it wasn't because of last night?' He moves closer and leans over the breakfast bar.

'Well, I was a bit upset. I bought a new dress and everything.'

'Yes, I saw.' He suddenly sounds tense. I chop onions with my back to him.

'I was worried when you didn't turn up at the party.'

'But you had a good time, right?'

'Yeah, but…'

He sighs. 'Okay, sorry, if that's what you want. Only I didn't think there were any rules. I didn't think it was crime of the century to get drunk with some mates from work.'

'Which pizza place was it?' I blurt it out. I can't help it. The flame inside grows stronger and I turn to face him. He tenses.

'Bloody hell, Kate. It was Rudy's, if you have to know. Do you want to see the bloody receipt? Shall I get a note from my boss?'

I shake my head and return to the onions. Rudy's is on the way to his office. I would have seen his car in the car park. Or would I?

'No, it's fine. I don't know what got into me.' I put the knife down slowly. My voice sounds crisp and businesslike and I kick my shoes off. I grab a bottle of wine and open it, pouring two glasses. 'Just need the loo then I'll get cooking. No harm done. Sorry if I got the wrong end of the stick.'

I brush my hand across his arm as I pass, and smile, but once upstairs I open the first spare room door. Its sunshine orange quilt cover is still tucked under the end of the bed. Not slept in. I pass Polly's room and open the second spare room door. Again, the quilt cover is tucked under, something Jake would never do if he had remade the bed.

I go into our room and change into sweatpants and a zipper top. I take my office clothes back to the kitchen and open the washer. It's empty. He has washed the blue shirt with the birds on the cuffs and his clothes from yesterday. I open the dryer and there they are.

I pass him his wine. He looks sheepish.

'I'm sorry. I'm stupid. I just got trashed and didn't think about you when I should have. Can we start again?' He grins at me.

It was his grin that first attracted me. Lopsided and charming. Even after years of knowing him, I feel a shiver every time I look at him. I could be wrong about him not coming home. He could have been in the spare room. His car could have been at Rudy's, and he could have tucked the quilt under. But I am not sure about this. Something deep inside tells me something isn't right.

I cup his face in my hands. I could be wrong, but I am not wrong about something being different about my husband. The dark circles under his eyes that have taken more than one night on the lash to materialise. His almost permafrown.

I kiss him again and nod. 'Course we can. But you would tell me if anything was wrong, wouldn't you?'

He laughs and I feel deep relief. He pulls me onto the sofa beside him.

'I would. And there isn't. Nothing serious. Just run-of-the-mill rubbish. Job pressure. And now a bloody hangover.'

'Yeah, me too. Whoever said champagne doesn't give you a hangover lied. And Clint was still drunk today. Didn't help this afternoon.'

I want to tell him what he said. How it hurt. But it can wait. He nods.

'Right. When will you find out about the bonus?'

'I'll give Suzie a ring later. I just needed to regroup.'

He takes my hand. 'Let's go to the coast. Get some fish and chips. One day out won't do any harm.'

His phone is beside him and it flashes. It's on silent but he sees it and grabs it faster than he really needs to. He looks at me to see if I have seen it. Then he answers.

'Hello? Hello?' I watch him. I can feel my heart beating faster. He raises his voice slightly, his tone more urgent. 'Hello? Who is this?'

The light fades and the call ends. He stares at the call register, just out of my line of vision. I go to the kitchen and check the pasta bake in the oven. I hear him run upstairs and drop down the loft ladders.

I log in to my phone and in to my smartwatch app. I can't help it. I'm not checking up on where he was, I just want to know that he was asleep before I came in last night. I log in to our shared account and tap on the J. His data appears and I tap 'analyse sleep'.

The moments tick by and I hear him walking around upstairs, each creaky floorboard increasing my guilt. I tell myself I'm just checking he is okay. That he isn't losing sleep or unwell. His resting heart rate is the same as it usually is. The cursor spins until the graph appears. I zoom in at the time sleep started. 00:45. And he was awake at 08:30.

It doesn't make sense. I run my mind over the app history to try to pinpoint another time when the sleep count has been wrong. Of course, there will be times it could have started late or early, say, when he was reading in bed or moving around in his sleep, and this is the problem. All the uncertainty. I can never say for sure that I am one hundred per cent accurate in my wonderings. He could always produce an excuse or an exception.

Except this isn't the real problem. My gorgeous husband reappears, now calm and smiling. I think about the agreement hanging on the hall wall. One line reads 'never go to bed on an argument' and I think that even if I wanted to, I am too tired to pursue this now. I have no actual proof he has done anything wrong, only a deep feeling that something isn't right.

He stands and takes my hand. I smile at him. Never go to bed on an argument.

I will talk to him tomorrow when I am less tired. I will ask him what is wrong. Ask him to trust me with whatever is bothering him.

CHAPTER SEVEN

I open my eyes and he isn't there. Somehow, I knew he wouldn't be. How has it come to this? I know I should be upset. In tears. Wondering where he is. I turn over and feel his side of the bed. It is cold. I listen to the house – each house has its own sounds – but there are no footsteps and no water running.

I can't put my finger on what was wrong last night. Maybe it was a gradual creep to this? One I hadn't noticed because I had been preoccupied with my job and getting the project finished? I know I should get up and see if his car has gone. But what's the point when I know it will have?

I know this feeling. I know it only too well. It's that hollow certainty of what you knew was happening. When you suspect something is amiss, then find out it is. The question here, though, is what? What is wrong?

I know full well Jake's car wasn't in the pizza place car park. I know he was acting strangely last night when he received that phone call. If it's another woman, why would he ask who it was? Unless it was her husband.

My thoughts race. I don't want to go into work after yesterday, and Jake's seaside suggestion had hit the right note.

41

Now I don't have that excuse, and I really need to face Clint. I check the time. It's eight o'clock. I marvel at how calm I am under the circumstances as I climb out of bed and go downstairs.

I scan for a note, a message to tell me where he is. I check the tumble dryer to see if he has changed into the newly laundered clothes from yesterday. No. They are still there. I pull back the curtains and his car has gone, as I expected.

I pick up my phone and log in to our shared phone account. The agreement looms above me and I wonder if he's just popped out somewhere. I snort at my delusion. Even now I was making excuses for him, but this still feels like a step too far. An invasion of his privacy.

I try to call him but it goes to voicemail. It irritates me and before I know it, I am deep into the phone account, scanning for his device. I find it easily and press on it. A blue circle spins on the screen for what seems an eternity and then I see the words 'device not found'.

I quickly backtrack and Google *device not found*. The wiki explains the device could be 'unavailable or removed'. I try it again. And again. But I know really. I know what is happening. He's disconnected his phone from the account. Revoked permissions.

My heart thumps and heat rises in my cheeks. Where is he?

I hate this feeling. I spent years living it vicariously through my mother as she waited behind half-closed curtains for my father to return from whatever nightclub he had deemed his second home that weekend. She was no stay-at-home-wife all of a sudden. No. They started to go out separately, and, on reflection, this was when the rot set in.

They had been bad enough together, but this surpassed anything that went before. It was just after the holiday when she had called me boring that he finally left. I had just turned fifteen, and she was going around with a woman called Sheila Phipps. Sheila had two little boys and they would leave me 'in charge' of them. Five boys crammed into a small bedroom. Me, downstairs waiting to see who came in first.

One particular night was the evening before my dress rehearsal for a school play. I had dreamed of this all my early life. A way I could finally have something of my own. Something I loved to do. Something to make them proud. I had to be there for eight o'clock for hair and make-up. Someone's mum had a beauty salon, and she was making sure we all looked professional.

I waited and waited. The clock ticked around to two o'clock. I knew the pub closing times and the club closing times. They had clearly both gone clubbing. I took her place behind the curtains and in that moment, I swore I would never do that in my life. I would never be the one waiting for someone.

Three o'clock came, and no one arrived home. I fell asleep on the sofa. I was awoken by a small boy called Joe crying for his mum at 6.37am. The rest of the boys followed, and I was soon sitting them down with a bowl of cereal.

I was worried. I considered calling the police. What if they had been in an accident? But I knew then, like I know now, that there was no accident. That they knew exactly what they were doing. They were adults.

I waited and waited and around ten she rolled in with Sheila. They were laughing, and I could tell from her brashness she was still drunk. I stood in front of her.

'I had my rehearsal.'

She looked at Sheila and pulled a face. 'So why aren't you there, then?'

I frowned at her. 'I couldn't leave these, could I? Not on their own.'

She blinked at me, not comprehending. Then I saw the flare of temper. The redness of her cheeks and the pressure-cooker eruption.

'Where is he?' She ran upstairs, all eyes watching her. Then she reappeared with a sock in her hand. She grabbed at me. 'When did he come back for his stuff?'

Patrick started to cry. Shouting 'Daddy'. I tried to go to him, but she held me.

'When? Cathy, when did he come back? What's he taken?'

I screamed at her. 'He didn't. He must have taken it before. I've been here on my own. As usual. And now I won't be in the show.'

She slapped me and I was silent and still. The whole room was silent. The tick of the clock that presided over who came and who went was super-loud as I tried to take in that my father was gone.

And he was gone. He never reappeared. She went looking for him but came back empty-handed. She was broken before the alcohol made a reappearance every day as aggression or screams in the night. And I almost expected what happened next.

One year almost to the day she went into the town. I often look back now to see if there was any show of love as she left our house that evening. Any faces touched or kissed. Any sadness. Any looks back.

She went out to the pub and never came back. She didn't take anything at all. Just the clothes she stood up in and her fake Gucci bag. No, there were no exaggerated shows of affection just before she went. Nothing obvious to indicate that she wouldn't come back. Perhaps she didn't know she was going to leave. That would make sense for Collette. There was no planning or strategy. She could have decided while she was out and just never returned.

Standing at my kitchen window now, I grasp at that feeling. I pull it towards me. I know it is in me too, that headstrong feeling of making changes. Of course, I've channelled it into taking business risks and, ironically, driving my own life forward and never even thinking about my mother.

But now that innate feeling is so close. I could just walk out of the door and forget about all these problems. No more insults from Clint. I could give Paula a wide berth for a while. And Jake. That's the deal breaker. I'm here because I care. I love him. I – we – have something more than Mum and Dad had. We have an agreement. We know what we are doing. This is just a blip. And I will get to the bottom of it.

I get dressed and drive to work. Once there, I go into my office and shut the door. I dial Jake's number. I wasn't going to, but now, away from the house, I feel more concerned. He doesn't answer and I don't leave a message. Instead, I WhatsApp him.

> Hi babe. I don't know what happened, but you were gone. I thought we were going out but... If there's something wrong, you know you can tell me anything. Anything.

When I look up Clint is standing in my office. I motion to him to sit down. He grimaces. I can see the remnants of tension on his face. Probably a hangover.

'I'll stand if it's all the same.'

I stand too. He just stares at me for a long moment.

'So... how can I help you?'

He laughs. 'Well, an apology would be good. For running off like that. Embarrassing.'

I breathe in. I feel my face contort into anger but, as usual, I hold it in.

'Look, Clint, it was the day after the office do. Can we put it all down to that?'

He is shaking his head and moving from foot to foot. 'No, we can't.' He leans forward. 'You cost your team the bonus, so it's them you need to apologise to.'

I grasp the seriousness of this, yet I start to laugh. Again, I am back in my childhood home. Back in the lounge on the morning of the second day my mother didn't come home. The hysteria of my brothers crying and me not knowing what to do. The deputy head coming round and telling me off for not being in school. The outburst just below the surface but never coming.

I held it down like I am holding it down now. Except for the laughter. Clint is unsure what to do, and I deflect by grabbing my bag and flicking off my laptop. I move closer to him. My voice spills out thick like treacle.

'I've got a lot going on at the moment. I'm taking some sickness leave.'

He starts to say that I can't, but I snigger at him. I turn slightly so that the rest of the office, who have now stopped to watch, can see what I am saying.

'I can. I have seven days without a sick note. After that I will send something in if I need to.' I lean closer still. 'You can't bully me anymore.' I feel the flame, strong inside me. 'Because if you try, I will leave and then you'll have to do some work. Think about it.'

And I think about it too. I love my job. Most of it, anyway. I love the creativity and the clients. I love the initial talks and the briefs. The teamwork and the ideas that float around in the air. The easy way my team push everything to its most extreme point to extract the design. All this flashes before my eyes now and I feel faint at the possibility that I might lose it because of Clint.

He's never been on my side. He's always resented me. Before I'd even settled in, he'd started transferring his workload to me. God only knows what he does during the day. I'd do all the work and then he'd lumber into the final meetings and take all the credit. He'd tell them he'd been supervising in the background and he'd come up with the baseline concepts. It was a shame because this could be something really special. But I'd carried him and right now was the moment I was going to drop him like a heavy stone sinking in deep water.

I step backwards. He is standing, open-mouthed, in the doorway. I raise my eyebrows and he steps sideways. I walk past the blue booths where the comms people sit towards the exit.

Pam is in the end booth and she mouths *are you okay?* I nod almost indiscernibly. But I am not okay.

Once out of the office I hurry through reception and into the car park. I fully expect a sense of guilt to descend, but it doesn't. All I feel is a sense of change. Now Clint was going to have a taste of his own medicine. He's going to have his own workload and more back. No one else is experienced enough to do it. He's loaded me high. I'm going to make him feel how I feel. Until he begs me to come back.

And he's not the only one.

CHAPTER EIGHT

She called me Cathy. My name is Catherine, and I shortened it to Kate, but she called me Cathy. She wasn't stupid. No. She read everything she could. Devoured it. But there was something inside her that overpowered everything else.

'After Cathy. You know, Cathy and Heathcliff.'

I did know. I loved *Wuthering Heights*. I often wondered why she didn't call one of my brothers Heath. Or Cliff. Or Heathcliff. It would make me giggle. My brothers are called Flynn, Michael and Patrick. Good old Irish names for a woman who comes from Ancoats.

'We are who we want to be...' she would drawl when I asked her about my grandparents and where they were from. 'You make your own life.'

She would suck on a cigarette and nod into the void, her mile-long stare confirming her words to herself. My dad was called Harold Palmer, and I half knew his mum. His dad died when he was a teenager and his mum, Grandma Jayne, would make an appearance at Christmas when she would look around disapprovingly until a row broke out. I shiver at my last memory of her and where all the wildness led.

But I knew *Wuthering Heights*. I knew the longing and the desire and the deep want. I loved the intensity and the drama. I knew she did too. Whether she was channelling Cathy, or she was already as wild as her, often played on my mind. One thing was for sure, though, I was not the daughter Collette wanted. She wanted a carbon copy of her.

Yet, inside, it was there. The flashes of wild and the sparks of mischief. It was as if all my spontaneity had been pushed down deeply by worry and responsibility. There were flashes, and her eyes shone on the rare occasions I had a tantrum or refused to do something.

There had been occasions at school when she had been called in. Once when I had walked out of a lesson because someone was kicking my chair continuously, and once when I felt sick. She interpreted both of these as major acts of rebellion and I had never seen her so proud. Her arm around my shoulder, she faced the deputy head with me. United in protest.

I grip the steering wheel. My phone flashes and it's Clint. I reject the call. I start the engine, but I don't want to go home. I don't want to wait around for my husband to come home when he fucking pleases. I don't want to phone Paula and wait until she has ten minutes free to talk to me.

Most of all, I don't want to be a target. Sitting there in my pristine home, waiting for someone to come along and expect a meal. Washing done. A quiet listener. Someone to do their work for them. God knows, Jake has been fair, but over the years he has begun to leave things for me to do.

I think about Polly. His daughter. Not my daughter. He made sure Polly was kept mostly separated from me. Even when she came to stay at weekends, he focused completely on her, leaving me to make endless meals and do washing. Book trips I wasn't going on. I am shocked at my resentment of this.

What else, Jake? What else have I pushed down because of my loyalty? My breathing quickens, and I know what else. I know full well. Veronica. He kept us completely separate and told me she was a horrible person. Yet, one night in bed when we were first married, he brought her into our relationship.

'So what's the best sex you've ever had?'

I'd laughed at first. We were having fun. But he'd never asked me about my past before.

'I don't know. I don't...'

He'd tickled me. Hands all over me. Lips on my neck.

'Mine's V. She was a bitch but hot. Not as hot as you though.'

I giggled even as my head spun with confusion. Why mention her. Why then? I knew it was some kind of game, something he wanted to introduce, but I rejected it by kissing him and climbing on top of him.

He never mentioned any other woman, but he did mention Veronica again. He told me she was a superb cook and a great mum. I'd immediately thought of Collette and her wish that I was something I wasn't. I wasn't a great cook, and I wasn't anyone's mum. I knew he was trying to shape me, but wasn't that what people did in a relationship? Didn't they gradually begin to understand what the other person wanted and needed? He never criticised me, but, I realise now, he did his work more discreetly. He made me feel bad. And I forgave him because I was so scared of fucking everything up again. Ian was a mistake. This time things would be perfect. The problem is, I don't, even now, know if Jake did it intentionally.

There's a burning inside me, a rage. This is the part where I usually swallow back the tears. Where I decide that it's not worth the hassle or the disruption that I know it will bring. The destruction that I saw first-hand. It burns in the pit of my stomach and races through my veins, heating my rage and clouding my head.

But this is different. This is more. Like the time I stood outside Paula's rehab centre where I had visited her every day for three months, only to find out she'd gone home with Luke

Parker, her dealer. Like the time Clint barefaced lied to a client that the big idea they loved was his. How he looked at me as he said it with an expression that told me there was nothing at all I could do. Suck it up, Kate. Suck. It. Up.

And I did. I went home and sat alone until the anger subsided. It sometimes took days. I'd ignored Paula's calls and avoided Clint at work. But eventually I went back to it all. Good old Kate. Always available. Always there with my hand up.

I start to drive. The only thing that stopped me from going mad with Jake was the fact that he might be in trouble. After what Paula said, it had hovered in the back of my mind, stopping me from asking and willing him to explain. But I know that this has been building up. Something is going on. If I am honest with myself, I have suspected it for ages.

He's had enough time to talk to me. Enough time to explain his lateness and, yes, absence. He's seen the single, lonely dish stacked on the draining board after he's come in late. He could have got into bed and told me whatever it was in the dark. I would have listened.

But he didn't. Instead, he's sneaking around and telling lies. I know full well he wasn't in the spare room. I would have known if he was in the house. He always leaves his shoes by the door and they were not there. And I know those messages weren't on my phone. I checked a thousand times and I absolutely know that they were not there. I also know that he's into software communications.

Jake's told me all about what he does. How he works with developers to find new methods of communicating digitally. I know he would be capable of making those messages look like they had arrived earlier. He's even told me how he'd done it for a client in a showcase presentation.

That's partly why I haven't Facebook stalked Veronica. Because I know he could see my phone history in our account. It's not because I haven't wanted to. I'd fantasised about getting another phone and setting up a fake account. But I didn't, and that was the important thing to me. The fact that I didn't want to hold too tightly on to Jake. Delve into his past. I asked myself over and over what was wrong with me, and I knew deep down that it was how he had made me feel. But wasn't someone allowed to mention their ex?

I know other women at work stalk their exes. Even when they are with someone else. They have them as Facebook friends and follow them on Twitter. Picking over the bones of old relationships and watching as they form new relationships. I'd congratulated myself on 'not having to do that'. I'm not even slightly interested in what Ian is doing. And how would that make Jake feel?

Jake, Jake, Jake. I thought about his feelings in everything I did. I made sure I consulted him on everything and had even given him the benefit of the doubt when he was talking about his ex-wife in our bed. All in the name of giving each other space. It's never been a problem until now because I have been fully subscribed to the agreement. But he obviously isn't. He thinks I'm stupid. And I suppose I've given him the impression that I will put up with anything.

I can feel the pressure building. I need someone to talk me down but there is no one. No one at all. Paula will be hungover from yesterday. Pam will be at work and I don't want to disturb her – or explain what happened with Clint. I have no one else. Everything has been for Jake.

I drive over to his office and pull up outside the gates. His car isn't there. I try to ring him one more time. It rings and rings and goes to answerphone, I can feel the words struggling to get out, to hurl themselves at him, but I end the call. I drive over to Rudy's pizza place and park up outside.

I stride up to the door and scan the room. Not Jake's kind of place, really, but we will see. I hurry over to one of the servers.

'Hi there. My husband was here the other night. His car was damaged outside.'

She nods at me. 'Which night?'

'Wednesday. The night before last. I wondered if…'

She looks up and smiles at me. It's a fixed smile and I know what is coming before she says it.

'Are you sure it was Wednesday?' I nod and side-glance at the opening hours on the glass door panel behind her. 'Only we are closed Tuesday and Wednesday. Are you sure he didn't mean Sally's over in town? They open Wednesdays.'

I blink at her. 'Oh, yes, thank you. Sorry. I must have misheard.'

She goes back to folding napkins in half and I go back to the list of lies and add another item.

My teeth clench and I get back in my car. What the hell was going on? He's clearly hiding something and lying about where he has been. I think about going back to the house and waiting. Pretending everything is normal. Making tea and eating a biscuit. Pulling washing out of the washer and putting it into the dryer. Tidying the garden and making the bed. Our bed. Polishing taps and smiling at the steamy messages on the bathroom mirror.

But I already know it isn't going to happen. I know I have passed the point of pushing down this feeling and making it so tiny I can ignore it. Instead, for once, I let it rage. I let it overtake me and demand its own space. This isn't about Jake, it's about me. I've dreaded this moment, the split second I give in to it and let Collette surface within me.

That hot mess of preoccupation with minute relationship issues. The magnification of tiny things and making them so big they overwhelm what is really important. Oh yes, I know what she did and how it works. I resisted it until now. I put myself second on purpose.

I increase speed as I head for home. Now it's here it isn't so bad. In fact, it makes everything feel a lot better. It's a feeling of sudden power, that, after all, it will all be okay because I am going to find out exactly what is going on.

There will be no more waiting for phone calls and messages. No more staring at my phone wondering where Jake is. No. This is where it all changes. He can wonder where I am for a while. I learned the hard way through my devastating marriage to Ian that people who play games need an audience at best, and an opponent at worst. It's hard to play when no one else is taking part.

I drive up the dual carriageway and stop at the traffic lights. I am so conditioned to Jake's little games that I automatically glance at my phone, waiting for the message he has trained me to accept. The little habit he has trained me into. The lights are on red, and I flex the tension out of my neck.

It would be easy to go home and have a hot bath and then just wait. Call in and apologise to Clint. Arrange to meet Paula to talk her down. And Jake. To talk to him and then understand what he needs. How I can help.

But I'm not going to do that. The lights turn to green, and I screech into the next lane. I don't slow down and turn the corner to the estate. Instead, I drive on, up the dual carriageway and out of town.

CHAPTER NINE

I drive past the supermarket where Jake and I do our shopping. Past the pizza place and Jake's office. Past the turnoff to the town centre where we buy our clothes. I drive past all the normality because none of this feels normal. I don't stop until I reach the place I grew up.

I stop at the end of our road. *Our* road. I always knew I would end up here. We moved here after they got evicted from the high rise for not paying the rent. I always knew I would one day sit here and look at the end terrace with my tiny bedroom at the front. The windowsill I would sit on watching the clouds. The gate my father made from pallets after he kicked the steel one until it was warped is long gone, replaced by spiral wrought iron to match the rest of the road.

We stood out. We were the troubled family. The ones who were always in a rush. Collette didn't keep house well. She half-cleaned and half-tidied and half-looked after us. As a result, we were half-feral during the balmy summers. As I grew-up the sense of shame for being different weighed ever-heavier, and I feel it press against me now.

I grip the steering wheel and stare at the windows. Clean now, with matching curtains. I've known a sense of calm since then. An intentional snubbing of drama. Of course, that means acquiescence, because anything else would make me like her. Any slight imbalance toward an argument or criticism would send me hurtling to my memories of this place.

Did I want this? *Did I?* Did I want the desperation and the screaming and the tears? The scratching around amongst the half-empty booze bottles for happiness? No, I did not. I pushed myself towards what I thought was normality. I turned down the heat to almost zero and found a million coping strategies to keep it under control. To not be like her.

But here I am. Burning with rage. Alight with all the injustice I have put up with. I've tried to tell myself it is my own fault. I have let my guard down. Jake is probably up to nothing. He's just stressed. He's just tired. He's just overworked. Still, I can't avoid the truth any longer. He's just lying.

He would probably say that he hadn't lied because he had said nothing. But the truth is, he's got so used to me being the allowing wife who puts up with anything that he can just do what he wants.

I stare at the front door and in my mind's eye I can see her. Flaming hair pinned up, half-dressed on the doorstep. Him, stalking towards the main road, hands in pockets. Her, screaming after him. Gesticulating, hyper-aware that the neighbours are watching through the curtain and pleased, because that is what she wanted. Affirmation that she was right.

'You think you can do what you want.'

The slamming door that, even if we didn't hear the argument, would alert us to the fact that she would be in bed for days now. My brothers sitting around the table and me pouring cornflakes into plastic dishes and splashing milk onto them. Dressing them and gathering together the reading books in zipped folders and the spelling tests we would practise on the way to school.

Even then I kept the anger inside. On the odd occasion as a

teenager, I would challenge her, ask her what she thought she was doing. Ask her why she wasn't like other mums. Her face would harden, and she would nod at me.

'Oh yeah, that's right. It's all my fault, is it? Why don't you ask him why all this has happened?'

I never did. Never. I just turned my back and ran. But it's as if there was always an invisible thread pulling me back. I did want to know. I craved normality, but now I am the odd one out again. The woman who can't talk about her family. The woman who doesn't get birthday cards or phone calls. Because acquiescence and sacrifice are bedfellows and, as Paula has reminded me in her drunken rages, very close to martyrdom.

However, I know I am not that person. Yet here I am. Somewhere inside me I had nurtured the nagging question of what would push me over the edge. What would make me snap back into the Collette-shaped mould that I had tried to avoid for so long. And now I know.

It hadn't worked out with Ian. I'd moved away from him because he had wound me up. I knew I needed something more structured. Someone who would agree to the life I needed. Someone who would not force me into anything, but who understood where my line was. When Jake and I made the agreement, it was for life. It was a serious moment, and we both cried. We had the templates of what we didn't want trailing behind us in our former marriages and this deep commitment to each other's freedom, but fidelity was based on truth.

Now he has broken it. I don't know what is going on. I don't know if it is another woman, or if he is in trouble, or if he wants to leave me. But I will find out.

The fire is burning now as I recall Collette storming into my bedroom at intervals throughout my childhood and throwing a single bin bag out the window. A signal between them that her line had been reached. He would stand below, hands upturned, pleading for forgiveness.

But her real strength was in getting to the bottom of things. She would eventually rise from her bed and get dressed. Then there would be phone calls and a full ashtray and whispers in the kitchen with her best friend Jean Smith. The two of them going out in the afternoon with their hair done and best clothes on. Uniformly marching up the street, handbags over arms.

Their return, and the tears and nods and sometimes tea and cake *because tea makes everything better.* I tear up as I hear her say it. Another sign that I am breaking. My last ounce of sympathy for her was weighed out long ago. Where will all this emotion take me? Where will this impulsive decision lead?

I start the car and do a screeching turn at the end of the street and drive away. I don't feel upset. I just feel different. I've heard people say that they just snapped. That they just decided to walk away and never come back. I'm not doing that. This time I'm making an agreement with myself. Something I will hold myself to and not be accountable to someone else.

I smile. It's the first time in my life I've done this. I've always thought I needed another person to sign, seal and deliver any agreement. Mum, Dad, Ian. Jake. But this is mine. I am going to leave and see who misses me. And I'm not going back until they do. Let's see how long it will take.

A tingle of excitement surprises me. I have left everything. All I have is what I stand up in. I have my credit cards and the contents of my bag. My car. Who *will* miss me? Who will wonder where I am? Not my family. That goes without saying. Not Paula. She is too involved with herself at the moment. Not work. I've taken sickness leave.

Not the man at the coffee shop. He probably won't notice I'm not there at exactly eight forty-five each workday. Not the car park security. They see me each day, but I am another anonymous parker. Not the guy in Greggs where I go each week to buy doughnuts for the team. Not my neighbours. I rarely talk to them. We all work, and they rarely show any interest in me and Jake.

So just Jake. I drive over the hills and north. Past the heather and the dry-stone walls, and past the pond that we have walked round holding hands. How long will it take him? I breathe in sharply as I realise he might call the police. He might ask them to search for me. *Good*. I shock myself.

After what happened, I have avoided any interaction with the police. I picture Jake, worried and fretting, calling Paula and work. Putting it all together and, finally, going to the police station. Telling them I didn't take anything except my car and my bag. Showing them my clothes. Them asking if we had argued. If there was any reason he could think of…

I stop myself. I am doing what she did. Making a big scene. Punishing. But something deep inside me releases the idea that I am finally standing up for myself. Not just with Jake. Not just with Paula, who, admittedly, would be worried when she finally realised I wasn't answering her calls. No, this was much more serious.

I drive into Huddersfield and find a Premier Inn. Not the one I stayed at for a marketing conference. This needs to be somewhere new. I park in the multi-storey car park beside the hotel and push the ticket into my bag. Once in the hotel, I go to the desk. A woman with a look of Amy Winehouse greets me.

'How can I help?'

I smile. It's fake, and I feel like telling her I am running away and why. 'Have you a double room for five days, please?'

She checks and nods. 'Yes. Could I take your name, please?'

I panic. My name. I want to make it difficult to find me.

'Kate. Kate Dooley.' I use Collette's name. Dooley. It just spilled out. It conjures up memories of internet searches years ago and the realisation that she built her life on a lie. But I use it anyway.

'Thanks, Mrs Dooley. Could I have your address, please?'

I give her the office address and she smiles.

'Thank you. That will be two hundred and forty-five pounds, please. We have an offer on breakfasts at the moment if you want to...'

'Yes, that would be great. Thank you.'

I push my savings account card into the machine and punch in my number. My heart races as I worry about the different names and addresses, but it completes. My savings account. The one account Jake has no access to. I opened it for the cheque that, in the end, I couldn't bear to cash. I put in odds and ends of my salary that I intended to save for presents for Jake. We were never short of money, and I bought them out of my salary instead. It is processing. The printer behind her whirrs. She looks up.

'Are you here for business or pleasure?'

I blink at her. I want to tell her I am here to put things right. I am here to find out what my husband is up to. I am here to find out if he loves me or not. Or if he even notices I am gone.

'Business. I'm here on business.'

I am. I am here on the business of the past. The waves of what happened ten years ago have lapped around my feet for long enough. I am here on business. Family business. I don't know where to start, or what I will find if I step back into that whirling ball of drama, but now I have to. Every second I am away from my life I have to both look at what just happened with Jake, and why.

It is the why that is at the root. I have known this for as long as I have avoided it. Now, it's like all the things I have pushed away are racing through me, beckoning to see, listen. Feel.

'Business? Great. We have a built-in business centre just behind the restaurant. You can use it with your room key.'

She hands me the key and the documents. I stop for a moment. Am I doing the right thing? Am I?

But there is no going back now. Even if I did, I would rage through my marriage with Jake and be a woman he would not recognise. I would whirl around him with my mother's wild accusations and never find out the truth. This way is better. My way.

I go to my room. Number fifty-six. It seems odd that I have no suitcase to unpack. No overnight bag. I sit on the double bed and look at my phone. No calls. No texts. No messages. I check my Facebook. Then I go to the phone account I share with Jake, the one he removed his phone from. He can still log in and see my phone and where I am, so I remove my device too. Then I switch off the phone and take out the battery.

My sensible self tells me I need a plan, but I know I don't, really. I already know what I have to do. I've gone over this so many times over the past decade, but feelings were pushed down and spontaneity pulled into the straight lines of rules.

It's scary and it's risky, but I just can't live in mediocrity anymore.

CHAPTER TEN

The first thing I do this morning is go back out and move my car. I drive it across town and park it on a backstreet. I catch a bus and pay cash for the ticket. I get off in the centre and buy a cheap mobile phone and a separate pay-as-you-go chip. I walk back to the hotel clutching my lifeline. I can search for anything with this. It strikes me that Jake always had the option to see my search history, as I did his. When exactly did he remove his device from our phone account? And why? What didn't he want me to see?

Back in the hotel room I wait for the phone to charge. I'll check my old phone twice a day to see if anyone has rung me, but I won't check it here. No, I will make it as difficult as possible for him to know where I am. Just like he has.

When my new phone is charged, I go into town again and I hire a car. I am the kind of person who always carries at least three types of ID just in case. I find the car hire place and the man is very accommodating.

'Here on business?'

I nod. It seems a popular question and allows me to build a story.

'Yeah, I'm at a conference. I didn't think I would need a car, but I'd like to look around.' I flick my thumb over my shoulder. 'He's got ours.'

He shows me a few cars and I choose a two-door hatchback. Blue. Something that no one will notice particularly. He helpfully lets me use their computer to get a DVLA code and completes all the forms for me. It stings my soul to act dizzy and helpless, but it's a means to an end. That's all. A way to find out what's happening. He even opens the car door for me and shows me where the key goes. I wave as I drive away and make my way back to the hotel car park.

As I walk through the hotel and back to my room I feel like I am getting somewhere. I don't know what I am going to do yet, but I do know that it will involve my deepest insecurity that has been eating away at my soul. Veronica. I realise now that she's been a constant, hanging over my head.

Jake never made a secret of her. He mentioned her regularly and I always thought it was because they had Polly. None of this is Polly's fault, and I did everything possible to welcome her. In fact, I have become fond of her. His constant complaining about *what a bitch V is* made me wonder if she was on his mind a little too much.

But no, good old Kate wouldn't say anything. Good old dependable Kate just made space for Jake's ex in their marriage. After all, everyone has a past, I told myself. But not everyone has to keep fucking mentioning it, do they? My face flushes and I grab my burner phone. It feels wrong but I suddenly don't care. And who will know? Maybe that was the problem. All my life there has been someone nosing around. Always someone seeing what I am doing so they can commandeer me to look after them. Do their dirty work.

I shock myself with this, but fuck it. I bring Facebook up on my phone. I dither about signing into my account and then don't.

No, it will show I have been active. Check later. Let them wonder.

I locate Veronica's account easily because I have looked at it before. However, it's not public. I spend some time making a Facebook profile. It feels like fraud, but who am I really? Who is Kate Clayton? I call myself Donna McBride and steal a random woman's profile picture. I almost steal that woman's family too – she has a public profile so is really open to it – but I stop. Instead, I find someone with a dog and download and reload the pictures into my account.

I go to town on the 'about me' section. I explain on Donna's behalf that she is newly divorced and new to Facebook and looking to hook up with old friends. I go back to Veronica's profile and, yes, of course she has left her friends list open. Some of them have St Mary's secondary school in common, so I make that mine too.

Then I start to add her friends. I make a coffee and wait. I've cut and pasted a message and I send it with the friend request.

Hi! Remember me? New to FB and looking to catch up about St Mary's.

I wait until a few of them have accepted, which is surprisingly quickly. And then I add her. Someone messages Donna asking how they know her, and I type some random shit about a school trip, and they add me. Bingo. I didn't know I had it in me.

While I am waiting, I scroll through her limited profile. There are some pictures of Polly and an old picture of her and Polly which has been edited to cut Jake off. I've seen it before in his photo album. When I first looked at her profile, I wondered why she would cut him off. I asked Jake, and he didn't look away from his phone.

'She's a cow. I was disposable. On to the next one.'

I blink at my phone, waiting for the notification telling me she has accepted. It takes two more hours. In that time, I have looked at Jake's socials. We are Facebook friends and I clicked on my own account. From Donna McBride's perspective I am someone who posts pictures of clothes and wishes people at work 'happy birthday'. There are some pictures of me and Jake and a few of works parties, but nothing exciting.

I look into my own face. My dull eyes and the fake smile I use to cover my fucked-up past. I am a yes woman. Someone who is just alive to avoid a problem reappearing. To avoid having to deal with a dreaded situation.

I am almost invisible, apart from the yes and the no, and the agreement. I just agree with everything. Give everyone leeway. By the time Veronica's notification arrives, tears are rolling down my cheeks and dripping onto the purple Premier Inn bedspread. I'd scoffed at all the TV programmes and documentaries and soap operas that played out the characters' problems that have a habit of reappearing. But I knew, really. I knew mine would.

I always thought it would be a phone call or a knock on the door. I never dreamed for one second I would snap and search out my problem myself. But back to the business of the day. I scroll through Veronica's Facebook profile. Picture after picture of her and Polly at kids' theatre productions and Polly's friends' parties.

Pictures of Veronica in overalls holding a paintbrush. I scroll back up to a recent photograph. I sneer at her, grinning into the camera. She is leaning forward and smiling. I am an expert at this. I have stalked all three of my brothers individually on social media.

Facebook didn't come a day too soon for me. I'd spent so long isolated from everyone I knew from back then that the day I discovered it, I was drunk on faces. Friends from school. People who lived near us when we were growing up. I looked them all up. I looked at their houses and their cars and their children, desperate to recapture the feeling of connection I took for granted back then.

When I first joined Facebook, none of my brothers had signed up. Flynn was the first. I'd got so used to typing in their names and nothing appearing that when his face popped up, I was shocked to the core. I was the oldest by three years. Back then, three years was the difference between thirteen and ten. Now, it's barely anything. She gave birth to them in quick succession, one per year.

She joked they were the happiest years of her life because Dad was always there. In reality, I realise now, they were happy because she couldn't drink, and she wasn't out all the time. For a short five years we had an almost normal life – there were still arguments, and she still stood at the curtains on Friday nights. But life was all nappies hanging over a rack in the kitchen and the smell of milk.

Flynn was the next child down from me. He had a shock of red hair and freckles. As a man, he had his hair tightly cut and he was tanned. That day my finger had hovered over the 'add friend' button while my stomach did backflips. My whole body shook with the memory of the last time I saw him, and I had no reason to believe it would be any different. I'd searched his profile for any clues about his life. He was engaged. His wife was Aleena, a beautiful, petite woman who wore gold jewellery. They looked happy, and I cried.

Patrick and Michael appeared shortly afterwards, and I added them to my daily family visit. I would look at their photographs and wonder who was on the other side of the camera. My nephew? Michael had a boy. Aleena, who I felt like I knew because her profile was open? Or had Flynn split with her? There were no recent photos. But I don't check them anymore. It's too painful.

Now I think about Veronica's photo. She is obviously in love with whoever is taking this one. She is glowing and has picked it out because it is one out of a million photographs that shows the feeling we would all love to bottle. Joy. The knowledge you are loved. I search the background for shadows. The shape of the person taking it. I enlarge the photo and look for a mirror image in her eyes, but it's too dark.

It creeps up on me. A feeling that I had seen laid bare on my mother's face. If she could have glowed green, she would have done every time she suspected where my father was holed up. Oh, I know how to search, all right. She would leave no stone unturned. I watched and learned as she started conversations with strangers that always led to one place. Harry Palmer. It was like a vocation for her. She would call up taxi companies claiming she was trying to find her husband's wallet that he had left in a cab. And what address had that taxi taken him to. Yes, yes, too drunk to remember. A roll of the eyes, even, to seal the deal. But underneath it all her hand shook, and she was white with shock.

I know that feeling. The realisation that something is going on behind your back. I would normally press it down with all the others. I would tell myself not to be silly, it would only cause trouble. I would end up not acting on my deepest intuition and… and… it hits me like a brick.

I would forgive him. It could have been Ian. Or the guy who ghosted me after three weeks of fun. But most of all, Jake. Our agreement meant that if I asked where he had been or who he was with, I was curtailing his freedom. It was unspoken, but the writing was on the wall. Literally. By the door where I had a constant reminder of what we had agreed.

I let the feeling ebb and flow and then rise into my throat as bile. We both stuck to the agreement. We both respected privacy and freedom. The difference was, I realise now, that I was doing it out of love. I was making sure I was strong and did not give in to anything that would break it. I wasn't the one acting strangely. I wasn't the one coming home late or staying out all night. I wasn't the one lying about messages. No, Jake was using it for a different purpose. He was using our agreement as a hiding place for something he wasn't telling me. And I wouldn't ask because then I would break it.

I've been a fool. I storm out in the clothes I've been wearing for almost two days, and I drive back across the moorland roads in my rented car at breakneck speed. In less than an hour I am parked opposite Veronica's house.

CHAPTER ELEVEN

The lights are out, and her car is not in the drive. I almost drive away but I can't. I need to know. I may be clutching at straws, but I swore I would trust my gut instinct. I've gone against my deepest feeling so much that it feels odd that I should trust myself.

In a second I am out of my car and hurrying up the drive. I've never been in the house, but I have stood at the back door with Polly. It strikes me that this is the house that they bought together. The family home. I wonder how often he comes here. How long he stays when he drops Polly off. All the questions I circled but avoided because I promised to trust him.

The gate is open. I push it and it squeaks loudly. The back garden has a high fence and Polly's trampoline blocks the view from the adjoining house. Perfect. I try the door and it is locked. Of course it is. I pull my shirt sleeve over my hand and feel at the glass side panel and press my cheek against it to see the inside lock. The key is in the door and a key ring with a picture of Polly dangles from it. A sinking feeling almost floors me as I realise where this is leading.

But I have to know. Something grips me and it's now or

never. I find a rock and take off my jumper. I wrap it around the rock and hurl it against the window. It cracks the first time and I push a long shard in. The hole is barely big enough to get my hand through, so I push at the rest of the pane. It falls and shatters. I turn to see if anyone appears.

My God, what am I doing? I am driven by a force that I have never felt before. A search for the truth and nothing can stop me. I reach through and turn the key. I push the handle down and lean on the door. She might have cameras. Or an alarm. But I know I am going to risk it.

I am in the kitchen. I push the broken glass to the side with my foot, pull back the mat and slide it all underneath. The fridge has pictures Polly has drawn stuck on it. I look around. It's homely, and a cardigan is hung around a dining chair. I hear a car and rush into the lounge, but it passes. I don't even know what I am looking for. Photographs. Of them together. His clothes? I don't know. I look around and find nothing obvious that my husband has been here. Is here?

I open a drawer and see some receipts. I search through them, but they are for clothes for Polly and some bathroom scales. I open more drawers and in the bottom one I find a folder. It's clear plastic, and it's got 'life admin' written in felt tip. That's what he calls it. My skin burns. He calls it life admin. All the documents that track an existence.

I rummage through it. Birth certificates for her and Polly. Her national insurance number. Some bills and an insurance document. I open it. It's her workplace pension. No mention of Jake at all. She's made a will and it stipulates that everything she owns goes directly to her daughter. It would anyway, wouldn't it?

Then I see it. A brown envelope with divorce documents scrawled on the front. I sit cross-legged on the floor and open it. I scan each page until I come to the key documents. Now we will see. I've been dying to know the ins and outs of it since Jake told me the bare details of what happened between them.

We were in bed. It was before he proposed, and we were still in the first flushes of love. He asked me about my divorce from Ian and if it was definitely final. He asked me a few details, and I answered honestly that Ian and I were finished and I would never see him again. I bypassed the injunction. I didn't want to alarm him and if anything happened in the future, I could tell him then.

'So what happened between you and Veronica, then?'

I tried to sound casual, but I was dying to know. He became serious.

'Oh, she was a piece of work. She bullied me and one of her male friends threatened me. It was all...' He'd buried his head on my shoulder. I wanted more, but I didn't want to push him. He recovered. 'Yeah, I had no choice in the end. She was awful and I couldn't live with her. So I divorced her for unreasonable behaviour.'

I wanted to ask him what kind of unreasonable behaviour, but it must have been bad because he was close to tears. He obliged.

'One night she came home with a bloke. She was drunk, as usual, and they were dancing in front of me. She called me some really insulting names, really hurtful. They were laughing. And that was just the start. Happened regularly after that. She was a lush.'

I hugged him. Poor baby. I stroked his hair as he continued.

'I went to see a solicitor. He told me I had grounds for a divorce, and that the best I could hope for with Polly was shared parenting unless I got social services involved. I told him how bad the house was – so bad it stunk at times – but he said it would need the family courts, and did I want to drag Polly through that.'

I look around. Veronica's house is not dirty. It's lived in, yes, but it's clean and tidy. Why had he told me it wasn't? But there was more.

'So he suggested I divorce her for unreasonable behaviour and cite the ridicule and bullying.' He'd looked deep into my eyes.

'Some of it was in public, about my size. So that's what I did. She was served with the papers and she argued at first, but she had no choice. She was out of control, and I had witnesses.'

Out. Of. Control. An echo from down the years hits my consciousness. Where had I heard that before? Where?

'The divorce went through, and she is allowed to keep the house until Polly leaves school or Veronica remarries. But I can borrow against it.'

He'd taken my hand and squeezed it. We'd already discussed buying a house but not the finances. I had half the equity from mine and Ian's house and some savings, and I was already approved for a mortgage. I'd been satisfied. I'd been happy that he had told me the truth and relieved that his marriage was as over as mine was.

I look around the lounge and sniff. It smells lovely. I spot a Jo Malone candle. This is not the dirty, stinking hovel that Jake had drawn a picture of with his descriptions. Perhaps she had changed. Perhaps she had to in order to keep Polly. I'd felt sorry for her, a child in the middle of a nasty divorce. It had made the time Jake spent with her on his own more acceptable. I'm sure he'd said that they'd had months of mediation. That there was a big argument in court. I rustle through the papers for anything from social services but find nothing. So I continue with the divorce petition.

I do a double take. The petitioner is Veronica, not Jake. I read it again, just to be sure. The dates are the same as he said, but she is divorcing him for unreasonable behaviour. Not the other way round. My heart thumps in my chest. I read on.

The petitioner will have joint custody of the child of the family, Polly Jane, with the respondent, and have made their own arrangements. The financial aspects of this case which are lengthy and complicated, were dealt with in a separate hearing.

The petitioner states that on several occasions and on the sample occasions cited in addendum 1, 1a and 2, the respondent caused an affray when asked to leave the marital home. The police statement is appended, although no action was taken at the request of the petitioner.

What? All this is new information. He told me Veronica would stay in the house until Polly left school. What's lengthy and complicated about that? And I cannot imagine Jake causing an affray. He is very calm and controlled. I suddenly feel sick. Jake had never, ever been abusive to me. He'd never even rolled his eyes or tutted. This must be wrong. Or I've got it all wrong. People make mistakes. Veronica wasn't right for him and I am, that's why he treats me better. Well, not like he treated her. But affray? Affray is serious.

I search through the rest of the papers for the financial case and the police statement, but they are missing. I read on. One sentence jumps out at me.

On three sample occasions the respondent sent abusive messages to the petitioner. This is evidenced in phone records.

Messages. I take a deep breath. Only a second ago I was sure that Jake wasn't doing anything wrong. But those messages. I go over it again. Could I have missed them? No. No, I couldn't. Is this the next step? Is this what he's going to do if I don't keep to the agreement?

I expect fear and tears, but instead something else rises. A strength. A resilience. A determination that I won't let this happen again. I won't. He can try if he likes. *He already is,* screams my more rational self. He can try but I won't back down. I will find out what he is up to.

I skip through the rest of it. It appears to be more of the same. I take out my phone and snap the page. I can hardly believe it. She divorced him. But why would he lie?

I fold the petition and push it back in the envelope. There is nothing else in the folder referring to Jake, but I dig deeper into the cupboard and pull out a bundle of papers. I recognise his handwriting immediately.

Then a beam of car headlights stream into the lounge. I slam the drawer shut and throw myself onto the floor. My skin burns as I crawl towards the kitchen. Once in there, I jump up and hurry into the garden. I reach through the pane and lock the door. Then I grab the rock and retrieve my jumper. I hear the front door bang and I duck around the corner. Have I touched anything with my bare hands? I don't think so. It's only in that moment I realise I am still holding the bundle of letters.

I peep around the windowpane and Veronica is in the lounge. She is talking to someone I can't see. I want to wait and see if it is Jake. I want to catch them in the act. And then I wonder why I don't just walk away. How I have become entrenched in this drama. Whatever is going on here, it is something I have worked hard to keep out of my life. It's complicated enough.

On the outside I'm cool, calm, collected Kate. But on the inside my thoughts are a constant game of cat and mouse. If outrunning your own memories was an Olympic sport, I'd have won gold many times over. But, as I hide outside my husband's ex's house, I realise I might be past my best. I've read dozens of articles about family traits and about people who had no contact with their families. How they thrive and find new faux families. But that hasn't happened to me, I realise, and the constant battle has weakened me.

I guess I had hoped that the upside to it would be that any similarities to my parents would diminish. The downside is too awful to think about, but I can feel it looming ever closer. All the things I have avoided thinking about. Everything my new life was meant to finally overlay. They are all rushing back full speed. I blink them away and peer around the door again. I hold my breath and pray she doesn't see the broken window before I can make it to the front.

Suddenly they are walking towards the dining room, and they are out of sight. I run around the house and up the drive and reach my car.

CHAPTER TWELVE

I 've never worn an item of clothing two days running as an adult. My clothes are starting to feel sticky and clammy, but that isn't the first thing on my mind. I peer at Veronica's house, willing her to come out with Jake. I don't want to be right, but at least I would know.

I am not a jealous person. I tell myself I never have been, but I wonder if I have forced myself into a straitjacket of trust. I did it with Ian. I thought the best of him. I bought into the story of 'it's only because I love you' and pushed myself harder and harder to fit into the shape he wanted me to be. And now this.

It's becoming clearer by the minute that Jake's life headed off at a tangent a while ago. Tears threaten as I think about the excuses and the stress on his face. Had he faked it? I just don't know. I suddenly feel like I don't know my own husband. Our relationship had been amazing. He was loving and attentive and we agreed on most things. Now all that is smashed and I'm sitting outside his ex's house.

I desperately want to check my phone to see if he has called, but I can't. I can't because I am worried he is tracking it. My insides shiver and my hands shake at what I have just done. Is this a throwback from my bad experience with Ian, or is this really happening again? But the messages. I go over and over whether I could have missed those messages in my head, but I know I didn't. Yes, it could have been the network. However, I received other texts and messages. But the divorce. I know what he said. I know what I heard.

No, something is wrong. And this is a process of elimination. If he isn't with her, he must be somewhere else. I drive around the narrow roads around Veronica's suburban semi-detached before I park up. I scan for his car too, just in case, but it isn't there. Her car is in the drive now, and I can see the reflection of her moving around through the window.

My heart quickens as she appears in almost exactly the same place as I was standing just a few minutes ago, then opens the front door and gets in her car again. She is followed by a woman carrying a dress over her arm. I finally breathe out. The woman kisses her on both cheeks and walks away, up the road and goes into a house four doors down.

Veronica is about my height and her hair is blonder than in her Facebook photos. Jake had said she had a taste for designer bags and clothes, but she seems to be wearing Primark's best offers. I recognise the tote bag. She is very pretty. I slide down so she doesn't see me as she drives past, then I start up my car. She might be going to meet him. But it is school time so she could be going to collect Polly. After what I saw in there, it seems unlikely that she is with Jake, but I need to know for sure. And I need to know more about her so I can see the extent of his lying.

I follow her, two cars back. She's driving towards the school where I have picked Polly up, but she goes past the turning and towards an old run-down shopping centre just outside Manchester. It's a 70s concrete monstrosity that screams 'don't come near me' – with one road in and out. I slow down. There are no lovely coffee shops or designer outlets here. It backs onto a huge sink estate and as she parks up, I see that the shops have steel grilles padlocked over the windows.

She grabs her bag and locks up then grabs a black bin bag out of the back of the car and strides towards the very end unit, a shop with the shutter half down. I strain my eyes to read it. The words hardly register at first, but I make out the words 'mother and baby'. She's pregnant; she must be. That's what all the secrecy has been about.

I'm out of the car and running towards the shop. I stop just short of the window and pretend to check my phone. I can see her in the rear of the shop, her back towards me, talking to the woman behind the counter. She hands the bin bag over, and I wait for her to make a move towards the door so I can hide round the corner. But she doesn't. Instead, she watches while the woman takes off her tabard and hands it to her.

Veronica pulls it over her head and stands behind the counter. I duck back into the shadows and the woman emerges.

'So I'll be about half an hour. Thanks so much for covering for me. You're an actual star, love.'

She walks away from me, and I watch as Veronica unpacks bin bags and hangs up second-hand baby clothes. A poster in the window catches my eye. It's individual pictures of 'the team' and an appeal for baby items. There she is, smiling and looking straight into the camera. Veronica is 'volunteer interim shop manager'.

I return to my car and bring up her Facebook profile. It makes more sense; the women in the pictures are her shop colleagues. The nights out look like charity events now I study them more closely, and there is not a designer item in sight. I scroll down and down, desperately trying to find some evidence of the woman Jake described. Greedy, uncaring, spoiled. But all I see is that woman behind the counter.

I wait in the car until the woman comes back. I have to be sure. Then I will let it drop. Veronica emerges and gets into her car. I follow her to a terraced house across town which she goes in and returns with Polly, who she is kissing and hugging. I feel a twinge of jealousy, both of her as a mother and of Polly. Collette barely touched me. Certainly there were no hugs.

I follow her home. It's getting late now, and I need to get back to the hotel, but I have to be sure. I need to know he isn't with her. It seems pretty unlikely, but I have to see with my own eyes. She turns into the drive. Polly jumps out of the car and runs to the door. My heart beats hard as I wait for Daddy to open it and sweep her up in his arms, but she waits and Veronica unlocks it. It's dark in the house and then some lights come on.

I feel stupid. He isn't here. In so many ways this would have been the easiest, most obvious answer to my questions, but I am wrong. Completely wrong. I get out of the car and walk along the pavement. I'm on the drive and I am almost in tears. I have a powerful urge to apologise to Veronica, but that would only make all this worse. Instead, I crouch behind a bush and angle myself at the window.

How do I know how to do this? How do I know how to follow someone? How do I know how to smash a window safely? How have I perfected the art of concealment? I learned from the best. There were many, many nights when all four of us were coaxed from our beds. Coats on, mittens if it was winter, and hats. She would tell us we were going on an adventure, but after the first time I knew exactly what it was. And I knew my role. It was recon. It was a mission. It was part of the battle manoeuvres in our parents' marriage.

She would hurry us down dark roads and across pathways until we arrived at the house in question. She would sit us backs-to-the-wall outside the house under the window or against the garden fence. Then she would carefully position herself in the darkness at an angle to the house and watch. Her face would be set into a determined frown, and she would shush us and tell us to keep still if we moved.

It would play out before us. People coming in and out. Her head following them and her leaning forward to get a better look. Them laughing and lots of *come in, come ins* while we blinked into the darkness. My brothers often fell asleep against each other, one leaning against the other and their breath clouding the air. I never fell asleep because I was in charge. Or that's how it felt. I was in charge of them. For her. She had other, more important things to take care of and I could not sleep.

Or play. I couldn't skip along carefree because I had to think about my brothers.

'You'll look after them, now, won't you, Cathy? No running up and down stairs. No running the bath. And get them some sandwiches for dinner. And pop.'

She would leave me in charge in the school holidays and I was never off duty. In the darkness outside those houses, I felt like I had to keep them quiet. Keep them warm. As a consequence, they would turn to me if they cut their knee, or if there was an argument. She was the last resort, because she was always looking for something. A job. Some dodgy cigarettes. Money off vouchers. Our father.

I would turn my head and peer into what were often scenes of family bliss. These were not the homes of the people who were sneaking around having affairs with my father. They were having meals together and watching TV and laughing. They were happy, in stark contrast to what was happening in our house.

On the odd occasion she lost it and confronted someone. She would tell us to stand up; four wobbly children, chilled to the bone, standing in a line.

'Well if you want him so much, have these as well.'

At the time I worried about the here and now. Would we have to go and live with this woman? In this house? What about my things? My bedroom? Later, it started to feel like I was something to barter with. A counter in the game of who had stolen my father, whose bed was he in and, ultimately, if they wanted to keep him, they would keep us too. I should have known how it would all play out then. But I was a child. It was so obvious that she had it wrong on most occasions and, eventually, around the age of twelve I refused to go.

Instead, I would lie in bed and recall all the warmth and closeness of the families she was watching and, of course, suspecting. It's only today that I realise what it was all about. She was searching for my father, but she didn't know where to start. She was trying everything and everywhere. We sat outside of dozens of houses watching. She had a little notebook that she would write in afterwards and shove back into her handbag. I'd see a glint of steel as she slammed the frame bag shut.

Occasionally she would explain.

'It's to keep me safe.' She would lean in. 'Keep us safe. You never know what could happen out there.' Her arm would swoop dramatically towards the window in general and I never questioned it back then. And on the occasions she was found out, when some woman's husband came around and told Dad she had been camped out in their garden and what the accusations were, he was angry. He would shout at her, and she would scream at him, 'Well, if you weren't such a bastard I wouldn't have to, would I?'

It just made her look more disturbed. More unbalanced. More mad. Their faces asked the question. What sort of woman drags her kids out at night? What sort of woman spies on her husband? All eyes on her.

Then the next day he would be back. In her bed. Eating at our table. The laughs and the jokes and the leg-touching. We would go on a road-trip holiday, and it would all be fine. For a while. Until we felt her pulling us out of bed again in the middle of the night.

Now I am there. In the suspect's garden, hunting down my husband. But I don't have a notebook or anything to keep me safe, because there is only me. I crane my neck and watch Polly and Veronica chase through the house. She catches her and Polly is laughing hard. She never does that with Jake or me. Jake's words echo through me.

'She's not a good person. Not a good mother.'

That's not what this looks like at all. She is brushing Polly's hair and they are chattering away. No TV needed to distract Polly like Jake does while he works. I watch Veronica's fingers work as she plaits Polly's hair and then she turns her round to face her and kisses her nose. Polly's arms are round her neck, and I catch a glimpse of an expression on Veronica's face that I recognise from the photograph on Facebook. The one I thought Jake had taken. It's pure love. Love for her daughter. Care and attention for the person who means the most in the world to her.

Then all of a sudden, she realises. She hurries from the kitchen, checking around the room to see if anything is missing. Clutching at herself in fear. Telling Polly to go upstairs and stay there. Grabbing her phone and nodding into it.

They will be here soon. The police. They will inevitably look around and see nothing has gone. Except the letters, but I doubt she will even notice. They might quiz her over why someone would do this and draw up a list of suspects. Would I be on it? No, I wouldn't. Because like everyone else, Veronica is more or less unaware of me.

I now know I am wasting my time here. It's a relief, although I feel ashamed of what I have done. I creep back to my car and look back at their home. The place where Jake used to live with them. I was completely wrong. He's not in their life anymore. They don't need him. That much is clear.

I drive away and start the journey back over the moors. I stop at a supermarket and load up my basket with brand-new underwear and a couple of outfits to see me through. I had been pretty sure that Veronica had something to do with this, but I am not so sure now. What I do know is that Jake lied about her too.

CHAPTER THIRTEEN

I wake up in a hot fever. Life isn't what I thought it was. I sit up in the soft bed and flick the TV on. Someone is talking about Christmas, and I shudder. Nothing is right. I've been living a lie. Holding everything in and making sure there are no clues to my turmoil, while Jake has pretty much constructed an alternative past for himself.

Is that what people do? Show their best side. I glance at the bundle of letters on the desk. I have a feeling that if I didn't already think he was being dishonest, those letters would seal the deal. I get out of bed and pad over to retrieve them. The paper is faded and brittle – it looks like one of the notepads Collette would write down all the particulars of her rivals. The letters are curled into a tube and secured with an elastic band. It snaps as soon as I pull at it, making me jump.

I start to read. I am expecting some degree of hurt as I read what my husband has written to another woman. Love letters. Declarations of their hope for the future. But it soon becomes clear that these are not love letters. They are threats.

... and if you don't, I'll tell everyone. Think about it.

I've got recordings. I've got everything. You give it to me now, or I'll send it to your parents...

It is Jake's handwriting, of that I am sure, but I could never imagine Jake saying these words to anyone. It just gets worse.

...no one will believe you. Pretty and dim. Pretty dim. That's you, Vee. Who would believe you over me? And I'll make sure you never see Polly again; I'll get full custody...

I am shocked. Polly? What an awful thing to say. All the letters are about what he will do to Veronica. Vague threats of how he will send some recordings to people if she doesn't do what he says. I skim read them, but I can't for the life of me see what she is supposed to do.

I am seeing now why he kept me away from Veronica. And Polly. He didn't really want me to be alone with her. The only time he allowed it was in an emergency, and then he would phone me and keep me talking. It was almost as if he didn't want Polly to tell me something. I'm starting to feel sorry for them. Guilt bites at me as I think about the window and how scared she must have been when she found out someone had broken into her home.

I promise myself that once I have found out what Jake is up to, I will apologise. Explain. I will face the consequences, but right now I need to keep going.

It's time to check my phone. He must have called by now. Maybe the police will have tried to call. I get dressed, leave the hotel and walk along to the top of the road and into the town centre. I buy a coffee and sit on a wall beside an oak tree. I pull out the phone and the battery and assemble it. I'm hot and shaky and the phone starts up.

There are a series of beeps as messages start to hurtle through. I scroll up and down. My bank. The DVLA. A reminder about my boiler service. Fifteen messages from Paula. One from Pam. I bring up the call register. Again, multiple calls from Paula and thirty-three calls from Clint. To be fair, some of them were from just after I stormed out.

There are no calls or messages from Jake. Nothing at all. I panic. What if he's in hospital? What if he's been in an accident and I've ransacked his ex's house? But if he had, someone would have called me. I'm his contact in his passport and they'd know I lived with him from the electoral register. I don't want to consider the other option. That he doesn't care. That he hasn't even noticed. That he's not contacting me because of that fucking agreement.

No, he's not dead in a ditch at all. I'm just making excuses for him. I switch on my burner phone. I am Donna McBride now, and I look up his Facebook account. Then I look at WhatsApp on my phone. It says he is online. Of course he is. He's online, but he's not messaging me.

The anger rises but now is not the time for it. I look at Paula's messages. At least she has missed me, even if it is because I am her echo chamber.

> Where are you, mate? Let me know you are OK?

Then later:

> Give me a call. Went round to yours but no one in. Have you gone on holiday? You never mentioned it.

She knows full well I haven't gone on holiday. I hate holidays. I almost believe she cares until I read the next message. But at least I know Jake's still not back.

> I need to talk to you. About John. Honestly, Kate,
> I never do this to you. I'm always there for you.

There are more messages, but I don't read them. Instead, I listen to my voicemail – Clint has left loads, each one more panicked, asking me to ring him. The final one makes me stand and hurry back to my car.

'Kate. If you hear this, please call me. Your office has been broken into. Someone has tried to get into your laptop. Call me back.'

In half an hour I am parking up outside Resner Platt. I look up to my floor and wish I didn't have to do this. Clint sounded serious and official and none of this sounds good. I have worked so hard to get here. To get a job like this in a respected company.

And it was all completely against the odds. Even before Collette left, my love of school and lessons faded away into the issues of childcare and lunches as my brothers' care transferred to me. I was overwhelmed by making sure everyone had everything they needed.

'Proper little mother, you!' she would say as she took a break from writing in her notebook or recovering from a hangover. But I wasn't; I was a child. I loved school. I loved the attention I got when my work was good. I tried my hardest at everything, but more often than not, I was late or had to leave early. Someone was sick, and I had to stay in and look after them while she 'went on an errand'.

I listen to the message again. Clint's office voice and the background noise. The chatter of my colleagues. I blink into the midday sun and there it is, the scene I wanted to push down, deep, deep down. The three boys in bunk beds. All sleeping in the same room even as they approached teenage years.

I knew what would happen. After she left, Grandma came round with a social worker. She couldn't take us. She didn't want to. She and Granddad knew that Mum or Dad could turn up at any moment and their lives would be disrupted for nothing. It had happened before. They had staged an intervention only to be rejected for years. Not allowed to see us. I understood but it hurt. And I wondered what would happen to us.

It was clear we couldn't live in the house. It wasn't allowed, even though I'd been looking after them single-handedly for years. Even though they turned to me for plasters and breakfast. They missed Mum and Dad, which made it all the worse for me.

I think back. Did I miss them? The benefit of hindsight has clouded my feelings, but yes. Yes, I missed them both. In fact, I didn't think they had left. Dad had been missing for days, sometimes weeks, before. I just expected him to roll back in until the next time, and every day I expected Collette to return. I thought she'd gone to find him. An icy shiver runs through me when I think about what happened.

I was torn between the inevitable of being taken somewhere with my brothers and my stand-in mothering continuing, or a life. A life and a job. A way to break free from everything – although back then I didn't have a sense of what that was. All I knew was that snippets of my life had been snatched away from me and replaced with beans on toast and pushing small feet into too-small shoes.

I loved my brothers. There had never been a time when they hadn't been around. But I was scared. I knew when social services turned up, I was on the brink of becoming a full-time mum or going into care. The latter were words that my friends whispered to explain all kinds of bad behaviour.

'She's in care.'

That was why someone had stolen an eyeliner from Boots or slept with their older boyfriend. Adults would nod in agreement, confirming my belief that without parents around things went bad. I hadn't seen that they were already bad.

I knew that one of my friends had a job. She'd told me they were taking on office juniors. I had just turned sixteen and taken my exams even through what had happened. I still believed that I could succeed. I wanted a job. I wanted to work. I wanted a life. So, I reached to the back of the kitchen cupboard and pulled out Collette's money tin. It occurred to me it was strange she hadn't taken it, and I almost told an adult.

But even then, somewhere inside me, I knew I would need it. I knew that, at some point, this would all blow up and nothing would be the same anymore. So I took the money, and I pushed most of my clothes into a carrier bag. I left my dolls and my books and even my honeysuckle perfume that Collette bought me for my birthday. I thought I would be back. I somehow thought that it would all still be there, frozen in time and waiting for me.

I crept out in the middle of the night. I knew what the next day held. Grandma had stayed over until social services returned and took us to a 'safe place'. The fact that they were not alone eased my exit, but I knew what it meant, really. I knew they would go without me. And me without them. I went into the tiny room they shared and watched them from the door. Flynn sleeping across Patrick, and Michael snoring through his nose and twitching. I thought I would see them again. I thought I would go back when I had made my fortune like some fucked up Dick Whittington and rescue them. But that's not how I saw them again. No, not at all.

My friend got me the office junior job. I lied and said I was seventeen. She had too. Her parents let me stay with them in the spare bedroom – I told them I lived across town, and it was easier for work. I know now that I dodged a bullet. I could have been homeless. I could have had nowhere at all to go. I was lucky in one way, but not in another because I was haunted.

As the weeks and months went by, the guilt set in. With some distance I realised what had happened. I'd left my brothers. I would have nightmares about them crying when they realised I had gone. Shouting after me. *Cathy. Where are you, Cathy?* Waking up and I wasn't there. I realised that I had done exactly what *they* had done. What *she* had done. I'd walked away.

That she was part of me. Her DNA inside me. The traits I might have in common with her. As I moved jobs, I took HR personality tests. I always excelled because I was driven by what would happen if I didn't. What I would have to go back to. But every time, it brought up imaginings of what I shared with her. It was bad enough that she'd gone, but what happened after that changed my life.

I push it away. This is not the time. I can't afford to stand so close to it right now. I switch my phone off and take out the battery again. Why hadn't he called? Did he really not care? Or was he with another woman? I was clearly wrong about Veronica, but it could be someone else.

Or maybe he just didn't care? People say they don't care, but there is always a fragment of it left inside. Can you love someone and hate them at the same time? If he does have someone else and he is doing this on purpose, then it is just cruel. And that's the way this is looking.

I said I will wait, and I will. I told myself I will find out what's going on. If Jake can't be honest with me, then I am going to have to take matters into my own hands. But one thing is certain; I cannot lose my job. Otherwise, the pain I went through when I deserted my brothers will be all for nothing.

CHAPTER FOURTEEN

I stand in reception and take a deep breath. My office has been broken into. Who would want to do such a thing? I glance up at the security cameras. They were all over the building; surely they would see who it was? I wait for the lift. I watch the light flit across the buttons and wonder what kind of Clint I will see today. Drunk Clint. Hungover Clint. Sober Clint. Over friendly, touchy Clint.

It's like an epiphany when I finally realise I've been putting up with his behaviour for years. I could get another job in another agency. But I've been clinging on to this because it's... what? Safe? Dependable? As the door pings I see sixteen-year-old me running through a field of corn, free as a bird. Except for the guilt. A voice deep inside me tells me again that everything has its price, even freedom.

I can see into my office from the doorway. All the side offices are partitioned off from the big open-plan office with half-glass panels and as I walk through, I look up at the cameras. If someone had been here, they would have picked them up. I stride past Pam and the blue screens, and Clint turns and spots me. He picks up his phone, says something and then stands outside his office door.

'Kate, thanks for coming.'

He waves me into my office. I glance at the lock, which is intact. Drawers are in disarray and my laptop lid is open when I left it closed. I turn to face him. He waits for me to say something, but I don't. I stare at him. He shifts from foot to foot and looks behind him at Alex Volt, our manager, who strides through the office.

'Clint.' He nods at him. 'Kate, thanks for coming in when you are on sick leave. Clint tells me your office was broken into. Someone has been looking in the drawers for something and the laptop has been tampered with.'

I look around and wait for more. But both men stare at me.

'Okay. So... I wasn't here. I'm not sure...'

Clint rolls his eyes. 'The thing is, Kate, your exit was rather... unbalanced. You rushed off and we...' he points between himself and Alex, 'we just wanted to check that everything was okay.'

I nod. Is everything okay? No, it isn't, but not in the way he means. Under normal circumstances I would say as little as possible in case I put myself in the firing line, but I feel myself gearing up for something else. Something completely different.

'So, what did the police say?'

Clint smirks. 'We didn't call the police. Nothing was missing.'

I walk around my desk. There are papers on the floor. Nothing is missing.

'When did it happen? Obviously not in office hours? So whose pass was used out of hours?'

Clint blinks at me. Alex looks at him.

'Well, I haven't...'

I look up at the cameras. 'So have you looked at the footage?'

They look at each other. It's too much for me. I step closer to them.

'Why am I here? Do you think it's me who has done this?'

Clint reddens. Alex's eyes narrow.

'Clint suggested you might know who would be interested in whatever was here. Or you might have forgotten something.'

'So you think I have broken into my own office?' They stare at me. 'Okay, okay, if you won't call the police, I will. There needs to be a proper investigation, not just what Clint thinks.' I fold my arms.

Clint looks out at the office. 'The thing is, Kate, you have been acting strangely. All that the other day and you've been a bit distant. And what you said when you stormed out. Well...' He shrugs dramatically at Alex. 'It was quite disturbing.'

And there it is. He's playing the 'she's mad' card. The unbalanced harpy. I'm surprised he doesn't ask me if it's my time of the month – it's in his range because he's done it before.

Alex frowns and looks at his watch. 'Okay, let's sort this out. Kate, have you been here since you left the other day? Or do you know who has?'

'No, I haven't been here. I've been on a... mini break. In Huddersfield. I'm stressed because of him. I needed to get away.'

Clint feigns injury. 'Oh come on, we both know it was you. You need help.'

I sigh. 'Okay, let's look at the footage. Clint, you have the code, let's have a look.'

Alex nods. 'Yes, that should clear it up. Let's look.'

Clint blushes crimson. 'I erm... I haven't really kept it up to date... I mean, we don't really need it on this floor. People find it intrusive.'

I perch on the edge of my desk. 'So let me get this right, you got me in here when I'm on sick leave to accuse me of breaking into my own office, and you haven't even got the CCTV footage for that time period. Is that right?'

Alex looks impressed. Clint is in defensive mode. Hands in pockets, chin up.

'People don't like being filmed. Privacy issues. It's not right.'

I pause. I know full well why he turned off those cameras. It would be so easy to walk out of here and never come back, but before I do, I will tell the truth. I will make sure everyone knows where they are in this scenario.

I jump off the desk and hurry through to Clint's office. They stare after me. I kick open the door and pull the drawers open. I drag out some files and hear the familiar clink of bottles. I pull them out, one after another, and line them up on the desk just in time for Clint to arrive with Alex behind him.

'Ta-da!' I stand with my hands on my hips. 'Is this why you don't want the CCTV on? And is this why you were drunk at the presentation?'

Alex turns to face him. 'Clint...' He moves closer to me.

'You planted them there.' He turns to Alex. 'She wants my job. She planted those bottles. She knew where to find them.'

'I didn't. And what about the other day? Ask anyone out there, they were all there when he called me boring. When he heckled my presentation. Some were filming it.'

Clint launches into a very detailed explanation of how he couldn't have been drunk and if he was, it was because of medication he was on. I suddenly realise what had happened. He had ransacked my office. He had made it look like I had gone crazy. He wanted me out of the way.

I look at them both.

'No one used my pass. No one hacked my laptop. No one has gone through my files. There was no footage, and you didn't call the police. Yet you wanted me to come all the way here so you could abuse me and accuse me.' I wait for them to speak, but they stand there in silence. 'Great. Just brilliant. You'll be hearing from my solicitor.'

Alex catches my arm as I try to leave. I freeze. I catch the panic in his eyes as he realises what he has done and lets me go. I look around. Everyone in the office has stopped work and turned to look. Several people are filming on their phones. I shake my head and take a step away. He apologises.

'Kate, I'm so sorry. I just don't want you to–'

I laugh. 'Get the wrong idea? It's a bit late for that.'

Clint is sullen in the background, probably thinking of a way to wriggle out of this. Alex continues.

'We can work something out.'

But I am already on my way out of the office, leaving the blue and the grey and heading towards something else that will be much, much brighter. I wait in reception until I have caught my breath. I've been playing a stupid cat-and-mouse game with Clint for years. I'd try to avoid being better at the job than he was, and his awful throwaway comments. He'd up the game every time I excelled and threatened to get a promotion. I marvel I hadn't said anything. That I'd just sat there and taken it.

But that's been my modus operandi. *That's just Kate.*

Even so, I hope I haven't lost my job. I think about the series of steps on my career ladder, each more difficult than the last, and what this would mean for our finances? Our? I remember in that moment that Jake hasn't even tried to contact me. No text. No call. Nothing. I almost ask at reception if he has been here to see me at work, but why would he? He would call.

Paula's message said she had been to the house, but he wasn't there. And I wasn't there. Had he been back at all?

I jump into my car and drive to Lynton Grove. It seems strange, even after a couple of days. Like I don't belong there. I wait at the traffic lights and glance at my phone, a bitter reminder of what started all this in the first place. I turn the corner and his car is not there. But he might be. It wasn't there the other day, after the party. I brake too fast and hurtle forward. Then I remember this isn't my car. No, it's a tacky rental that he won't recognise. I drive a little closer.

So he's not home, and he hasn't tried to contact me. I go over what we said. I try to think if I've given him any hint that I might go away. Maybe he thinks I went to the coast on my own? Or that I need some space? Or maybe he just doesn't fucking care.

We've been together nearly five years and we have hardly had a disagreement. I'd always thought it was because we laid down the ground rules before we moved in together, but it was more than that. He was kind and attentive. There have been times on birthdays and anniversaries that I got upset and he asked me what happened. It took me two years to even tell him about my childhood, let alone what happened ten years ago.

He always listened and asked all the right questions. He would hug me and tell me I could tell him anything. And I did. I told him everything. He is the only person who knows what happened and what I had to go through. It only makes it more painful. I pull the battery and my phone out of my bag and assemble it. The screen lights up and there is a beep of a message. But it's from Pam asking me if I'm okay.

I scroll down but there is nothing at all from Jake. I read the last messages he sent me and try to understand what is happening. All the lies. All the deceit. I thought we were so close. I bring up a picture of us together, him looking at me as I laugh into the camera. Us in Scotland two years ago when we went to Tim's wedding. We look happy. I never imagined in a million years that I would be stalking my own husband.

I see a sudden movement and duck down. I peek over the dashboard and our neighbour, Sam Jarrod, is outside our home. I don't want him to see me here and tell Jake. My heart beats fast as the seconds tick by and I wait for him to appear at the window above my hiding place. But he doesn't. I wait and wait and finally look up. He has gone.

I wait another fifteen minutes and then start the engine. I desperately want to turn the key in my own front door, step inside and have this out with him. Or just be in my own home.

But I won't. Not yet. I'll find out more. I'll find out where he is and what he is up to. I need to eat, change, calm down a little and think about what I have to do next.

CHAPTER FIFTEEN

I'd searched for her. Once I'd settled in a proper job and moved into a flat share, I tried to get in touch with Grandma. I wanted to make sure my brothers were okay. I thought about them every day. I rang first, but it rang out, so I went round. They had moved out. One of the neighbours told me they had gone into sheltered accommodation somewhere but didn't have a forwarding address.

It had only been two years since I left. I hadn't even considered that other people would leave too. I'd clung to the fact that it would all be the same. I rushed around to our old house. It had been sold, of course. New people were sitting in our lounge. New children playing. New curtains in my old bedroom. I wondered what had happened to my dolls and my honeysuckle perfume.

Until that day I had a background. A family. Stuff. Suddenly I had very little. I rang social services, but they wouldn't tell me where my brothers were. It was a dead end. There was no social networking like Facebook. Nowhere to look and plenty of places to hide. But I knew where Collette hung out. I knew the places she went because I'd listened to her and her friends talk about them. I knew she wouldn't have left town because I knew why she had left us. To look for him.

I went to a few of the bars she hung out at. I started to realise that I knew nothing about her, really. She never spoke about her parents, and she only alluded to the fact that she was Irish. So I asked around. Did anyone know Collette Dooley? Collette Palmer? Had anyone seen her?

It turned out they had. Plenty of people in the Frog and Jockey knew her. She came and went. Sometimes it would be weeks, but she always came back. And in another bar, The Grapes, I found Lizzy Bennett. Lizzy was one of Collette's Friday night friends. She would come round to our house and drink booze with Mum and other women. She didn't recognise me immediately. I'd tapped her on the shoulder.

'Lizzy?'

She'd half turned. 'Who wants to know?'

'It's me, Kate. Cathy? Collette's daughter.'

She'd stared at me, wide-eyed. 'Bloody hell. We all thought you were dead. Police were out looking for you, lady.'

I smiled to myself at my success. They hadn't found me though, had they? That was swiftly followed by surprise that anyone had cared.

'I'm looking for her. Collette. Is she around?'

She'd laughed loudly and shook her bottle-blonde curls. 'You'll be lucky. She's all over the place. What do you want her for, anyway?'

It was hard to believe she had asked me that question. She was my mother. I missed her. It made me feel awkward and small in this adult world where no one seemed to care about anyone else. Where the fact that I wanted to see my mother was viewed as suspicious.

'I just wanted to make sure she was all right. I thought she might have gone back to Ireland.'

Lizzy frowned and slugged back her vodka and Coke. 'Ireland? Why would she go there?'

I nodded and smiled. This I was sure of. 'She's Irish, isn't she? You know, my brothers' names. Her name. She told us.'

Lizzy started to laugh. Deep belly laughs. Roaring until the whole pub looked around at us.

'Irish? Jesus Christ, love. I'm more Irish than she is. She was born in Bolton. Her mam and dad had a pie shop. She came over here when she had a bit of bother. Then she met Harry. Your da.' She stopped laughing and looked at me to see if I reacted. 'She's not fucking Irish, love. You haven't seen him, have you? Harry?'

I stared at her. 'You know she left me, don't you? Us. You do know that?'

'I do. But it was for the best. All all right, aren't you?'

I wasn't all right, but this seemed to be the way things were. No one really cared that Collette had left her kids. I wondered if she did. If she ever wondered what I was doing or how I was? I went back to that bar as often as I could for over a year. I went to all the places I thought she might be, but she was never around. She had been, or might be later, or she was last week. But she never turned up when I was around.

That was twelve years ago, and I wish I had carried on. I might have been able to change things. But I didn't. It's this that drives me on now. I can't give up. I need to know, and I will find out. I had a plan then and I have one now.

As I drive back across the moorland roads, I wonder why I didn't just get a hotel in town. Only a few days ago I was brittle with suspicion that Jake was fucking his ex. Now I am bold with the bravado of having put Clint in his place. And mortified that I broke into Veronica's house. I have the radio on loud and David Coverdale is leading Whitesnake into a rousing chorus of 'Here I Go Again'. It reminds me of Dad. He used to hum it as he left with his bin bag over his shoulder after a particularly bad row.

The sarcasm was lost on me then, but now I have to smile. And sometimes cry.

Today I am not crying. I am going to speak to Jake. I am going to the one place I know he will be. His office. He's spent so much time there recently that he will inevitably be there now. And if he isn't, I'll talk to Dave Lord, his director. It occurs to me that I could phone ahead, but why should I? I've always kept out of Jake's business, worried that it will look clingy. And it might have done before, but now I have every right to know.

I keep that in mind as my legs shake when I get out of the car outside his office. His car isn't there and I am beginning to wonder if I have imagined him. I pull out my phone and put it together. He will know I am here in a minute so here is the ideal place to check – even if he isn't here someone will tell him I have been. It flashes into life, and I check my messages. Nothing from Jake. Two from Paula.

> Kate, I'm worried. Call me. Where are you, mate?

I look at Jake's office window. The light is on. Good. I walk across the gravel car park and arrive in reception. The woman behind the desk smiles.

'Can I help you, madam?'

I smile too. A tight, nervous smile. 'Yes. May I see Jake Clayton, please?'

'Are you a client of Mr Clayton only he's–'

I interrupt. 'Look, if Ja… Mr Clayton isn't available, I'd like to see Dave Lord. Tell him it's Kate. Jake's wife.'

She nods and goes into the back office, leaving me wondering why she didn't just ring Jake or Dave. I watch as she talks to another woman, and they both look at me. She picks up an internal phone and returns.

'Mr Lord will see you. Follow me.'

Her whole demeanour has changed, and she is guarded. I

follow her up some steps and she knocks on a door. Dave gets up and comes towards me. He hugs me tightly then lets me go.

'Kate, it's not bad news, is it?'

I stare at him. 'I don't know what you mean. I came to–'

He interrupts. 'It was all so sudden. None of us knew what had happened. One minute everything was fine, we were all working on the enormous project. Then... nothing.' He grabs my hand. 'Was it pressure of work, because if it was...'

I shake my head. 'Slow down. Let's start from the beginning. I'm here to see Jake.'

He sits down hard. 'Jake? When did you last see him? Is he okay?'

'A couple of days ago and he was fine then, but I need to speak to him. We've had a bit of a...' I was going to say row, but that doesn't seem enough. Trouble? No. Rift? 'Upset.'

He is silent. He stares at me. He is thinking how to tell me something.

'The thing is, Kate, and I don't really know how to tell you this. He left Jenkins Stuart three months ago. He just walked out one day and never came back. No goodbye. No discussion. I assumed he was ill. I tried to phone. We all did, but he never answered.' He breathes out heavily. 'Thank goodness you are here, though, I thought you'd come to tell me he was...'

'Dead?'

I almost laugh as I say it. Three months. He hasn't been to work for three months. Where was he going every morning then? Where was he when he said he was working late? I scan my memory for the times he had chatted about the office and even Dave. He'd even mentioned him last week in some story about going to a bar after work.

Dave sighed. 'We were worried. We thought he might be depressed or ill or something. It didn't make sense.'

I sit down heavily. 'Tell me about it. None of this makes sense. He never told me, Dave. He'd been going to work every day.'

Alarm bells ring in my mind. Had I got it wrong? Was there something that I had missed? In my jealousy had I missed the truth? Dave continues.

'Has he seen a doctor? I mean, and I don't know how to say this, but he isn't suicidal, is he?'

I gasp. Suicidal? Is that it? Is it? Oh my God.

'He was going to work every single day. Coming home later on, sometimes saying he was working overtime. How was he when he was here?'

Dave shrugs. 'Just normal. Fine, work was excellent. He was always on time and never left until he was finished. Model employee, until he never turned up again. We considered calling the police, but he's a grown man. We knew if something had happened you would let us know.'

I consider telling him he had been troubled the other night. That he hadn't come home. But I need to think. I need to go over the possibilities. I stand to leave.

'Yes, I would have.'

Dave stands and goes over to a cupboard. 'He might have just got another job. But it seems strange.'

He's right. He might have just got another job. But why didn't he tell me, and why did he pretend he'd been out with his Jenkins colleagues on the night of the party?

He pulls out a black holdall and hands it to me. 'This was in his office. I didn't look inside, looked like personal stuff when I opened it to put his jacket in.'

I take it from him. 'Thanks. Sorry to have made this worse. I'll let you know what happens.'

He nods and walks me to the door. The receptionists scatter and I want to tell them it's okay, he's not dead, even if I do feel like I have just collected his personal effects. But I have a different concern now. As well as questioning my judgement about Veronica and the possibility that something is wrong with Jake, I am wondering how he has been living for these past three months. We contribute equally to the bills and the mortgage. He hasn't missed a beat. How the hell has he done that without a salary?

I throw the holdall in the car. Under normal circumstances I would go through it for clues, but I have a more urgent mission. Jake and I have four joint accounts. The bills account, which I check every day. The 'love fund' for special anniversary and birthday treats. The holiday fund for, well, holidays, and another account where we do our serious saving. I have a record of the balances on my phone. I check them intermittently, maybe every quarter. The bills account is fine. I checked it a couple of days ago on my phone. The others are with a different bank. We looked at interest rates and chose carefully. I never set them up on my phone or on my laptop because they were just for putting money in. The only way I can check them is by going to the HSBC in town and using the cards I stored carefully in my purse.

In ten minutes I am standing on the high street outside the bank, my hand shaking as I push the first card into the cashpoint machine.

CHAPTER SIXTEEN

I push the first card in. It's the one for the Love Fund. I mentally check the balance and I know it would be a couple of thousand pounds. I am hot as I punch in the pin. The balance flashes up and I breathe out. It's correct. I move on to the holiday account and that is also correct. Then the savings account.

The number displays and I blink at it. We had seventeen thousand pounds saved. Jake wanted an orangery, and we have been saving hard. I mentally check that I am right then check the display. Twelve thousand and twenty-five pounds and eighty-four pence.

I put out a hand to steady myself. Bile rises in my throat. He's withdrawn thousands. He doesn't even have a card on that account. I gather my senses and take a printout of the balance. Then I go inside the bank and wait in the queue for the counter service.

My mind races over the scenarios. Has he taken my card? He can't have, because I have them all in my possession. Where has that money gone? Obviously into his account, because he still transferred the money to me for the bills. I try to remember if he seemed flustered or upset or... anything. He's been distracted and absent, but he never once mentioned money. Not when I bought the new dresses and bag for the party. Not at all.

Am I so unapproachable? Am I so distant from him that he can't tell me he is in trouble. That he has left his job and had to take money from our savings to keep up a pretence? He must have been paying for petrol and lunches to do whatever he was doing during the day. And evenings. Maybe he has another job, but I can't get past him saying he went to Rudy's with the Jenkins crew.

I move up the queue. I am impatient and I wonder again why I booked into a hotel in Huddersfield. Why didn't I just book into a hotel in town? But I already know the answer. I needed to get away. I needed to have some space to work out what is going on. And now I have I don't like it.

It's my turn. I smile at the cashier. 'Hi there. I wondered if I could have a printout of this account, please? Last three months, if possible. It's in joint names with one card. Have you issued another card recently?'

She clicks the keyboard. 'No. Just the one card.'

The printer whirrs and she passes me an A4 paper with the transactions on. I study it. I made some deposits at the bank. And there are some withdrawals. I point to them. She stares at me through the Perspex. I feel stupid not knowing what is going on in my own bank accounts. 'How were these withdrawals made?'

She fixes a smile. 'May I see some ID, please?'

I pass my passport through the till.

She takes it and studies it.

'It's my husband. The other person on the account.'

Her eyebrows raise and she leans in. 'Oh. I see. Well, as you can see, they are mostly in five-hundred-pound amounts and were withdrawn by card.'

I nod. I have had my card all the time. I've never left it lying around. And no other cards have been issued. It doesn't make sense. I sigh.

'Is there any way I can change the account to two signatures?'

She shakes her head. 'You would both need to be present to do that.'

I smile and look again at the A4 sheet. 'Thank you. Can I query those withdrawals, please? I just don't see how...'

I circle the transactions. I draw big circles around them. I know it's Jake but I need to know how. Where. Why. She takes the sheet from me.

'Do you think they are fraudulent? Someone may have used your card? Only there are quite a few transactions here. And they are made on dates quite far apart?'

I think. Is it fraud if it's a joint account? Maybe he just couldn't tell me. I suddenly feel a deep guilt. My own husband couldn't tell me. A million scenarios cascade through my mind. A man in the queue behind me sighs heavily. This is not the place. I need to think.

'No, no. Look, I'll have a think, and I'll call if my husband doesn't remember either. Thank you. That's all for now.'

Back in the car I look at the sheet again. I try to think if the dates are significant, but they aren't. It strikes me he would have had plenty of money in his own current account. He barely spends anything. What did he want the money for? None of the dates make sense. They aren't even weekly, just random. I sit in the town centre car park surrounded by shoppers and workers, and I start to cry.

It's a mixture of frustration and sadness. Frustration that I don't know what is going on. And sadness that my lovely husband could do this. It feels like I am missing something big. That he may have been trying to tell me something but couldn't. The phone call the other night that he took somewhere else. His mood changes.

I pull his holdall from the back seat and open the zip. I pull out a T-shirt. It's the spare that he took to work in case they went out to eat afterwards. The burgundy one I bought him for his birthday. He'd opened it and kissed me hard. Jake loved presents. He loved fuss and birthdays and any kind of celebration. Jake loved date nights. He loved this T-shirt. I thought he loved me, but right at this moment, I am not sure.

Is it me? Is it? Or has something else happened. Something that made him leave his job and need extra money? My mind whirrs into overdrive. What if he's in trouble? Or what if he really has another woman? Not Veronica. No. Someone else. Someone younger and prettier. Someone exciting. I hold the T-shirt up to my cheek. I can still smell him. The musky scent I am so used to.

I reach into the bag. Deodorant. A mini bottle of aftershave from a Christmas present. A pair of socks and an Ian Rankin novel that had got a bit wet at some point. I reach in further. Petrol receipts and slips from the gym he goes to with times and dates stamped on them. All stopping when he walked out of his job. And right at the bottom, another phone.

I pull it out and press at the button on the side. It flashes into life and shows twenty-three per cent battery. I scroll through as messages beep their arrival. One after another, and I can't keep up. There is only one number, and it's marked N. Just N. All the texts are from this number and I hurry to read them.

They are all times and dates. A few of them tell him to 'bring the money'. Only one is more detailed.

> Don't even think about telling anyone. Or you know what happens.

Oh my God. He's been living a double life. He's been under all this pressure, and he couldn't tell me. And Jake does not cope well with pressure. In fact, it was work pressure that made us have our only row. It was just after we got married, and he'd been working on a project for months. I was still in the first flushes of honeymoon home making and I was over-invested in curtains and blinds.

I'd asked his opinion a couple of times and he had just nodded.

'It's fine, Kate. You do what you think.'

I didn't get the hint. I kept on and on about it, and I could see the pulse in his temple throb. I'd never seen him really angry before. He didn't get angry. That was one of the reasons I agreed to marry him. He was so calm and patient and, well, like me. We appeared to be on the same wavelength.

But that day he became quiet and withdrawn. His cheeks flushed and his eyes narrowed. I hadn't realised what was happening.

'I like the wooden blinds. What do you think? Or would that be too cold in winter?'

Deep down I was disappointed at how little he had contributed to the interior design. On one hand, I had a blank canvas and a free rein; on the other I had wanted us both to be involved. I tut at myself now. I was doing exactly what I agreed not to do in the agreement we made. I was pushing him. But it was a lot of money to spend, and I wanted him to make the decision with me. I must have mentioned it twenty times before he finally faced me.

'Do what you like, Kate. Seriously, it doesn't matter.'

He was staring at me. I felt instantly uncomfortable.

'Of course it matters. It's *our* home. We should...'

He leaned forward on his leather work chair at his temporary workstation. He was calm at first. 'Look, I'm trying to get this finished. Just do what you have to do. None of this will matter...'

He swung the chair round, and I felt tears threaten.

'What do you mean? None of this will matter? What...'

He didn't face me. He just blew. 'Just fucking leave it, will you? On and fucking on about stupid things that you want to buy. Just buy them.'

I stood up. 'No need for this, Jakey. No need. I was just...'

He swung around again. 'Just what? You wanted this. You

107

were up for it. House, garden, furniture. I honestly don't know what is fucking wrong with you. You want to live like this. Yeah, I like this place. Course I do. But it's...'

I didn't know what he was going to say. Temporary? Not important? I didn't know, and I suddenly realised I was holding my arms over my head just like I did when I was a child. Just like I did when Dad was shouting at Collette. She would give as good as she got, but I didn't want to. I didn't want to build those walls of bitterness and uncertainty.

I'd rarely been shouted at since then. Ian didn't argue, he was very factual, laying out all the evidence – or what he thought was evidence. He would slam doors and sleep in the other room to punish me for something I wasn't doing. Something that existed only in his mind. I could have argued and protested, but where would that have got me? Into a screaming match I had purposely avoided.

That day with Jake was the same. He'd screamed more instructions for the future that I added to my list of things I could not do.

'And don't call me Jakey. Jake. It's fucking Jake. Stop asking stupid questions about soft furnishings.'

Oh yes, I had them all stored alongside *don't go to school events because you might be needed at home* and *don't react to other people shouting because you know where that leads* and countless other rules that other people had made for me. All those things I had silently collected and applied to my life had led me here, today, to the NCP car park, unable to ask my husband why all this was happening.

That one row had scared me. I had crumpled into a sobbing ball instead of letting that anger out. Instead of telling him to fuck off and just buying what I wanted. I'd gone to lie on the bed until the sobs subsided and soon, he had lain beside me, his fingers touching mine. It was almost as if he had forgotten to be himself for a moment. He murmured into the darkness.

'I didn't mean to scare you.'

But he had scared me. I didn't know what he meant by *it doesn't matter*. I was scared that I had jumped into another uneven relationship, where I cared much more than the other person who had a different agenda altogether. I didn't want my parents' relationship, where all they could see was each other. That was more Ian's territory. But I didn't want a chasm between us, either.

However, I was more scared that we would descend into a couple who rows. And that would get worse until…

That was the day I told him. That was the day I explained about Collette and about what happened. It was hard to form my mouth around those awful words because I had never been able to tell anyone before. I had, I realised, told no one what happened. But I did tell Jake. And we promised to tell each other everything. Which is why what I have found out over the past few days is slowly destroying me. And now he could be in danger.

CHAPTER SEVENTEEN

I dial Paula's number. She answers almost immediately, and it sounds like she has just woken up. No matter how annoyed or upset we are with each other, we will always rock up in an emergency. And I have a feeling it is. I hear her yawn and stretch.

'Where the fuck have you been?' She is laughing.

'You won't believe it, but I had a big row with Clint–'

'Yeah, I heard. Jesus Christ. He deserved that. Have they let you go?'

I laugh involuntarily. Somewhere inside me still petulantly says *what if they have? Who gives a shit*, but I try to push it down. For now. 'No idea. It isn't about that. Look, can we meet up? I really need to speak to you.'

She yawns again. 'Give me an hour.'

'Great. I'll come round to yours.'

She coughs. 'No. No, I'll meet you at the coffee shop in town.'

She ends the call. It takes me a minute to wonder why she isn't at work. She's obviously with someone, and she doesn't want me round there to see the aftermath of overflowing ashtrays and wine bottles.

I push all Jake's stuff back into the holdall but keep the phone. I wonder whether I should go to the police. But what would I say? I have no actual proof of anything. No crime has been committed. My heart thumps at the thought of it. No, I need to talk to someone about it. Paula might not be the right person at the moment, but she will have some advice. She knows me well and she will pull out all my biases and tell me when I am being overcautious.

But as I sit here in the car on a cloudy day, something inside me still burns. Something telling me that I will not let this go and I will keep going no matter what. I call it loyalty, but I saw the destruction it caused for Collette. Her line was in a different place to other people's. Even before that final time, I knew that. I looked back down the years, and I saw the place where she might have stepped back and let him go. Where she might have drawn a firm line in the sand to indicate that yes, this was the last time he would leave and no, he wasn't coming back.

But she never did. Neither did he. Instead, they clung on to each end of an invisible cord that bound them together with perpetual drama and a need to keep finding each other. She knew he had left that day. Every other time he had stayed out late or not come home. But that day he took his things. There was no throwing bin bags out of the bedroom window and shouting after him as he flicked the Vs back at her and laughed. No. He was gone for good, and she knew it.

And the heartbreaking truth was that her need to find him was stronger than her need to look after us. It devastates me even now. Every time I miss her or I think about how she would brush my hair from my face or read me a story and do all the voices, I remind myself of how I felt when I realised she wasn't coming back. In some ways it is worse than what happened after that.

I can see it in myself now. Her nothing-will-get-in-my-way persistence channelled into a dogged determination to make my marriage work and to succeed at work. Like her, at any cost. I think about Clint and how I let him bully me and taunt me. It would be easy to blame myself, but Paula would tell me it's never the victim's fault. It's always the fault of the abuser.

I go through the messages on Jake's burner phone again, then I log on to my own as Donna McBride. I check Jake's Facebook and then, out of habit, Veronica's. There is no activity on either. So I look up Flynn. I haven't gone down this road for a long time. Seeing my brother's face brings back all the guilt and love and terror that still trickles through me after all these years. But I need to feel everything now. I pushed it all down for a long time.

He is first on the list of Flynn Palmers. I touch the screen and click, careful not to friend him. I don't want him to realise it's me or he might expect me to one day try to make contact. I don't know him now. I don't know Patrick or Michael or their children. I gauge how bad the pain is and whether I can bear it as I see them all together on a photograph. Flynn's cover image is a birthday party. I click on the image and the caption says: *All the family together again.*

I go to message him but stop when I remember the last time I did this. And what happened then? How he had asked me for proof it was me. For ID. How he was cool and precise and only passed on information I asked for. How he made his Facebook pictures private soon afterwards. It was as if he knew I had been searching through them for clues about his family, trying to piece together his life and glimpse what I could have had.

I don't blame him, or Patrick or Michael, for being upset with me. I was there one day and gone the next. With the passing of time, I began to see what it would look like to them. I realised they could never know what I was thinking. How I wanted a job like other girls my age and how staying would have meant I could never have it. All they would know was that I left. And they would do what we all do when things like that happen. Painful, confusing things. They would search for another situation like that and compare it.

And they would have searched back, and they would have thought I was just like her. Just like Collette. There one minute, gone the next. As time went on, they would have realised that neither of us were ever coming back. I toy again with the idea of messaging him as Donna McBride and finding out how he was doing. Pretending I know him from school like I did with Veronica. Drawing out the gaps in what happened. But it wouldn't be right. It would be just another layer of fucked-up dysfunction in an already chaotic situation.

I take my finger off the message button and close Facebook on my phone. I'm going to delete that account when I get back to the hotel tonight. It's clear Jake isn't going to ring me on my phone. He obviously has too much on his mind to track me anywhere. I see Paula crossing the road in front of me.

She is wearing a long brown skirt and sandals. Her hair is swept up in a swirl and her beige cardigan is falling off one shoulder over a camisole. She looks pale and skinny, but somehow glowing. I wait a moment until she disappears into the café opposite the car park. For once I have no urge to be early. I'm not even sure if discussing all this with Paula is the way forward, but I need another perspective.

As I open the café door, she is checking her phone and smiling. She stops and places it face down on the table as I take a seat.

'Anyone interesting?'

She blushes and looks at me though her eyelashes. 'I met this guy.'

I know what this means. Sleep deprivation and warped thinking. She would have been with him. I'm wondering now if I will get the chance to say my piece as this is where she usually gushes about her new bloke. I make the correct noises and wait for the onslaught.

'Oh? Who is he then?'

She waves my comment away and summons the server. 'Tea, please, no milk. And a coffee for Kate?' I nod and wait for her to get started. She takes a breath. 'Oh, just this guy. Early days but… any way. What's the emergency?'

I swear her eyes are glistening. Her cheeks are flushed as she pulls at the sleeves of her cardigan like she did when we were first friends. I don't know where to start. She helps me out.

'Is it about Jake? Only, when I went round the other day, he said you'd gone away for a couple of days.'

I stop cold in my tracks. 'You went round? You saw him?'

She frowns. 'Yeah. He was at yours. Like I said. Why?'

I swallow. 'I haven't gone away for a couple of days. Well, I have, but he didn't come home. So after work I just kept on driving. I haven't been back since. Or spoken to him.'

She stares at me. 'So you've left him?'

'No. I just wanted to see…'

I can't say it. I can't. I can't admit that I have run away to a neighbouring town to see if he phones me. It suddenly seems infantile and stupid. But she nods. She knows me. She knows I hate this sort of thing. Drama. Fuss.

'Right, so you buggered off, and he hasn't got in touch?'

I nod. A tear escapes and falls onto my saucer. 'What did he say when you went round?'

She pulls a face. 'Nothing much. He just stood outside and told me you weren't there. That you'd gone away for a couple of days.'

I pause. I try to form the right words, sort through the confusion.

'It's not just that. There's some other stuff. He left his job. And he lied.'

She blinks at me. The server brings our drinks, and Paula studies me as she stirs in two sachets of sugar.

'Okay. And you haven't discussed this with him?'

'No.'

'Have you tried to phone him?'

A sob escapes. 'Not since before I left. I had that row with Clint and… it's all got too much. I wanted to see if he cared. He's been all over the place. Then he didn't come home. Then he wasn't there in the morning.'

She reaches out and touches my arm. 'Mate, this doesn't sound good. Not at all. Maybe you should–'

I interrupt. 'I went round to see his ex.'

She almost spits out her tea. 'Veronica? You didn't think…'

'Yes. Yes, I did. He talked about her a lot. But he lied about their divorce.'

She weighs it up. 'So you spoke to her?'

I remember the glass smashing and the look on her face later when she realised. The charity shop and her lovely home. The shard underneath the mat.

'No. I… went in her house when she wasn't there.'

Paula's eyes are wide and she half smiles. 'Oh my fucking God. You did not.' She goes to fist bump me. 'I didn't think you had it in you.'

'The thing is, I smashed a window, and she might have called the police.'

She snorts. 'Is that why you're scared of going home?'

I think. No, I'm not scared of going home. Not for that reason, anyway. I'm worried about going home because I am not the same Kate. I'm not the same woman who went to work that day. And I don't know what that means in the light of what I know about Jake.

'I'm not scared. I just don't know what's going on.' I slide the phone across the table. 'It gets worse. This was in his workbag. I went to find him, and they told me everything. And there's money missing from our savings account.'

She reads the texts then tilts her head to one side. She might look all fresh but her bloodshot eyes tell me that she's still drinking, and I remember that she is not the most reliable advisor. I remember all the crazy shit we have done down the years and how we have grown into the nemesis of each other. Not by design, but by circumstance. She never knew my family. I met her way after all that happened and then, ten years ago, I dropped out of her life while I dealt with the heartbreak. I never told her then, and I'm not going to tell her now. One thing at a time. She speaks now.

'None of this sounds good, Kate, but none of it is your fault. If he hasn't told you, it's his choice. It sounds to me like the only option you have is to go home and see what he has to say about it all. But be careful. It sounds like he is in some kind of trouble. Have you thought about the cops?'

'Yeah. But then I'd have to explain how I found all this out. And they might put it together with Veronica's broken window.'

She winces. 'Right, right. Look, do you want me to come with you? I can sit with you while you confront him?'

She is checking out the clock on the café wall. I almost laugh at what a reversal this is. It's usually me refereeing between her and some guy who never called or robbed her purse. I know she doesn't really want to. She's checking her phone and smiling as she types a message.

'No, it's fine. I need to think it through and then I will. I'm in a Premier Inn in Huddersfield.'

She laughs loudly. 'You run away to Huddersfield to a budget hotel? Bloody hell, Kate, I would have at least gone to London. Or Manchester centre in a decent hotel.'

I smile and think about why I did it. I don't want Jake to find me. I wanted to beat him at his own game. I wanted to find out what was going on. Mission accomplished. But not exactly in the way I had imagined.

'I know. But I will go home. I'll talk to him, and I'll let you know what happens.'

She touches my hand. 'I got to go. Things to do, people to see.'

She winks and hugs herself. She takes a hurried selfie of us both and leaves. It's only when she has gone that the server brings the bill for me to pay. Nothing changes with Paula. But me? Well...

CHAPTER EIGHTEEN

For once Paula is right. I need to go home and talk to him. But I know something is wrong. It's obvious. And now I have added to it. Instead of going home and waiting for him, I sped off into the distance and lost the plot.

I think I know more, but I have a feeling I know less. I know he's lied to me and I know he's being blackmailed. But why? And more to the point, why am I not at home supporting him? Why am I still absent? And why hasn't he tried to contact me?

I search back over the months and years we have been together. Has there been anything I was unsure about? Has there? It all swirls around me, all the synchronicity of making meals. All the laughter and just doing everyday things together. Nothing fancy, just living.

My mind rests on a time just before our wedding. Because we'd both been married before we had agreed on a low-key affair. But he wanted family there. He started to tell Polly she would be a bridesmaid. My heart had lifted. Nothing about my marriage to Ian had been right. The wedding had been a regimented we-can-only-afford-forty-guests affair with me in a meringue dress and plastic tiara.

Second time around I had expected a very small affair. And I didn't care. I just wanted to be with Jake. But when he suggested something tasteful, I got a little bit carried away and started to look at Vivienne Westwood gowns. Then I found out he had already booked the registry office and the hotel reception. I say found out, because I glanced at an open spreadsheet on his laptop. He'd quickly closed the lid.

'It was supposed to be a surprise. I wanted it all sorted for you.'

That was Jake all over. He wasn't controlling. Most things were free and easy, but anything that involved money was tightly controlled. I remember the alarm bells ringing, the Ian-esque way he presented the facts to me without wavering. He showed me the spreadsheet. It was tightly budgeted.

'But we've saved more than this. Much more.'

He nodded. 'But that's for our life together. This is just one day.'

I knew he was right, but we hadn't discussed it. I wanted a relationship with someone who would talk about things.

'Okay. It looks great. But I've got some ideas as well.'

'Course. But these are booked. I was going to surprise you. But you can dress it up.'

I tap my fingers on the table and finish my coffee. That's what a lot of our marriage has been. Him directing and me dressing it up. The house. Our wedding. Holidays. I suddenly have an awful feeling that there is a lot more to Jake's life than I had realised. He talked about work, but I didn't know what he was involved in. He is good with finances, but now someone is blackmailing him.

Why had I done this? Why the hell had I not gone home that day? Partly because of Collette. Because of the burning inside me to let nothing go. But also because something was missing. And that had got much, much worse over the past couple of months. The acquiescence of maintaining calm because you're afraid of the alternative is one thing, but it's a vicious cycle. The alternative, which is buried deep inside, means it is impossible once the high bar of suspicion is raised not to act.

I'd reacted to something I had no proof of. I'd thought he was having an affair. I almost laugh. Those heady days of the worst thing that could happen being your husband shacking up with his ex. Not a thought that something else could have been wrong. No. Me, me, me. 'What I thought' was king and following up a line of inquiry that led to a dead end was my queen. Just like her.

I'd carried on searching for her, but she was nowhere. People had seen her, but she was never around when I visited those bars. Which I did for almost a year before I tried another avenue. My naivety told me she would wonder what had happened to us. She would eventually return and expect to walk back in. So I went to find the only other person who knew what had happened.

In my imagination I had reassured myself that, with me gone, Grandma had taken my brothers in, and they were all living happily ever after. I wondered if this was what Collette thought would happen too, and if she had been back to see them. With more grown-up eyes, I saw that the house they lived in would not have accommodated three near-teenage boys. It was a tiny two-up two-down. My childhood memories were of us all crammed into a tiny kitchen eating rice pudding, which was lovely, but not a living arrangement.

But I knocked on the door all the same. She answered and stared at me.

'What do you want?' All the pain resurfaced, and I started to cry. She folded her arms. 'Where have you been?'

I sobbed on her doorstep. She didn't let me in. She closed the door behind her. Eventually I managed to speak.

'Has she been here? My mum? Are my brothers here?'

She snorted and shook her head. 'What about yer dad? My son? Aren't you going to ask after him?'

'Yeah, him too. Where are they?'

She stared at me. 'You went. As if we didn't have enough to do, we had to look for you as well.'

I remember wanting to shout in her face that I was a child. I was on my own, left with three younger children. I was scared. That it wasn't up to me to look after them. It was up to her precious son and Collette. It was a mashed-up mess in my emotions but one thing I knew was that I had to keep it in.

I don't know now if it was respect or fear, but I was again standing in Collette's shoes. I could feel her there, searching for Dad and screaming at Grandma that Harry needed to come home. She needed him there. I didn't want her to think I was like that. So I just stayed quiet. She didn't unfold her arms, and she didn't hug me. Her eyes were warm but the rest of her recoiled.

'Where you living? I hope you're not...'

She pulled the door behind her. I could hear the TV. I wanted to see Grandad, but I knew I couldn't. I knew he wouldn't want to see me.

'No, no. I was staying with one of my friends. Now I'm sharing a place.'

Her features softened into something I didn't recognise then, but I now know it was relief.

'Good, good. Look, just leave it now. Her. She's no good. She left her kids. She'll be pissed in some bar. Just leave it, love, and get on with your life.'

I wanted to tell her Dad left his kids too. But I didn't because then I would be in the firing line. Because we all left.

'Where are they? My brothers?' I looked at my shoes. 'I had to go, Gran, I had to. If not, I would have had to look after them and it wasn't my job.'

The words hung between us silently.

It was hers. Her job.

She just nodded. 'Aye, I daresay. But what's done's done. Don't worry about them. Social services sorted it out. They're okay.'

She looked behind her at the closed door. 'He won't have any of it. He won't see none of you. Go and live your life, love.'

I couldn't leave it there. I had to ask again. I had to try harder. 'Where are my brothers?'

It came out hard and flat. Not my voice, more that of an older version of me. Someone who was in control of a situation. She nodded and stepped onto the path. She grabbed my arm and pulled me around the corner and behind the coal shed. Then she spun me round to face her.

'Now you listen to me. I have had enough, lady. She was nothing but trouble, and if you think I'm going to start all that again, you are bloody wrong. You listen good now. You thought it was a good idea to come around here asking me what's going on? Right?'

I nodded. She was hissing at me, and I could feel droplets of spit on my face. This wasn't the woman who had dried my tears and sung me to sleep. She continued.

'Well did you stop to think about what this had done to me? How I had to watch them little boys taken away crying. I always bloody knew it would come to that. Or worse. It almost killed me. Not that it's your fault. No. But you picked your bloody time to have a tantrum. Made it worse, because I knew where they were. Safe.' She pointed in my face. 'But you. I didn't know where you were. Can you imagine how that feels?'

I could imagine. I knew. Because I felt it too. I felt it every day. I shook my head. 'I didn't think anyone cared about me.'

As quick as a flash she slapped my face. 'No, you didn't, did you? Because all you could see was her. Like him. Like everyone else. But no one took my bloody feelings into account. And didn't today. I haven't seen my son or my grandsons. Or you, till now. But I'll get over it. And to do that I need it to be just me and him in there. He's the only one who gives a toss about me. And no, I don't know where they are. Ask their social workers.'

She went inside and shut the door. I stood at the gate and

looked at the place that was once my second home. Another dead end. I almost laugh at how long it took me to realise that I had no family anymore. That it had disintegrated, and the fragments were scattered in places I could not go. The only time it ever threatened to reform was under extreme pressure and, even then, I was too scared to. Because I knew it stirred something in me. And I am the same kind of scared now. Scared that I will go back and fuck it all up. Even more, if that is possible.

But tomorrow I will face this. If Jake is in trouble, I will offer my help. If it's another woman, I will let him go. The one thing I can't understand is why he hasn't phoned me. Or even messaged me. He told Paula I had gone away for a few days.

It's only now I realise what it could be. What if he thinks something has happened to me? If it's something to do with the messages on his phone? I pull it out and read it again.

> Don't even think about telling anyone. Or you know what happens.

What if he thinks someone has taken me and he can't tell anyone for fear of what will happen? I am suddenly hot. I flush with the fear that I have got this all wrong and I am making his situation worse. He must have been going out each day and pretending he was at work. Was I so unapproachable? Was I trying to make our life so perfect that he couldn't tell me he was in trouble?

The last few days have shaken me, and I don't know what is real anymore. I thought my worst problem was my husband being late for a party, but now it has avalanched into something much bigger. Now it's much more complicated. I need to make a decision about my marriage. I need to decide if I will face this with him, make him tell me what is going on. Help him.

I hurry to my car and drive back over to Huddersfield. By the time I get there the car hire shop is closed and I will have to stay another night. But first thing in the morning I will go back home and help my husband.

CHAPTER NINETEEN

I wake up at five and lay in the purple Premier Inn bedroom staring at the ceiling. The past days have been an eye opener for sure. I still don't know if I did the right thing, but I have a vague feeling I don't care. What I have learned about my husband has worn away the steely determination to be perfect. I snort to myself. As if I ever were perfect.

Far from it, but at least I tried. At least I was honest. There had been lots of times in our marriage when I had made mistakes. Everyone does. Paula would rather walk over hot coals than admit hers, but I am different. Or I came to be, because I thought Jake made me a better person. This was my chance to get it all right. To make sure my marriage was authentic. I had become fond of that word, because it implied something real and honest.

I'd told Jake if I ever messed up. Like when I washed his very expensive sweater and it shrunk. Or the time I got a speeding fine – he hated anything to do with fines or courts. He would nod and smile. If it was something about spending, he would just laugh and tell me *you can't take it with you*. It kind of took the fun out of spending and it became a bit boring.

But now there are so many things I haven't told him. My job. Veronica. His work. Hiding in a hotel. I wonder how much more he hasn't told me. I try to imagine how I would have felt if I had read those divorce papers earlier. Or he had lain there that night and told me what really happened. Would I still have married him? I don't know. I can understand but not forgive him not telling me about that, but what about his job? Why keep that from me? I told him everything. All about Collette. All about my dad. And all about Flynn and the insurance money. Everything.

I am beyond tears now. I blink into the morning sunshine that streams through the hotel curtains that don't quite meet. Nothing feels right. I won't rest until I have spoken to Jake and found out what is going on.

At nine I am parked outside the car rental shop. I watch as the employees arrive and in my mind's eye, I can see my colleagues streaming into the office. I don't even know if I still have a job. But that can wait. I need to go home. I need to be amongst my own things. I need to understand what the future holds for me and Jake.

I've already considered the options. I know what happens only too well because I went through it with Ian. If Jake's lying and pretence is because he is in trouble financially, I'll try to help him. If it's because he is unhappy in our marriage then it will mean splitting and selling the house. There is no option to do nothing. That has passed now. I know today will decide the rest of my life.

I realise I am squeezing my hands into a tight fist. I used to do that as a kid. Lying in bed listening to either the laughter or shouting coming from downstairs. Holding myself in a ball of stress because I had learned that whatever happened meant trouble. It meant upheaval and possibly me stepping up and doing things out of my comfort zone.

Even downstairs in the house, as a child, I set my jaw in tight determination. I often find myself clenching my teeth when I want to say something but don't. Locking those words in and swallowing them down until they turned to an acrid bile swirling in my stomach. Making sure that what you saw was what you got and that my face did not give away one ounce of my sadness. Because anything else would make everything worse.

It's only then I realise. Maybe that's why she struggled too. Maybe Collette wanted a quiet life. Maybe the reason she ran was because she couldn't handle the constant trouble? My mind fights against it. I don't want to make excuses for her behaviour. No. This is me, not her. I've become someone who is used to an even road, not the bumpy, twisty chaos of marital problems.

The man in the shop turns the sign from closed to open, and I go in and hand the keys back. I call a cab and it takes me to where I have parked my car. I push the carrier bags of new clothes into the boot, and I am back where I started. I suddenly wish I could erase the past few days and just turn the corner at the traffic lights and go home. But I know deep down that I would have found out about Jake another way.

I have to face it. I force myself to drive back over the moors for the final time. The road is quiet, and I watch the heather and the ponds turn into rows of houses as I approach the town. Soon I am driving past Jake's office that he suddenly left, and past my own office. The pull to go inside and find out about my job is strong. I know my team will have started a new project now and I wonder if they have used my project notes, or if Clint has been put in charge in my absence.

I am still technically on sick leave and I know this is pure avoidance tactics. So I carry on driving and eventually I reach the traffic lights where all this started. I glance at my phone and laugh. No messages now. My stomach does somersaults as I turn the corner and see Jake's car there. This is it. This is where I face him.

My mind races as I park up outside the house where I thought we were happy. I try to smooth it over, to tell myself it will be fine, I will help him if he's in trouble. Stand by him. But what about the lies? What about Veronica's divorce papers? And how am I going to explain how I found out about them?

I start to get out of the car but stop in my tracks. What if she called the police? Of course she would have. Someone broke into her home. But what if they know it was me? What if the police are looking for me? I brush this to one side. I am going to have to face whatever happens. I make a plan. I will focus on asking Jake about his job and why he left. What the messages were about. The rest can come later when I know what is going on.

I glance inside his car as I pass. He has moved all the maps and his signature Costa Coffee cup in the drinks holder. He must have had it valeted. Brilliant. His wife is missing, and he gets his car cleaned. Then I remember my marriage is on the line. He stayed out. He lied. He quit his job and never told me.

The lounge curtains are open, and I can see the alarm is set. The red light flashes through the glass panel at our front door. Our door. Our house. The pain of what I have to lose almost pushes me over the edge, but I steady myself. I've been here before. My heart thuds and I think about the agreement on the wall in the hallway. My absolute dedication to it and where it got me.

I lift my key and push it into the lock. I step inside and punch in the alarm code. There is mail behind the door and Jake's shoes are not neatly placed on the shoe rack.

'Jake? Are you there?'

I pick up the letters and shove them into my bag. I glance up at our agreement, once a thing of optimism and motivation but now just a reminder of our problems. Something isn't right. I can feel it. The house sounds hollow and cold. I check for his coat, and it isn't there. I check again that his car is there just in case he was going out the back door as I came in. It is. I walk through to the kitchen and feel the kettle. It is cold. Stone cold. The kitchen clock ticks behind me and I look out into the garden to see if he is in the shed.

Its padlock is on. He isn't there.

'Jake? We need to talk.'

I take off my shoes and pad through to the lounge. Something is missing. It takes me a moment for my brain to identify the gaps, the empty spaces. The bookshelf is thinner, with a gap at the end, the elephant bookends moved along. His speaker bar is gone. I panic and wonder if we have been burgled.

I rush upstairs into our bedroom. The bed is neatly made and everything seems to be in its place. Except Jake's sliders are gone. And his dressing gown. Gone. I fling open the wardrobe doors and his side is completely empty. I check through the few expensive dresses I have to reassure myself that someone hasn't just taken the designer stuff he loved to buy. I feel along the top shelf on his wardrobe for his watches. Gone. All the gold watches I had bought him, the ones he collected.

I sprint to the bathroom. Even his shampoo and conditioner are gone. All his care and grooming equipment. Everything has gone, and the bathroom is wiped sparkling clean. The hand weights he keeps in the hallway are now just an impression in the carpet.

It is as if he were never here. And the entire house is spotlessly clean. Someone has gone right through and erased any trace of Jake. I've held it together until now, but I sink onto my bed. What the hell is going on? Has he left me? Has he? Is this what all this was about? So he can leave when I am not around? But it makes no sense, because eventually we would have to divorce and sell our beautiful home. He can't avoid me forever.

I feel sick. None of my jewellery is missing. Nothing at all. I check the spare rooms and even his exercise bike has gone. I feel under the bed, and he's even used his half of our matching luggage to pack his things. I am suddenly sobbing. It's the shock and the pain of realising my husband has gone. It is so out of character for him to do this.

Then I remember the phone. What if something has happened to him? What if this was something to do with those texts? None of this is right. I pull the phone out of my bag and switch it on. I read the messages again. I should have called the police.

> Don't even think about telling anyone. Or you know what happens.

What if he told someone? Oh my God, what if they know that I have read those messages? What if my snooping around has caused this? I hurry to the end of the landing and pull down the loft ladders. Maybe I can find something in his office, something to explain. But I already know before I reach the top of the ladders. I can tell from the echo of the noise from outside, the unfamiliar sound of the room. Even in complete inner silence, a room has a sound. This room sounded of distant traffic and aeroplanes and the click, click, click of disk drives. He kept an array of old laptops and desktops in here. An archive of his tech past.

But they are all gone. The machines. The printers. All the pictures from the walls. All the one-year calendars and all the sticky notes he used to plan. Notebooks and diaries. Business books and a few novels. All gone. I climb into the roof space and stand on the very expensive flooring. I look around. It's bigger than I remember now it is completely empty.

Completely empty except for one trestle table holding a single laptop. I move closer. The screen has a map on it and the map has red lines criss-crossing it. The red lines record routes through a town. And I my blood runs cold as I realise that town is Huddersfield.

CHAPTER TWENTY

What the hell is this? Jake's gone. All his things are gone. And someone is watching me. Oh, my God. How could I have been so stupid? I should have acted straight away when I knew something was wrong. I shouldn't have run away. I should have called the police when I saw those messages on his burner phone. But how could I? What if it put him in more danger? My God. Where is he?

I lean in and look closer. The red line is like a scribble of activity as I walked around Huddersfield, with straight lines leading off the screen. I scroll down the screen, down, down, until I reach my hometown. I zoom in and see the lines lead to the places I have visited over the past few days. My old street. My office. Jake's office. Veronica's. Whoever this is has been monitoring my movements.

I reach into my bag for my phone. I hurry down the loft ladders and, once in the lounge, I call 999.

The operator answers. 'Which service, please? Police, fire or ambulance?'

My heart thuds in my chest. Why is this happening? Why? Where is Jake? 'Police, please.'

There is a pause as it connects to another line.

'Greater Manchester Police. How can we help?'

I take a deep breath. 'My husband's been kidnapped.'

The officer is tapping on a keyboard. 'Your name and address, please.'

'Kate Clayton. 17 Lynton Grove, Oldham, OL23 2LP. And my husband is Jake. Jackson. Please, I don't know what's going on.'

She taps some more. 'Okay, Kate. Is this happening now?'

'Yes. I mean, well, I'm not sure. But he's been threatened and now they've taken him and his things.'

There is a long pause. 'What kind of threat?'

I feel tears on my face. The shock ripples through me. 'His phone. Someone messaging him. He's been blackmailed. And now… please.'

She records the details. 'Is there forced entry to the property? Is anything missing?'

'Everything is missing. All his things except a laptop. They've left a message. But no forced entry. His car is still here, though.'

She clicks away. 'Everything? Meaning…'

'Everything he owned. Every single thing. And the house has been totally cleaned.' I sniff at the lemony smell. Not my scented cleaning fluid. This is different. 'And his car. Cleared out and left on the drive. The messages. And he left his job. He was clearly scared.'

'Okay, we'll send someone round.'

I panic. 'When will it be? I'm scared. They might come back.'

'Within the hour, probably before. They'll be with you soon.'

I thank her. She reads out a crime number that I don't write it down because I am too shocked and end the call. Nothing is out of place. And none of my things have been moved. But all evidence of Jake has been removed.

I go outside and look up and down the street. Someone must have seen him. Someone must have seen something. Everyone will have left for work. But Lee Cressey's car is on the drive across the road. I hurry over and knock on the door. I mentally calculate when this could have happened. Paula saw him two days ago, so it must have been yesterday or the day before. The door opens and Lee smiles.

'Oh, hello, Kate. What can I do for you?'

I frown at him. 'Jake... did you see anything yesterday or the day before? A van or anything? Or Jake...?'

He is suddenly serious. 'Are you okay, Kate? Is everything okay?'

I shake my head. No, I am not okay. My mouth is dry, and I look up the road for the police. 'Look, something has happened to Jake. I...' He is staring at my feet, and I realise I have no shoes on. And I have walked through my garden. This is all falling apart. I am falling apart. Finally, I start to cry. 'He's been kidnapped. He's gone. Someone's taken his office apart and...'

Lee steps forward and hugs me awkwardly then lets me go. 'Do you want a cup of tea or something? I can...' He points inside the house, but I see a police car turning the corner.

'No, no thanks. They're here. I have to...'

I hurry back in bare feet and stand on my drive waving frantically. I am suddenly me ten years ago who opened the door to the police in another desperate situation. Waited to give my statement and felt the same helplessness as I watched the worst situation of my life unfold. Its familiar creep unnerves me more and I recognise the same erratic behaviour threatening. I need to check myself. Keep it under control. But I couldn't then, and I am struggling now.

The officers park up and get out of the car. They walk around Jake's car and up the drive.

'Kate Clayton?'

I nod and beckon them in, my dirty feet making marks on the ultra-clean carpet as I walk in front of them. We sit. I can hardly breathe with fear. I hear the crackle of one of the officer's radios as he listens. Then he speaks.

'Okay, Kate. We're just waiting for DS Bradley. She'll be here to take your statement.'

I stare at them. 'What will happen?'

I remember the last time. The cold, grey interview room. The terrible grief even though I'd been alone for years. The fog of remembering and hoping I had remembered correctly. I'd never seen a dead body before. The shock. The implication that I was somehow involved. And, when I got home, the rage of not being able to do anything about it.

'We'll have a look round and take a statement. Then we'll take it from there. So how did they get in?'

They both look around. I have a horrible feeling they were expecting chaos. Upturned furniture and emptied drawers. The only chaos here is inside me.

'I don't know. I wasn't here.'

'You weren't here? Where were you?'

'I was away for a few days.' I suddenly realise I am going to have to explain why I was in a hotel in Huddersfield. 'He was here when I went away and then...'

Out of the corner of my eye I see a brown car park on the pavement outside my house. A red-haired woman gets out and looks up at our house. A man gets out of the driver's side and stands beside her. He doesn't look like he is a police officer; he would be more at home in one of the indie bars in Manchester. The officers stand.

'Here's DS Bradley now.'

She walks over our lawn, following almost the same trajectory as I did earlier. The man walks up the drive. My heart beats faster and faster and soon they are standing in front of me. I'm the only person sitting down, so I stand. She blinks at me.

'Rebekah Bradley.' She pushes her hands in her trouser pockets to make it clear we are not shaking hands and avoids eye contact. 'And this is DC Sharples. What happened here then?'

DC Sharples steps closer. He speaks and his accent has a hint of received pronunciation, which surprises me. 'I'll be assisting Bekah. DS Bradley.'

The first officer fills in. 'Kate tells us her husband Jake Clayton has been abducted.'

She looks around. 'What makes you think that, Kate?'

My stomach somersaults. I need to get this right. Not like last time. 'So I've been away for a few days. And when I came back, he was gone, and all his things are gone. Everything. During those days I went to his office to find him. He left his job months ago and his boss gave me his workbag. It had this phone in it. It's got some… threatening messages on it. And there's money missing from our savings account.'

'I see. Is there any forced entry? And evidence of a struggle?'

I shake my head.

The second police officer speaks. 'No, ma'am. No forced entry. I've had a quick look around. No struggle.'

She looks from him to me. She sits on my beautiful sofa, and I sit beside her.

'So were you away with work, Kate? Why did you go to your husband's workplace?'

I hesitate. I know where this is going. But I can't avoid it. 'He's been working late, or so I thought. Then on Tuesday he didn't come home. He was here when I got home from work, but he'd gone again when I woke up the next day. I just needed some space.'

I almost add *to find out what the fuck was going on*, but I don't. She nods deeply.

'So, things weren't going well between you?'

I sigh. I pick up the phone beside me and hand it to her. 'Read the messages. This isn't his main phone. I… I… didn't know about it. And he had a full office upstairs. It's all gone except for one laptop.'

She reads the messages. 'Okay. May I look at the laptop?'

I show her to the loft and follow her up the ladders. The men stand at the bottom. She looks around the loft space. Then at the laptop. She moves closer to it and my heart thuds.

'Whoever has moved his things has cleaned up.' The floor is spotless. No marks or dust from the furniture that was removed. I point at the map. 'And whoever it is has been tracking me. That's where I was. Huddersfield. They know where I am. I think I'm in danger too.'

I desperately want to tell her that my phone hasn't been tracked as I dismantled it. Or my car. Because I hired one. But I am starting to see how disjointed it makes me look. She scrolls the map up and down. Then she walks towards the loft ladders and climbs down. I follow and we all stand in the lounge. She smiles tightly.

'Okay, boys, you can go and wait outside. I just want a word with Kate.' I start to speak but she moves very close to me. 'Look, Kate, I don't know how to say this, but this doesn't look like an abduction. I'm going to be really honest here. I only came out because it's the second time Jake Clayton's name has come up in the past few days.' She pauses. I swallow hard. Veronica. 'Do you know Jake's ex-wife?'

I shrug. 'Not really. I know Polly, his daughter. She stays with us. But I've never met Veronica.'

'It seems there was an incident at her home the other day. His name came up and when I saw this I wondered... but I think it's becoming clear what's happened here. I'm sorry, Kate, but this just looks like Jake has left. There's no real evidence of foul play and–'

I interrupt. I am desperate to tell her that Jake isn't involved in Veronica's break-in, but how can I? Instead, I blurt out my words a little too loudly. 'But the messages? And the laptop? They know where I am. And where was he when he wasn't at work?'

She sighs. 'The messages are not recent and they appear to have stopped. He would need to report them for us to act. And the laptop, well. Look, Kate, is it that you two haven't been getting on? You left and he suspects you are up to no good? He followed you and – well I don't know what you were doing in Huddersfield…' I start to speak but she holds her hand up. 'And I don't need to. Mr Clayton appears to have left the property. I suggest you see a solicitor.' She hands me a card. 'But if anything else comes up, a crime committed, give me a call.'

She steps away. She looks around the room, up at the ceilings. 'You might want to have a think about how he has tracked you, but my money is on your phone or a smart device. I would change your passwords. I'm really sorry, Kate, I know this is upsetting, but we can't investigate something with no real evidence.'

I stare at her. I consider what she has said for a second. She turns to leave.

'What about his car? He's left his car.'

She reaches the door and looks at it. She gives me a look that says *maybe his girlfriend has a better one.*

I sound desperate, I know I do. And she thinks Jake has left me and broken into Veronica's house. But deep down I know neither of those things are true.

CHAPTER TWENTY-ONE

I watch as the police car leaves, followed by Rebekah Bradley and her sidekick. I want to feel numb, like she is right, and I am wrong. That Jake has left and has, for reasons unknown, broken into Veronica's house. Because that would mean I am safe. And he is safe.

But this isn't the case. It can't be. The agreement looms above me. If I hadn't been so wedded to carrying out its every word, I would have spoken to Jake before all this blew up. I would have made him tell me what was wrong. I would have argued with him about coming home late and demanded to know what was going on.

I didn't want to crowd him, though. I didn't want him to think I was clingy. All the while I was deluding myself because deep inside I was as angry as I am now. I had crushed the anger and frustration down so I wouldn't break our agreement. And all the while he was lying. It's just more and more confusing the more I think about it. But one thing is clear, Jake, my husband Jake, is a serial liar. And perhaps that is how he got into this trouble he's in. By lying.

Anyway, it doesn't matter now. The fire is lit inside me. I can still see DS Bradley's car at the corner of the avenue. The indicator is blinking right, and its slow metronome calms the surface of me but I can feel the rage building. The injustice and the 'here we go again' and the hollow feeling of less than that comes from not being believed.

The car turns the corner and I feel the scream escape before I hear it. I lash out and I am suddenly back in a place buried so deep that it is blurry and fuzzy in my mind's eye. But I can feel it. Oh yes, I can feel *her*. The loudness and the deafening shrieks that made us cover our ears. The hidey-hole under the stairs where she kept her high heels and her faux fur coats. We would squeeze in and cocoon ourselves against what was about to happen.

Then the destruction. I sat at the front. Front row and centre of my brothers to block the view of the horror show. The door closed with a latch on the outside and I had to pull it shut on the inside. It never closed fully, and I would see flashes of her pass and the crashes around her. Plates, cups, cutlery. Family photographs in second-hand frames smashing onto the terracotta tiles of the kitchen floor.

Her screaming obscenities at life and tearing at her hair and her clothes. I may have only glimpsed it but I felt it. Another lesson in how not to be, even if I felt like it myself sometimes. My brothers' faces told me the price of it.

But they are not here now, and I feel myself stretched to the farthest limit of control. I know tears will diffuse it, but they won't come. They are dammed by a solid wall of something I barely recognise in myself but have experienced vicariously. Now it is here, I am relieved. I am up for it. I am finally, *finally* letting go. I sweep my arm across the worktop and my set of cups clatter to the floor. None of them break but I do not care. All I care about is the years of control flowing out of me and swirling in this space.

I rip the shared calendar from the wall and tear it into tiny pieces. I know I am shrieking but I don't care. I don't care if the neighbours hear, or if Jake suddenly appears, or if DS Bradley comes back Columbo-style and asks me another question. I almost laugh. Suddenly this has taken a comical turn. My emotions are lurching and swelling and falling, and I pull all the papers out of our 'life admin' file and tear them apart. The duplicity is not lost on me. He's carried over this and probably a lot more from Veronica to me.

The shreds of paper cover the carpet, and I pull the coats from the rack behind the door and kick at them until I am exhausted. The vase of flowers in the hallway, that withered while I was away, are swept across the wooden flooring. I stamp in the damp stems and scream. I can hear myself asking the eternal rhetorical questions – *why am I so stupid* and *why did I believe him* and *I knew this was going to happen?*

Even underneath it all I can still remember my twelve-year-old self sitting in a cupboard wondering why, when she knew this was going to happen again because, after all, it kept happening, she didn't just stop. Just stop. Why didn't she stop this? Later, I wondered if it was because she had us as an audience. Because she needed to show us how she was feeling, how bad it was for her.

But now – today – I know the truth. It made her feel better. It made everyone else feel worse, but Collette needed these violent interludes to be able to go back and cope with the everyday. It was just that she couldn't do it in front of anyone. Because we all knew it was wrong. Bad. Mad. Just like everyone called her. Crazy. And look where it got her.

But I have no audience. I have no one to upset. I have been very careful not to get close enough to someone in case this happened. In case *she* happened. Because I always knew. But I got too close to Jake. Now he is in trouble and instead of trying to find a way to help him or understand what is going on, I am trashing my home. I am hurt. DS Bradley's words stung me and are seeping inside me, snaking their way into me.

Has he left me? Has he? That didn't explain the phone and his job and the messages. However, it did fit with Veronica's letters and the lying about their divorce. Had he just been waiting for the right time? Had he pitied me? Felt so sorry for me he couldn't tell me? It doesn't make sense. I push it away. He would have just told me. If he has, he would have to face me eventually, so why do it in such a sneaky way? Why follow me? Jake isn't Ian. He's much more confident. Much more self-assured. No, this is something else.

I tip out my handbag. I shake the items all over the sofa and rummage through them. I need to find out how they have tracked me. I feel the lining and inside all the zipped pockets. I search through my mini make-up bag and inside the lipsticks and brushes.

It can't be the phones. I sprint through the house and fetch the laptop. I zoom out so I can see the whole of the route. It starts when I leave town and ends when I came back today. It can't be Jake's secret phone I picked up from his office. It started before that. Or my burner phone. I push them to one side and stare at my own phone.

I snatch it up and run outside. I hurry to my car, leaving the front door wide open, and I turn the key in the ignition. I speed off in my bare feet, screeching around the corner and up to the bypass. I speed around the roundabout and then back home. I rush back in to see if another red line has appeared on the screen. And there it is. A short line with a bobble on the end of it where I flung my car round the roundabout.

I throw the phone onto the sofa and run outside again. I am out of breath and strips of paper stick to my feet. I will get to the bottom of this. I repeat my route, but in the opposite direction. I am almost at my office then I spin my car in the middle of an empty road. Screeching tyres and dust match my inner turmoil. Then I drive home.

Inside again, there is another short red line. I look around at the contents of my bag. It is nothing in there. It isn't the bag itself. I rush to the bathroom and take off my clothes. I jump in the shower and scrub at my hair. Then I go into our bedroom. The room we spent so much time in. The love and the hugs and telling each other our secrets. His book is gone from his side of the bed, and I don't need to open the drawers to know that everything will have been removed. I hug myself. I take out my earrings and pull off my necklace. I can't see how those could have been tampered with as I always wear them. Always. I am naked, and I stand in front of the full-length mirror.

It was only a week ago I stood here excited for the party. My biggest problem was Jake being late. I stare at my reflection. I look after myself. I make sure I am the best I can be, inside and out. Yoga, massage, good food. Reading. Learning. All to maintain a level. All to keep a lid on who I really am. Someone who can flow out of control then ebb back to complete silence. Jake isn't who I thought he was. But neither am I.

I dress and hurry downstairs. I am still on fire and my skin tingles with fury. I rush to the end of our long garden and back again. There is another short red line. How am I being tracked? How? I just don't understand. I try to think but my mind is filled with *what ifs* and deep wonderings of how I could have missed this. The magnitude of it. It's eerie. It's just like he's never been here. I am alone, and that thought sends my anger soaring again. I fell for it. I did everything to make sure I made no mistakes. I made sure I never put my marriage in danger. Because I love him.

I let out a loud scream that ends in a sob. But there are no tears. No, not for this. He is in danger. I know it, but he never told me. He just let it happen and excluded me. He must have known it would put me in danger too. Yet he still didn't tell me. I dutifully held his hand and at any time he could have whispered his fear. I pivot onto his fear now. Onto the kind of desperation he must have felt at those messages. I both understand and blame him in the same moment, and it tips me over the edge.

Then I see it. The fucking agreement. It seemed like such a good idea at the time. I am suddenly angrier than I have ever been. I should have been myself. I should never have agreed to all of that. I shouldn't have held it all in and made myself so steady and inaccessible that Jake couldn't talk to me for fear of rocking the boat. The lies about his divorce rip at me, but don't lots of people reframe their past? I hadn't told him everything. I told him about Collette and what happened, but I didn't tell him my deep guilt. I didn't tell him how what I said changed everything.

Jake is missing. My Jake. The police think he's left me. I know he is in danger. I just know it. I pull the agreement from the wall and try to smash it on the coat hooks. My expensive Habitat coat hooks that seemed essential to have at the time. But the frame is plastic – the printed agreement held in place and the block sealed.

'To last forever...' he had told me as he gave it to me. No, he hasn't left me. This is something else. I suddenly feel calmer. I feel the tide of anger pull back and I let it. I place the heavy plastic block face down on the coffee table. And then I see it. Tiny writing in the corner of the frame. I lean down.

KATE. THERE ISN'T MUCH TIME. THEY ARE EVERYWHERE. IF YOU HAVE FOUND THIS, I MUST BE GONE. POLLY AND V. KEEP THEM SAFE. YOU MUST...

The ink scrawls across the plastic and smudges. What the hell is going on? I am suddenly very calm. I look around at the chaos. I hang the agreement back on the wall. I was right. I was right. He is in trouble. He hasn't left me. He has been taken. I rush upstairs and turn on the shower. I breathe on the bathroom mirror, the place we secretly communicated with each other every single day. As the steam forms and my breath hits the glass, I see words emerge.

HELP. HELP ME.

CHAPTER TWENTY-TWO

Twenty minutes later I am sitting outside Veronica's house again. I want to call DS Bradley and tell her something new has happened, but what is the point? She won't believe me, just like they didn't back then. I called and called to try to tell them I had made a mistake. I rang them over and over again to try to put things right. Tell them I could have been mistaken.

They told me I was upset. I'd given my statement, and that was all. That the matter had concluded, and it had been closed. I could see my solicitor. And the mumbled warnings about contempt of court and wasting police time. It was the wax seal on my determination to start again. Forget about it. Live my life. Never mention what had happened to anyone. But I knew really. I knew I was a coward. I knew that I should have gone to see my solicitor and put things right.

Instead, I hid it deep down. I thought it had gone away. I thought by playing it safe it would never resurface. Never trigger the thoughts I had back then about her. Never remind me I didn't do what I should have done. I avoided any situation that might bring me into contact with my family or the police. I started again.

But, sitting here outside my husband's ex's home, I realise you can't start again. You can surround yourself with different things, but you cannot erase memories. You cannot erase family ties, even if those ties were rotten and fraying. The truth of it is that all families have their difficulties and secrets. All the drama and arguments and happiness and hurt. The only time the police become involved is when a crime is committed – even though serious wrongs are done in families, few of them are chargeable.

I look at Veronica's home. How am I going to explain this? I feel for the bundle of letters in my bag. I'll tell her I had taken them. That I broke into her home. I thought only I knew, but whoever has been tracking me knows too. And they know I am here. I brought the laptop. It is slotted inside my handbag, but I dare not look at it. No, they won't stop me.

Knocking on Veronica's door is the right thing to do. I will myself to do it and I am out of the car. On her drive. I know it is the right thing. Like Jake scribbled, it will keep her safe. And there is safety in numbers. If she believes me, we can call DS Bradley and ask her to look again. I stand stock-still on the drive. I know what is holding me back. The knowledge that she might shut the door in my face and that I will be alone. That she will be as scared as I am and run.

But I have to do it. I step up to the door and knock hard. Her car is here, so she must be in. For a split second, I think that they have taken her too, but then I see movement behind the dimpled glass porthole. She pauses, then opens the door. A flash of recognition registers and she steps backwards.

'Veronica. I'm…'

She fills in. 'Kate. Yes, I know. What can I do for you?'

She isn't smiling. I can see Polly behind her watching TV.

'It's Jake.'

She pulls the door shut and her hand goes to her mouth. 'Oh. He's not… is he?'

I shake my head. Shit. I don't want to scare her. I desperately don't want to scare her.

'No. No, I don't think so. But something has happened. Can I come in?'

She hesitates. 'Look, I don't want any trouble. I don't want to get involved in anything to do with him.'

I want to tell her she might already be involved. That she could be being watched. That Jake warned me. I step closer.

'I'm just the messenger. I just need to talk to you, then I will go if you want me to.'

She opens the door slightly and looks at Polly. 'Okay. But we're going out soon.'

I follow her into her home. We go through to the kitchen. The window I smashed has been temporarily boarded. She sees me look.

'Someone tried to get in.' I nod. She sits at the kitchen table and waves at me to sit too. 'So, what's happened?'

I take a breath. 'Jake's in trouble.'

She makes a small noise of derision. 'Oh, really?'

It's sarcastic. It's a *what's new?* And *that's why you are with him and not me* moment all rolled into one. I lick my lips. She's going to be hard to convince. I realise I am hugging my bag with her letters in it with both hands. I begin.

'He's missing. I went away and when I got back today, he was gone.' She is nodding, arms folded, eyebrows raised. I continue. 'All his things are gone. Every. Single. Thing. He left his job.' I place his phone in front of her. 'Messages implying blackmail. I found them in his workbag when I went there...'

She holds up her hand. 'Hang on. Back up. You went away. When you got back, he was gone? So when did you go to his office?'

She is smart. But I guess she has had to be. I sigh. 'Okay, he was late. Stayed out. I left to... to...' I don't want to say it, but I have to. 'To teach him a lesson. To make him feel how I had felt.

But he didn't contact me. So I wanted to find out what he was up to.'

'So, you stalked him?'

'No. Well, kind of. I thought...' Oh my God. I thought he was with you, Veronica. This is fucked up. I feel fear rise. Fear that I am suddenly wrong. To blame. Bad. Again. I need to level with her. I look her straight in the eye. 'I thought he was with you.'

She lets out a hollow laugh. 'You've got to be kidding.'

'No. I thought... well, I was wrong. I'm sorry. But I had to find out what was going on. And I did.'

She reads the messages and places the phone back on the table. 'So what's this got to do with me? You do know what happened between us, don't you? And the police think he's been here and...' She glances at the window. This is it. This is where I need to tell her what I have done. I take a deep breath.

'It's not him. It wasn't him.'

She laughs. 'Ah, protecting him... Yes. I went through that as well.'

I shake my head. 'No, I'm not. I'm well past that. He's lied to me. There's something going on and he didn't tell me. He let me suffer. He let me wonder. He made me think it was me.'

She studies me. 'Yes, I'm familiar with that. But you're still covering for him. And helping him.'

I reach into my bag and bring out the laptop. My heart beats fast. My fingers wrap around the letters, and I pause for a moment. She blinks at me.

'I called the police when I got home and found all his things gone. I told them everything, but they think I'm... misreading the situation. They think he's left me. I lost the plot. I ripped the house up. Not like me at all.' I feel tears rise. It feels good to get it out. 'We had this agreement...'

She laughs out loud. 'You've really got to be bloody kidding me.' I frown at her. 'An agreement. Bloody hell. He never changes.'

I register his duplicity again but push it to one side. I open the laptop. It still shows the map and another red line has been added. One that leads from my house to Veronica's. She leans in.

'I went off to Huddersfield. Someone was tracking me. I don't know how. They still are.' I point at the line. She is suddenly serious. 'He left his job ages ago. Money has gone out of our savings account. Someone's been blackmailing him. I tried to smash the agreement, but he'd written on the back of it.' I bring up a photo on my phone of the message. She looks at it. And then the mirror. 'I'm here because I'm worried you are in danger.'

She flushes. 'Oh my God, he's finally done it. He's finally pissed people off so much that they want to kill him.' She looks at the door. 'I thought it was him. But it was them, wasn't it? Wasn't it?'

I glance at Polly watching TV in the lounge. She has a snack and a toy. I pull the letters out of my bag. I am breathless and afraid, but I have to tell her the truth.

'No, it was me.' She stands up, scraping her chair. I place the letters on the table. 'I'm sorry. He made me feel like I was mad. He made me feel like I was in competition with you. And everyone else for his time. He separated me from Polly, made me feel like I wasn't good enough. He made me feel...'

She sits again. She takes the letters and shakes her head, deflated. 'I wanted to warn you. I wanted to tell you what he'd done to me. No one believed me because he is the standard nice guy. Good old Jake. But I'd sent the text messages he sent me to my friend. She persuaded me to get help. To get a solicitor and a divorce. When he met you, I wanted to tell you.' She looks at the laptop. 'But this is next-level. He's clearly pissed the wrong people off.'

I breathe out. 'I'm so sorry about your window. I was desperate. I followed you.' The words spill out thick and fast and I can't stop them. 'I saw you at your work and I saw you pick Polly up. I was here when you came in with your friend.'

She sighs. 'Well, you've seen that I'm nothing exciting then.'

I smile. Then I sober. 'I came here to tell you that you could be in danger. We should call the police.'

She nods. 'Yes, yes. Unless… no. No, ignore me.'

I frown. 'No, go on.'

'Well, unless he's set this up himself – it's within his range. Problem is though…' she turns and looks at Polly. 'He might be a complete bastard, but she's his soft spot. He pushed for me to sell the house so he could have his half, despite the courts saying I could stay until she grew up. He tried to bully me into it, but when she said she loved it here, he dropped it like a stone. Polly is his princess. If he's in trouble, and those people know him… oh my God. They'll know only one thing matters to him.' She picks up my phone and looks at the photo of the agreement. 'This. He doesn't care what happens to me or you. We're disposable. But Polly. You're right, shit got real for him. He would never do this otherwise. And he would never involve Polly if he was working alone. That much I know.'

She moves to pick up her phone, but I am staring at the screen of the laptop. A timer appears. A countdown of five days that has already ticked down to four days, twenty-three hours and fifty-eight minutes as we stare at it. My phone beeps a message.

> If you want to see Jake Clayton alive again, you need to send 100k GBP in five days' time. Do not involve the police or we will take Polly.

CHAPTER TWENTY-THREE

Veronica shakes her head violently.

"That's not him. He would never do that. Not to Polly. We need to call the police."

I stare at the ticking clock. How the hell are they tracking me? But it doesn't matter now. All that matters is that we find a way to do this.

'We can't call the police.' I point at the map. 'They know where we are they're watching. They might be able to hear us.'

Her face clouds. 'But… but what are we going to do? I don't have that kind of money.' I nod. I am surprisingly calm. But she isn't finished. 'My God, this is just an extension of what a bastard he is. You know what's happened here, don't you? He's tried to get smart with someone and they've outsmarted him. Not that it's that difficult.'

I immediately feel defensive. Her words stab at my heart. 'Hang on, he's been bloody kidnapped. Not really his fault.'

She faux laughs. 'Oh, it will be. It'll be another money-making venture gone wrong. Let's just hope it's not drugs or anything.' All the while her eyes are on her daughter.

I feel my panic mount. 'We need to make a plan.'

She snorts. 'For what?'

'We have to find that money. Whatever he's done, it doesn't just involve him now, does it? It's leaked out to us and... Polly. We have to.'

She stares at me for a long moment. She really is nothing like Jake described to me. Harsh. Cocky. Unpleasant. She is gentle and sweet, and she clearly loves her daughter. The clock on the screen ticks down and I feel a flutter of panic. A mental counting up of what I have and what I can sell. On one hand it is right here in front of me, a task to be completed. On the other, it is ludicrous. I want to pick up my phone and call DS Bradley again. I want to believe it is all a hoax.

But my mind runs through the evidence to the contrary. The things I have discovered over the past week, culminating in my half-empty house, and the desperation of the message on the agreement and the mirror tell me that this is real. I half want to believe that, like DS Bradley thinks, Jake has left. Left of his own free will. I want to think he is capable of this, but I know his love for his daughter is strong. I've seen his face when he is with her. His hand constantly on her. Veronica speaks.

'I don't have anything, really. I have a part-time job and I survive on that and Jake's maintenance. Which he didn't pay last month.' She thinks. 'But there is equity in the house. Not much. It's worth about two hundred thousand. But there is really only the deposit and what we've paid off.' She corrects herself. 'What I've paid off. So, about 50k.'

I stare at her. 'So much?'

'Yeah. He put down 25k. The rest has just been chipped away at. There was a time when I had to freeze the payments when he wasn't paying me initially, but...'

'I've got about 25k in total in savings. Our house, Lynton Grove, worth about three hundred thousand. We put down ten per cent, so with what's paid off, about 40k. But I'm not sure they will remortgage the full amount. For either of us. Even if they did, we're still short.'

She sighs. 'Polly's got a trust fund with ten thousand in it. From my parents. They're…'

I nod. We shouldn't have to be doing this. I stare at the maps and the ticking clock. 'How do we know they won't want something else afterwards? How do we know all this is going to get him back?' *And what if he comes back* asks a small voice somewhere inside me? *What then?*

She nods her agreement. 'It's like some awful movie.' She leans over the table. 'Look, you shouldn't have done that.' She points to the window. 'But I just want you to know that I know how you feel. I know how he made you feel.' She points at the papers. 'Did he…?'

'No. No, he didn't. It was more…' What? More subtle? More hidden? Less obvious. 'I don't know. More in my head.'

I think about it. It wasn't what he did. It was more what he didn't do. What he left me to do. Things that took up my time. Making me so aware that the house wasn't safe unless properly secured. The clarity that while he loved to cook with me, and he laughed and joked, he didn't want to clear up. So it was left to me. He liked a clean bathroom, but never, ever cleaned it. I hadn't complained because I was too busy holding myself rigid and hiding from my past. It had been a fait accompli, really. But I'd called it synchronicity. I hadn't seen the creep towards more and more of my time being occupied, leaving him free.

'But I did start to wonder about the late nights and then he didn't come home. Now I see that was all part of this.' *Maybe he does love you,* chimes in the small voice. Then I remember the look on DS Bradley's face that told me I am imagining it. All of it.

Veronica slams the laptop shut. 'I can't stand the thought of them watching.'

I touch her arm. 'Believe me, I searched everything. And I mean everything.' I feel my bare ears and neck. It feels strange not to have my earrings and necklace. This is truly awful. 'I'm not seeing many options here at all. For either of us. But if you'd rather, I'll go and do this on my own. It's me who is being tracked.'

She thinks for a moment. She considers it, and I hold my breath. She looks at Polly and her home. She would have no chance if someone came for Polly. At least with two of us here...

'No. Stay. I'll write down everything I can think of. Every way to get money. And you do the same. Then we'll see where we are. I know from before, when I suggested to my solicitor that me and Polly go into hiding, when he was harassing me, that it has to be a complete break.' I think about my feeble attempt at going into hiding. Laughable, because all the while someone was watching. Although none of this is laughable. She mirrors my thoughts. 'But this is worse, much worse. If I go to the police and ask for protection, then it's forever.' She looks into her garden. Into the distance. And I know it is the same distance as I am peering into. Something completely unknown and terrifying.

She gets to work writing down anything she has of value. I do the same, but I know my monetary worth already. I'd constantly kept it at the forefront of my mind as some fucked-up accolade for leaving my working-class roots and ascending to the middle classes. The equity in the house is 44k. Maybe 45k now. My savings account totals 25k. No, 20k with the money Jake withdrew.

I log in to my phone to check the amount and glance at our joint mortgage account. There must be some mistake. We borrowed two hundred and twenty thousand pounds. This balance shows two hundred and fifty thousand pounds. I press on the screen over and over to bring up recent transactions. And I see it. The word 'remortgage' a year ago. My God. This has been going on longer than I thought. I am irked that he'd done this without me – and probably forged my signature – but he must have been desperate.

There would be no chance of me borrowing against the house – unless… yes. Unless it had increased in value. I quickly bring up Rightmove and a house four doors down that had been up for sale recently. It flashes on the screen, and I focus in on the asking price. Three hundred and ten thousand pounds. I can ask for a loan on the equity. But even if that is possible it wouldn't be enough.

I weigh up what else I have. I could sell clothes and jewellery. But who am I kidding? My wardrobe is functional and I hardly have any jewellery of the kind of value I need. Except… I look at my wedding ring. And my engagement ring. Jake had produced it out of nowhere on a walk in the country. He got down on one knee in the gravel and begged me to marry him. It felt right. And when I saw the ring, I wondered where he had got something so expensive.

I twist it around now, along with the matching wedding ring. I'd peered into jewellers' windows at similar pieces. Eventually I spotted exactly the same ring in a Manchester jeweller for an extortionate sum. The diamond was so big that I wondered if it was real. But it is. I swallow hard. He might not be perfect, but we have had good times. I don't want anything to happen to him, and I can tell Veronica feels the same. She is thinking and listing and looking in drawers for documents. I add my rings to the list. But it still isn't enough. And even if it was, five days is not enough time to get loans and arrange mortgages. No, I know where I have to go with this. The one thing I vowed I would never do.

I didn't hear from any of my brothers until one day a text message popped up. I'd thought I was getting over it all, and then this bolt from the blue. Flynn contacted me on a Monday morning. But it took me until Friday to see it, because I kept my phone switched off most of the time. Ian would call me at work and on the train and everywhere, really, to see where I was. What

I was doing. Who I was with. So I sacrificed the convenience of having instant communication for freedom.

It wasn't until I was settled in front of the TV with a cup of tea after work that I turned my phone on. I was only in my twenties, but Ian kept me like an old woman, waiting in while he went out. If I did go out with him, he would sit stiffly in pubs and restaurants as if I was somehow stifling him. So I stayed in alone. And that night I was grateful he wasn't there. Because the shock of Flynn getting in touch ricocheted through me as I read the message.

None of what had happened that previous year had really sunk in. I was still numb with grief and pain and disbelief, and my own marriage problems stopped me from processing anything but everyday tasks. I had distanced myself from everything except what was absolutely necessary but suddenly it was all there in front of me again.

> Hi Kate. This is Flynn. I got your number from my solicitor. I hope you don't mind me contacting you. To cut to the chase, I have the insurance money and a cheque for your share of it. Let me know how you want to collect it.

I'd stared at the message for a long time. Flynn. My little brother. It seemed so grown up for him to text me and tell me he had something for me. The insurance money. I remember a shiver down my spine and my hand shaking as I held my mobile phone. The last time I had seen him he was asleep in his bunk bed, his eye twitching in his sleep. He was a young teenager, the eldest of them. The others slept in the same bunk, end to end.

I debated about calling him. I had his number now and I could call him or text him. But I didn't. It would be the easiest thing to just punch in his number and press the green phone. Green for go. But I didn't. I typed in a thousand responses over the next week and sent none of them. Then I just did nothing. I was too busy fielding Ian and thinking about the day I left them and how much I had missed them.

The next thing I knew, a white envelope dropped onto my doormat. It was from my solicitor and when I opened it, I saw a cheque for fifty-two thousand pounds. That was nine years ago. It would have gained interest now because I never cashed it. I opened an account, one of my own, separate from Ian, especially for it. It would be my business. I already knew, deep down, that Ian and I would not last. The surveillance got much worse, and he suspected everything. I knew things were coming to an end and this would help me escape.

But I couldn't cash it. I'd got as far as the door of my bank with it in my handbag, but something stopped me every time. I didn't know what it was then. Now I know it was my conscience. I open my Facebook app and look at Flynn's profile. I could message him right now and ask for the money. I'd have to do it direct because my solicitor had retired, and his practice ceased. All his records were transferred to another practice, and it would take too long to explain. Or it would be too painful to go through it all again and things are bad enough already.

His latest status tells me he's had a barbecue and his brothers all turned up with beer. They are all in the picture, arms around each other. I used to fantasise that he was posting these photographs for me, to let me know they survived. *Everything is okay, Kate, despite you and her and him.* I wondered if I could go back and if I would then be in the pictures. I could explain and tell them why I did it. Why I left and why I said what I said later. But I never did. Because I am a coward. I never did what I should have done.

Now I might have to, I realise. My finger hovers over Flynn's face. I imagine him at the weekend round of family get-togethers. Him seeing my message and suddenly sobering. Blinking into the distance and remembering that day from his eyes. Waking up alone. Mum and Dad gone. And now Kate. What did it do to him and Patrick and Michael? I don't know what he would remember because I wasn't there. I don't know what happened when the social worker took them from our house. Did they take their toys? The scruffy Action Men and the Lego? Their favourite pyjamas? Were they allowed something to remember Mum by? Or Dad? Or me? Did they even want to?

Who made them breakfast? Did they cry? Were they afraid? All the questions I cannot process flood my senses, and I slam my phone down on the table. Veronica looks up and Polly turns round quickly. Veronica jumps up.

'Kate? Are you okay? Has something happened?'

I shake my head. No. No, it hasn't. It's all exactly the same as it was all those years ago.

CHAPTER TWENTY-FOUR

I slept at Veronica's last night. She was too scared to stay there on her own and told me she would go to Scotland to her mother's house. I convinced her to stay, and she slept in Polly's room. I found myself sleeping in her bedroom. Their bedroom. I lay awake thinking about the ridiculous and terrifying situation I find myself in.

But Veronica is right. Safety in numbers. We made a long list of things we could try to get the money together. We've already looked at Veronica's bank accounts online to see how much she can scrape together. It's less than we thought. She insisted we go to the bank and sit in front of someone to make it all real. We'd driven there in silence in her car. I took the laptop and watched as the line snaked with us, despite not being in my own car. That's when I realised it was me. I am the tracker.

It wasn't a wasted journey, but Veronica was disappointed. She would only be able to borrow half the equity and the process would be long. It would involve a valuation of the house and a short legal underwriting process.

The lady we spoke to didn't notice our pale, scared faces as she trotted out her sales pitch. But I saw my expression reflected in the glass partition. It was an expression I hadn't seen for just short of a decade. Focused. Fearful. Wide-eyed and blinking fast as I struggle to take in the information overlaying the sheer volume of thoughts darting around my mind.

'Of course, you could always take out an initial loan to cover the sum. Then, when it's finalised, pay it off.'

Veronica held on to Polly tightly. It was the first appointment of the day. Polly had complained about not going to school. Veronica sighed.

'How long will it take?'

The woman tapped on her computer keys. 'We'd have to run a credit check and subject to earnings, the loan could be in your account within twenty-four hours of signing.'

She looked deflated. 'I only have a part-time job. But the security of the house…'

The woman shook her head. 'I'm really sorry. It doesn't work like that. The two are separate. You would need to show you can pay it back. You would need payslips or a letter from your employer on headed…'

Her voice fades away as I think about the lengths we are going to need to go to. To save someone who lied to us both. And probably got himself into this mess by lying, too. But I look at Polly: she's the real reason. The threats against her have dulled both our anger. Jake can take care of himself. And we must now, too.

She borrowed as much as she could and started the remortgage process. She had a few payslips, and the amount was much smaller than we needed, but I almost cried with relief when she was approved for the loan.

And I did the same. I signed up for a loan to borrow against the equity. It was slightly different for me as the house is in both our names. I need a copy of our marriage certificate, my own and Jake's ID and/or Jake to sign the application form all scanned and sent to the bank's head office. I had to think quickly. I had a scan of his driving licence and my passport. I could forge his signature on the form. Not something I would normally do, but needs must. But our marriage certificate. I rerun my rage and the state of our lounge afterwards. The shards of paper from our 'life admin' file – including our marriage certificate.

I could get another one. This was day two of five days. I could get another one.

So now Veronica and I are outside the pawn shop. She took Polly to school. She told the teachers that Polly must not go with anyone else. She asked them to show her the security system. They were concerned, but she brushed it off as a 'domestic', implying that she and Jake had had an argument, and she was just worried. They told her they had to let her go with Jake because of the 'family arrangements' but assured her that no one else would be able to collect Polly. The deputy head looked at me as she said it. She recognised me from the school yard. Veronica half turned and smiled tightly.

'Of course, Kate is okay. She's Polly's step-mum. She can collect Polly. Of course she can.'

It meant a lot. And as we watched Polly run along with the other children, laughing and oblivious to our terror, I knew this was the best thing. Stay in public, no one is going abduct her from a full classroom. Or us from a high street, together.

I twist my wedding and engagement rings on my finger. Veronica sees me.

'No, you can't. You're not going to…?'

But I am. I am going to pawn the most precious things in the world to me after Jake. Or the man I thought he was. I don't even know if our marriage is over. I don't really know what has happened. But I know I have to do this.

I peer into the shop. There is a queue of five people. We park just down the road and go inside. Veronica stands by the window checking her phone. I wait. And wait. A woman is arguing over a gold chain and telling one assistant that she needs the money to pay her gas bill. Finally, a manager takes over and the queue shuffles up a place.

I take off the rings. They are heavy and my hand suddenly feels light. Or is it my soul? Our wedding hadn't been the fairy-tale event I had envisaged. I'd gone along with the arrangements Jake had booked and, as he said, dressed them up. In fact, I'd project managed it. Everything matched.

It wasn't until we were sitting in the hotel in front of the event organiser that I realised. He'd shown us the room plan. We were to walk through an arch of cherry blossom with white wooden benches on each side for guests. I'd chosen a garden theme because that is how I wanted ours to look like. Then, after the ceremony, the arch would be moved to the back of the room for photo opportunities and tables would be placed between the benches.

'So let's look at the top table. Kate, who are your top table guests?'

All eyes on me. The event organiser; his secretary, who was taking notes; the menu designer; and Jake. I searched for names. I searched for the right words to tell them I had no family. We'd already established that Polly would be bridesmaid and Paula maid of honour. All I could see was black spaces on a table plan. Empty spaces on one side of a wedding hall. Jake had stepped in.

'I'd like the guests to mingle. Could we enter via the arch already at the end of the room? That way the photographer has a perfect backdrop. And Kate and I discussed mixing our guests. I know it's not traditional, but…'

I blurted it out. Right out. 'Could we sit on thrones? His and hers thrones?'

Everyone blinked at me. Jake bowed his head and smiled. There was a long minute of visualisation and then the manager clapped his hands with glee.

'Yes! Yes! Thrones. Like Katy Price?'

I nodded. Jake gripped my hand, and the day was saved.

Except the actual day wasn't. Because no matter how much I swapped and changed and merged and mingled, my family were not there. A couple of people from work turned up at the night reception, but no family at all. It would have been the perfect time to get in touch. Invite them.

Jake knew most of what happened, and he told me to make contact with my brothers. But I didn't. I kept meaning to, but all I could see was trouble. Bad feeling about the distant past and recriminations about what happened later. My wedding was not the place for it.

The man in front of me is tired of waiting and leaves. The queue moves up one and it is me next. Nearly there. I close my hand over the shiny rings. My engagement ring that I wore so proudly. And my diamond studded wedding ring. I'd never had them valued, although I had wanted to. But it felt wrong. It felt like I was somehow questioning his intentions. His promise. It felt like it would break the agreement we had made. I snort to myself. The irony of it. Now I have to sell them to save him from himself.

The woman in front of me has several items and they are going through them all. I know that the money my rings fetch will not be enough, I feel a wave of bravery run through me. I need the insurance money. It goes against everything I decided, and it will inevitably bring up issues I don't want to – need to – think about right now. But what choice do I have? It seems ludicrous, but this is spiralling out of control. Even now I wonder if I have to do it, if I have to get this money together. But I can't see another option. If we call the police, we are in even more danger.

I've watched hundreds of TV dramas and almost screamed for people to call the police. My hands shake as I take out my phone and type. I don't know if this will solve anything or make it worse. Panic overrides these thoughts and I bring up Flynn's

Facebook. I press 'message' and type out the words I swore I never would.

Hi Flynn. This is Kate

I type 'your sister' then delete it.

I wondered if the insurance money could be transferred to me by bank transfer, please. I know it's been a long time but there was a lot to think about.

I type 'and regret' and delete that too.

Let me know. Kate.

I do not hesitate. I press send and watch as the two grey ticks emerge and then two blue ticks. I feel sick. He has seen the message. I grip my phone and will him to respond. When I look up, the woman in front of me has gone and I am next. I push the phone into my pocket.

'Hi. Hi. I have these rings. I'd like to sell them.'

She stares at me. 'Sell or pawn?'

I lean forward. My voice is a tortured whisper. 'Whichever brings most money and is quickest.'

She nods. I guess she has seen it all before. I push the rings into the metal tray underneath the security screen and she pulls them towards her. I suddenly want to shout at her to give them back. That I'd made a mistake. My wedding ring finger feels bare and odd. But I watch as she looks at them.

'Okay, these are very nice pieces. I'd like to get a second opinion. Could you leave them with us, and I will ask my manager to take a look? It'll only take an hour or two. He's very knowledgeable in this area.' I'm unsure. I lick my lips and stumble for words. She senses it and speaks again. 'He has buyers for this kind of thing. Otherwise, you are looking at just the gold value.'

I nod and she weighs the rings, takes my details and issues a receipt.

'I'll message you when we're ready for you.'

We leave. Once in the car, I look at the laptop. The clock is ticking, and I feel a renewed panic. Veronica is looking out of the window. She suddenly speaks.

'You know, I didn't like you at first. I thought you were stand-offish. Jake told me you were very serious. That you had a serious job in the media.'

'Yeah, he told me you were a bitch.'

She laughs. I feel the laughter rise and we sit in the car howling. None of this is funny. It's beyond any emotion I have felt before, and I didn't think that was possible. She finally stops.

'The weird thing is, we're more like each other than different.'

I know what she means. We're both pushovers. We're both gullible. We both believed him. But I don't say it. Instead, I look at my phone. No messages from Flynn. No messages at all.

'Well, I hope so, Veronica, because you're not half as bad as he painted you. Come on, I'll go home and get my ID and send the loan applications. I need to get that marriage certificate so I can try to remortgage.'

I slam the laptop shut and drive up the high street. We're running out of time.

CHAPTER TWENTY-FIVE

We turn the corner to Lynton Grove, and I see it. A 'for sale' sign in the middle of our lawn. My lawn. Someone has dug a huge hole and the beautiful grass is churned around it. The estate agent is Dyer and Francis and I start to ring them. But as I turn the key and go to switch the alarm off, I realise it isn't on. I end the call and look around. Veronica is behind me.

'It's… it's…'

She looks into our home. She hasn't been here before. 'It's very nice,' she offers. Her eyes wander to the agreement which is back on the wall. I lift it down. The message has gone, and the surface wiped clean. Her voice breaks. 'It's exactly the same. Exactly.'

I could have guessed it would be. And she is right. The house is very nice. Very nice and tidy. There isn't a shred of paper or anything out of place to suggest I'd had a huge blow out in here yesterday. It is pristine. I check everything and nothing is gone, save the stuff I destroyed. I grab my ID from the drawer. Then I redial the estate agent. I am held in a queue and there is not time for this. I end the call again.

'He's put the house up for sale. Or someone has.'

She shakes her head. 'Oh my God, they must have made him. What are we going to do? I'm scared, Kate.'

I look at her. She is scared. She is pale and tearful. I, on the other hand, am fuming. I'm not scared. I am angry and it's only because Veronica is here that I don't completely lose it again. But I can feel it coming. Pressure from all sides and my past sprinting towards me.

I fire up my laptop and upload my ID to the bank application file. A cheery pop-up, which is completely at odds with how I feel right, now tells me my evidence is complete and the loan will be processed. All I need to do now is take my marriage certificate to the bank and start off the process of remortgaging. If I can, because it looks like the house could be sold at any moment.

Once done we drive back into town, and I hurry into the registry office. Veronica is behind me. I tap my fingers on the reception desk as the clerk files some papers in no particular hurry. I am wound tightly now. But all I know is that I must complete this in time for the countdown on the laptop.

Finally, she walks towards us. 'Good morning. What can I do for you today?'

I keep it under control. Just. 'I'd like a copy of my marriage certificate, please.'

'I'm very sorry, you can only order them online. Unless you have a priority appointment.'

I stare at her. 'Can I have a priority appointment for now, please, then?'

She opens her mouth to speak, and I can tell she is going to refuse. I take a deep breath.

'It's really important. It's time limited.' I look behind me. 'And it's not busy. Please?'

I am blinking fast and ready to blow. She licks her lips. She is used to dealing with people. She can tell I'm on the edge. I see her making the decisions. Does she press her panic button or just do what we ask?

'May I have you full name, please, and that of your husband?'

'Yes, thank you. Catherine Mary Clayton. And Jackson Hewett Taylor Clayton.'

She smiles tightly. 'Oh, what an unusual name. No need to ask for dates. Here it is.'

I side eye the screen. I see my name next to his, and the entry below it is Veronica and Jake. I blink at the screen as she turns around and fetches a book of blank certificates from the back office. I turn it slightly towards me and wave at Veronica, who is sitting biting her nails in the corner.

'This.' I point at a third entry. 'Is this fucking him?'

My voice doesn't sound like my own. I am so angry at the depth of his omissions that I almost explode. Of course it's him. Of course it is. Veronica's eyes widen.

'First I've seen of it. Or heard. Holly Marie Brierly. Maybe it's another...'

I shake my head and snort. 'No. It's him.'

The receptionist is back. I stare at her.

'Actually, can I get all three of those? We're doing a family history project for our children, and we wanted to do Daddy's family tree.' The lies slip from my tongue thick and fast as I turn sugary sweet. I make my voice break slightly at 'daddy'. She pulls a sympathetic face.

'Of course. It's an upsetting time. It's so important that children know who their family are.'

She thinks we're filling in the gaps. She thinks he's dead. And there it is. A small voice somewhere inside me that confirms everything I ever suspected about myself. *I wish he was dead.* I steady myself on the counter and the woman looks at me in sympathy, as if I am overcome by emotion about my dead husband. But I know I am on the slow march to where I never wanted to be. *Like* I never wanted to be. Like Collette.

She prints the certificates onto the official templates and then slowly signs them with an ink pen, blotting the words as she goes. I watch her, willing her to hurry. She completes mine and Veronica's and finally Holly's.

The mysterious Holly who no one has heard of. We've both been married to a man who decided not to tell us he had been previously married too. I hand Veronica her certificate and she shakes her head. It does not escape my notice that all three of us were married at the same hotel.

'That will be one hundred and five pounds, please.'

She hands over a card machine. I push in the card and punch in my number. I look her in the eyes.

'Thank you.'

She nods. 'It's okay. We don't usually issue certificates here but… well. I hope whatever it is, is worth it.'

Worth my silent threat to her. That's what she means. But before I can apologise my phone rings. I answer it quickly.

'Mrs Clayton? It's the jewellers. Mr Greene is back now if you'd like to come over. Any time before three.'

Her casual tone is at odds with my panic. Veronica is staring at me.

'Was it them?'

I shake my head. 'No. The jewellers.'

I retrieve my card and the marriage certificates and hurry out of the registry office. Back in the car I open Facebook on my phone. The anticipation of Flynn responding to my message is overwhelming and my hands shake. But he hasn't. So I search for Holly Brierly. Veronica snorts beside me.

'Like looking for a needle in a haystack. She'll have remarried. Or she might still be called Clayton. Bloody hell, three Mrs Claytons.'

She laughs, but we both know nothing is funny about this. There are lots of Holly Brierlys but only one near Manchester. She looks the right age. I scroll through her photographs. No man or children. I see she lives in the red-brick flats in Hulme. I recognise the entrance she is standing outside because one of my friends from university lived there. I check her friends list just in case he is there. He isn't, but I do recognise some names. Ben Stokes. Len Crowe. Both ex-workmates of Jake's. I look at a recent photo of her with her dog. I zoom in to see who this woman is – this woman who has been married to my husband – and the rage rises.

I close Facebook, start the car and drive to the pawn shop. No good can come of ogling Holly Brierly right now. I mentally calculate how much we have got together. The two loans against the remortgages come to fifty-five thousand pounds. My savings add twenty-five thousand to it. It's not enough. I think hard about how I can raise more money. I could ask Paula, but she's got enough on her plate at the moment.

I think about messaging Flynn again. The hard fact is that the insurance money is rightfully mine, but the complex emotions attached to taking it hold me back. I may have no choice. I count through my credit cards and think about transferring the available balances into cash, just as insurance in case there is a problem with the loans. But first, my wedding rings.

We stride into the pawn shop and the counter assistant nods. A tall man in a grey suit appears.

'Ah, Mrs Clayton. And…' He looks at Veronica.

'Veronica Clayton.'

'Ah, sisters. Delightful. Come this way, ladies.'

I roll my eyes. Veronica and I bear no resemblance to each other. None. But I'll take it as it means not having to explain the real reason we are here. He points to a bench at the back of the shop, out of sight from the busy street. I follow him into his cosy office.

He opens a huge safe adjacent to us and takes out my rings. He places them on a black velvet cushion and clasps his hands together.

'I do understand. This is a difficult time and the

circumstances of you selling such delightful pieces are, well, upsetting. I'm here to make it as easy as possible.'

I stare at him. Every nuance of this whole bloody escapade seems to be designed to rub in the fact that Jake has deceived me. Us. Yet, and although I would happily divorce him tomorrow, I now have to rescue him. Selling my rings is painful enough, but to have to act upset over my non-existent divorce is almost too much. My hands are shaking as the fire threatens to escape but I just nod. He continues.

'Well, I have some good news. I'm not certain, but I suspect I have a private buyer. Of course, they will need a good clean.' He raises a loupe to his eye and inspects my wedding ring, polishing it with a cloth. Then he places it on a scale and records the weight. He looks again at each individual diamond. My heart aches with each movement. He finally speaks. 'Lovely piece. Do you have proof of ownership?'

'Yes. My husband had it valued for the insurance. It's on the policy along with the other ring.'

My mind races through the debris of the lounge after my angry whirlwind of destruction. Then I remember the policy is stored online in our account. I search for the email while he picks up my engagement ring. I click and he studies the ring. I find the email and show him the policy and the photographs of the pieces.

But he has a pair of long tweezers in his hand.

'I'm afraid you'll get nowhere near what it's insured for there. And it needs a good clean, as I said. But they always do, because they are rarely removed.' He scrapes at it and pokes around behind the stones. 'Looks like there's a backing on the stone. Unusual.' He scrapes again and a silver dot drops onto the black cushion. He holds the ring up to a lamp beside him. 'Ah. Better. Clearer.'

I stand. 'Wait here.'

I rush to the car and grab the laptop. Veronica opens her mouth to speak as I sprint past her but there is no time. I rush back inside and open it. The clock is still ticking down and I enlarge the screen on the map. Bigger and bigger. Until I can see the last line. I go cold as I see it end right at the place we are now. But there is no line leading from the jewellers to my house. I think fast. I grab the rings from the cushion and pick up the silver dot carefully.

'Thank you so much. I'm afraid I can't go through with it. Too upsetting.'

We are out of the shop before he can say anything. I hurry into the McDonald's next door. Veronica runs after me. I hurry through to the toilets and almost throw the silver dot into the pan and flush. But then I think better of it. Instead, I look for a dusty ledge. One that is never wiped down. I stand on the toilet lid and reach up to the very top of the window. It's thick with grime and grease, and I stick the dot onto it.

I am gripping the rings so hard they make indents in my hand. I sit on the toilet seat and scream loudly. Veronica just stares at me.

'My rings. That was the first time I've taken them off since we married. The first time. I swore I would never take them off. It was part of the agreement. But you know what that means, don't you?'

CHAPTER TWENTY-SIX

I am running. Running to my car now no one is following me.
I suddenly feel so angry I could hunt Jake down and rip him
apart. It is a familiar feeling I have only ever felt vicariously
before, one that says, 'This is it'. One that is unstoppable.

Veronica hurries behind me. 'Shouldn't we call the police
now?'

We get into the car. I cannot believe it. Even after all I told
him about Ian and my family, Jake still chose to follow me. I've
had the engagement ring for four years. He's known my every
single move the whole time. I bang my hands on the steering
wheel and she jumps.

'Sorry. Sorry. I just...'

She fills in for me. 'Can't believe it? No, neither could I. He
was so convincing. So lovely at first. But...' She covers her face
with her hands. 'Look, I have to go and collect Polly in an hour
and a half. We should go back to mine and have a think–'

I interrupt her. I am starting the car and screeching down the
high street. Shoppers turn and look, and Veronica grips the door
handle and pulls on her seat belt. 'This won't take long. I just
need the final piece of the puzzle.'

I speed along the Mancunian Way and over the bypass. I pull over at the Red Bricks and park outside a block of flats with flowers streaming over the balconies. I open Facebook and check this is the right block. The cherry tree sapling outside tells me it is. I start at the first flat. I buzz the doorbell. A woman's voice crackles. 'Yeah, who is it?'

'I'm looking for Holly. I'm an acquaintance.'

She is silent. 'Are you the police?'

I step backwards so she can see me through her window. I shrug and force a smile. Veronica does the same.

'No. I'm just wanting to ask her something about... this bloke.'

She is silent again. Then she speaks. 'I'm not buzzing you in. But she's number four.'

I press the buzzer for number four, marvelling that people's lives are so open on social media. So findable. Seconds pass and I resign myself to the fact that she's at work. Or just out. But then she speaks. 'Hello?'

I swallow hard. I don't know what I want. I don't know what I will do. But I know that I want to find out more about Jake and his past.

'Hi. I'm Kate Clayton. I'm married to Jake. I'm with Veronica Clayton. Who was previously married to Jake. Can we talk to you, please?'

She is silent. I hear rustling. 'Has something happened to him? Not that I give a shit.'

'No. I just wanted to... I don't know...'

She is silent again. Then I hear rustling. 'Let me guess. He's fucked you over?'

I sense the bitterness. The distant hurt being brought back into focus.

'That's just it. We don't know what's going on. Neither of us knew about you until today. Can we just talk to you?'

Seconds tick by. The buzzer sounds. I grab the door and we duck inside. The corridor is concrete, but there are plant pots and some wicker hearts. I face her door just as she opens it. She is tall and willowy but looks tired. She waves us in.

Her flat is tidy and very beige and yellow. It reminds me of sunshine and is a complete contrast to the outside of the building. She motions us to sit. Veronica sits near the door, but I sit on a dining chair in the tiny lounge. She doesn't offer us a cup of tea or ask how we are. This is not polite conversation. She knows what we are here for.

'So, what do you want?'

Her eyes mock me. I suddenly realise I am no longer the child waiting outside in the bushes. I am here, where the reality of the situation hides. Behind closed doors and hidden in unspoken words.

I take a deep breath. It's hard to know where to start. But I have no need to because Veronica speaks now.

'So, I married him and we have a child.' I see a slight wince, less than a tick, cross Holly's face. 'Almost immediately he started to bully me and then he...' Holly is nodding and hugging herself, her knees tight against each other. Veronica continues, a little louder and stronger. 'It was hard to see what he was doing. It was a collection of small things rather than anything I could really grab at. Lies I couldn't prove. Staying out. Supporting me to finish work when I had Polly. Then taking away any housekeeping he promised to give me. And if I challenged it, he was just... awful. But the final straw came when I realised he had remortgaged the house.'

She turns to me, a tear running down her face.

'And now he's been kidnapped or something. He's obviously done something wrong. Upset someone. And they mentioned Polly. And the truth is, Kate, the equity on the house is only what had built up since then. I had to take on the full mortgage. I'm sorry.'

Holly holds her hand up. 'Wait, wait. Please don't tell me

you've given him money? Have you called the police? Not that they will be interested.'

I nod. 'Yeah. I… erm… went away to have a think. I found out some stuff then went home to challenge him, and he was gone. With all his things. I knew something was wrong because of some messages on a phone in his workbag. So, I called the police, and they just said he'd left me.' Unexpected tears. I can feel the sorrow force its way up into my throat and I swallow it back down. 'But then I found a message on the back of our agreement…'

Holly lets out a loud, exaggerated 'Ha!' She is nodding and smiling. 'Ah, yes. The agreement. Let me guess. All about being in each other's pockets. Own space. All that shit. Oh yes, I know all about that.' She leans forward. 'Let me tell you what he did to me.' She reaches behind her and picks up a lever arch file that is bulging with papers. 'So, this is everything. All the loans he took out in my name. All the bank statements where he withdrew money. We were living at my mum's while we bought a house, I already had some savings before I met him. Quite a lot. I'd worked abroad for a while. Then we saved and saved and… well, then it was gone. We'd only been married a year, and he wiped me out. When he disappeared, the loan payment demands started to arrive.'

She throws the file onto the rug between us.

'It took me ten years to pay them off and to get sorted. I lived with my parents for a while, but then my friend was renting this place out so…' She sighs. 'He took everything. It wasn't just the money. It was… well, I guess you know what it was.'

It's completely silent in Holly's lounge. Yes. Yes, we do know. And it's becoming clearer by the minute. I feel completely stupid. I'd believed him. I'd hung on his every word. I'd made excuses for him. I'd slept with him. A thousand questions teem through my mind. Did he love me? Did he always intend to do this? I know the answer, really, but I still explain.

'Yes, I do know. The problem is, we can't understand now if this is him or if he is really in trouble. They asked for a ransom. But my ring–'

She jumps in. 'Ring? What about it? Did he sell it?'

I look at Veronica.

'No, no. He put a tracker in my engagement ring. I just had it valued and the jeweller found it. He's been tracking me since...' I struggle with the words. I can't even think about it.

But Holly is on her feet. 'Tracking? Tracking? Does he know you're here? I don't want him here...' She is genuinely terrified. 'He told me if I ever told anyone he would...'

Veronica stands. 'I think we should call the police. Whatever's happened, they will be able to help. And this has gone further than money now. Following someone is illegal. It's harassment.'

Holly scoffs. 'Yeah, if you can prove it's him. He'll deny and deny until he's blue in the face.'

I feel myself falling. The shock of what I am realising shows on both Veronica's and Holly's faces. And I've seen it before. I only recognise it now as abject helplessness as Collette walked away from the women she had been arguing with. On the occasions she had left us outside houses when the object of her suspicion had let her in and explained the situation.

She became quiet and withdrawn. The calm before the storm of her getting blind drunk and first dancing with us then sending us scattering to our cubbyhole hiding place as she destroyed the house in her rage. It is boiling inside me, that rage.

No one speaks. We are wondering what to do next, but I am wondering how much more I can take before I blow. Before I go to find him. But I can't let this get the better of me.

Holly rocks a little and then speaks. 'My money would be on him pulling a fucking fast one. I've never seen him since. Never looked for him. But I see he's been busy with you two. And now he'll be on to the next one. Lining her up for the kill as you lick your wounds.' She's staring at me, a smile on her lips. 'You still love him, don't you? You still don't believe he's capable of this? Maybe this is someone else, but you can bet your bottom dollar that if it is, he's fucked up badly somewhere and they're out to get him.'

I nod. She's right. But she's been there, hasn't she. 'I haven't had time. I haven't had enough time to understand. I knew something was going on but... I just didn't know what. This time last week I thought he was... I thought he was still in love with Veronica. He was acting strange.'

She tuts. 'Late for things? Staying out? Telling you nothing was wrong? Making you feel like you were imagining it?'

Veronica nods her agreement. 'It was more than that with me. It was... cruel. I think he expected me to do something. Kate ran off. I just sat there and took it because I had Polly.'

Holly wrings her hands. 'I didn't even notice. I was so young and besotted.' She still looks young, but she has worry lines and deep crow's feet. She has a concerned resting expression and searching eyes. 'It's ridiculous. I completely fell for it. He took over everything. "Looking after me" he called it. Joint bank accounts because we were married. And because, according to that fucking agreement, trust is everything.' She wipes a tear away. 'But he robbed me of the one thing I wanted so much. A baby. By the time I'd paid off his debts I was forty. Ticking clock. Forty and single.'

I stare at her. 'You don't look forty. Not at all. And forty isn't too late.'

She nods. 'I know, but I'd have to meet someone and get a place. He robbed me of years of my life.' I reach out to touch her arm, but she shrinks away. 'Anyway, now you know. What are you going to do?'

None of us have an answer. This is unfamiliar territory for me. I completely extracted myself from Ian's life. A loud buzzing pierces the silence. Veronica jumps out of her skin and answers her phone.

'Yes, this is Mrs Clayton.'

I watch her as her quiet expression twists into horror.

'What do you mean she isn't in class?'

I stand. Polly. I already know before she says it.

'But don't you have cameras?' She is shaking. Her face flushes and she is screaming into her phone. 'No, she is not with me. I told you not to let her go with anyone. I told you.'

She listens, blinking away tears. Holly and I gather around her. Finally, she ends the call. Her expression is haunted.

'We have to go. We have to meet the police back at mine. Polly's been taken out of school. They can't find her.'

CHAPTER TWENTY-SEVEN

She is no longer calm, collected and a little bit timid. Veronica hurries out of Holly's flat and strides towards the car. She waits for us, back turned. I stare at Holly.

'Are you coming?'

'Will he…'

'I don't know. But I need you to tell the police what you told me.' She is hesitant. I watch Veronica turn to see where I am. 'Please. We need to find him. Find out what's happened.'

She pulls on her coat, and I wait with Veronica while Holly locks up. She looks unlike herself. Her skin is tight, and she is hyper alert.

'Come on. We need to get back.'

I unlock the car and she gets in. Holly is on her way. Veronica stares straight ahead. She has one focus only. Her daughter. She speaks in almost a whisper.

'It's not him. He would have just picked her up. They don't have cameras inside the school. Just on the front and the yard. On the entrances. The police are checking them now. He wouldn't risk being caught on a camera. He knows they are there. He was on the fundraising team for them. This is someone else.'

Her knuckles are white gripping the edges of the seat. Holly sits quietly in the back. She's brought her file and has a small rucksack beside her. I drive fast. I can feel Veronica willing me to jump red lights and overtake on the pavement. We pass the school and I see a police car parked outside. She turns her head.

'I'd be picking her up in half an hour.'

I want to tell her it's okay. But it isn't. I know this is critical now and that we should have called the police earlier. I glance at the laptop. Through the rear-view mirror, I catch Holly's eye. 'Can you open it, please?'

She pulls up the top and turns the screen around. It's still ticking away and telling us we have little time left. Veronica's phone rings and she jumps out of her skin. She answers it on speakerphone.

'Hello?' Her voice is weak and drained.

'May I speak with Veronica Clayton, please?'

'This is Veronica speaking.'

There is a pause. I've heard that voice before.

'This is DS Bradley. How far are you from your home, Veronica?'

She looks out of the window. 'Two minutes.'

I can hear Bekah Bradley breathing through the car speakers.

'When you get there just enter the property as normal. We'll be around the back. Just walk through and let us in. Okay?'

She nods, even though she is on the phone. 'Yes. I'm with Kate. And Holly.'

Another longer pause. 'Kate Clayton?' She doesn't sound surprised. Just factual. 'And who is Holly?'

Veronica searches for the right words. 'Holly is Jake's first wife.'

Bekah sighs loudly. 'Okay. Right. Tell them to just walk in. Then we'll take it from there.'

We are turning into Veronica's road. There are no police cars and no cars at all parked anywhere near the house. I try to remember if she has a back gate or if there is a lane behind her house. But all I can remember is smashing glass.

I park and we sit in silence for a moment. Veronica murmurs her words. 'What if they... what if she's...'

Her eyes are steely cold. I sense she is playing out her thoughts behind them.

'The police will get them. We need to give them all the information we have. All of it.'

She nods. 'But we only have information about him. Not about the people who have him. Them.'

Her face contorts into pain. I have seen that look before. On my mother's face as she realised she had lost the thing that was most important to her in all the world. The pain she felt when all love was lost, and she couldn't see a way forward. Except the love wasn't for her children. It was for him. And there it is. Surfacing at the very moment I need to think about something else. Something serious and life threatening.

There it is. The realisation of why I did what I did and why, since then, I had been running around seeking everyone's approval. Being beyond reproach and never, ever saying anything that would make me seem less than agreeable. There it is. In Veronica's eyes, the overwhelming love for her daughter that was absent from Collette's. Her gaze was somewhere else entirely, and the scar is still on my soul.

I open the car door and grab the laptop from the back seat. Holly is unsure, but I ignore her. She can wait here if she wants, but I am going to support Veronica. We walk towards the house and after a few seconds Holly follows. Outside she seems taller and more ethereal. In her own environment she looked at home, but here, in the street, she looks slightly dishevelled, and her gait is clumsy. She squints at me.

'I haven't got any money to...'

I shake my head. 'No, no, it's okay. I just want the police to hear your story.'

Veronica is turning her key in the lock, and I will Polly to be inside, safe, running towards her like some wrap up in a crime series. But as we all enter, we see DS Bradley and DC Sharples standing by the boarded window. Two men in builders' clothes are bending over the wifi router on top of Veronica's bookcase. Bekah Bradley hurries towards us.

'We've met before...' She glances at both me and Veronica then turns to Holly. 'But I haven't met you. Have you got any ID?' Holly goes straight for a side pocket in her rucksack. She takes out her passport and hands it to her. 'Thanks. Okay, so this is where we are. We've got someone reviewing today's footage from the school. Nothing yet. And we're setting up an intercept over your landline.' She slams a piece of paper on the table in front of Veronica. 'We need you to sign here, here and here to give us permission, including your mobile.' She points to three crosses on the paper and Veronica picks up a pen and signs.

Holly glares at us. She throws the bulging file in front of Bekah Bradley. 'It's all in here. What he's done before. Look at your records.'

Bekah blinks at her. 'We need to find Polly.' She takes a deep breath. 'And when we establish what has happened here, we will collect the evidence.'

Holly is jittery. She eyes the back door and Bekah nods. I watch her storm outside and make a roll-up. My stomach is doing somersaults and my mind is racing, but I manage to count backwards. Polly is eight. Veronica was with Jake three years before they had her. All this must have happened over eleven years ago and she's still not over it.

Veronica is sorting through some photographs and giving them to Bekah. Her expression is solid, but her eyes give her away. I flick through Holly's file. It's a scrapbook of diary extracts, photographs, accounts and statements. Final demands and then, towards the end, solicitor's letters. I look at her, leaning against the fence. She sucks on her cigarette. She has waited more than a decade for this. She could have looked for him. Us. She could have done something about it. But she didn't.

I suddenly see Collette and Sheila in my mind's eye, laughing and drinking vodka. Sitting in our old dining room at half past seven on a Friday night. Collette never went out alone. She always had friends in tow. 'Safety in numbers!' They chinked glasses, got their stiletto heels and faux fur coats on, and left for whatever that night's mission was. I was left alone with all the fear that responsibility piled onto me. All the wondering about what would happen if something went wrong until I did not move for fear it would.

Holly was too scared to carry on. She sat perfectly still and waited and waited until someone came. I sit down heavily in Veronica's kitchen. Who the hell is this man I am married to?

The two plain clothes guys are examining the laptop. It ticks away and they push in a charger. I watch as they try to move away from the page, but nothing happens. They press buttons and type in lines of code, but the screen flashes back on each time. I intervene.

'He was tracking me. That map...' They enlarge the map. Criss-crossed with red lines. 'There was a tracker in my engagement ring. I tried to sell it today.'

Suddenly Bekah is behind me. 'Where is the ring now? Have you still got it?'

I feel the cold gold in my pocket. All my dreams tied up in two pieces of gold and some diamonds.

'Yes. But the tracker is safe. Somewhere he won't find it.'

One guy snorts. 'In Maccie D's on the high street.'

I stare at him. 'Yeah, but they'll never find it.'

They stand. The blond one shakes his head. 'Unless they go in there with a sweeper.'

Bekah weighs it up. 'So he was tracking you? And this is the laptop you showed me? So, whoever this is, they know about the tracker.' I swear she is going to say *unless it's him*, but she holds it in. 'And the ransom. That's from them too. What does this guy do for a job?'

I search back through the information he has given me. I know the basics but not the details.

'He works in software. Implementations. I'm not sure–'

She shouts over to DC Sharples. 'Posh, get someone over to his last place of work. I want a client list. This could be someone with a grudge. Someone he's upset.' She spins around to face me. 'Didn't you say he was acting strangely?'

I open my mouth to speak but Holly is behind me. I can feel her body heat and her fear. She jumps in.

'It's what he does. He keeps it all calm then bam! Makes you feel uncertain by acting freaky. Then he hits you with it.' She's animated and her eyes shine. 'It's just what he does. To keep you involved until it's too late.'

Bekah looks at me. 'Okay. You haven't paid any money, have you?'

'No. We were going to… well, we took out some loans until the remortgages come through and sold some stuff – that's what I was doing with my wedding rings.' I pull them from my pocket and show her. She whistles. 'But then…'

She flicks her hair and rubs her cheek. 'But you haven't paid any money to anyone?'

'No.'

She goes to sit next to Veronica on the sofa. Veronica is clearly in shock. So pale and still, arms folded over her knees. Holly and I follow her over. She makes sure we are all focused on her.

'Okay, this is what's going to happen. First, we've got people on the street searching for Polly. And Jake Clayton. There's an all-ports alert and we've been round to your property, Kate, and no one is there. So we wait. We wait for any further contact. We'll intercept calls and listen in. Veronica, you will need to speak.' She nods almost imperceptibly. Bekah continues. 'Do not offer any information. Just stick to one-word answers and don't be scared to show emotion. We'll trace any messages or calls. We'll take care of it.'

We look at the screen. The map and the ticker in the foreground and the ransom note in the background. The plain clothes officers are messing with the socket. The tall one stands.

'Back on now. We can pick up any calls on landlines and mobiles.'

I turn to look at him and when I look back another message appears on the screen. I feel my hand go to my mouth and I point at the screen. The men move round to read it.

You were warned. The price just went up to 200k.

Holly groans and covers her face with her hand. Bekah hurries over, and we all stare at the message. Veronica just stares ahead, blinking. Then, in the quietest voice possible, she speaks.

'Just find her. Find my baby. I don't care about him. Just get Polly back.'

CHAPTER TWENTY-EIGHT

My God, it is eight o'clock in the morning and DS Bradley's car pulls up outside Veronica hasn't slept. She has kept watch in her chair all night. I fell in and out of troubled sleep and jumped at any tiny noise. As she left late last night, Bekah Bradley told me and Holly to go home. To get some sleep.

I couldn't even consider being alone in my – our – house. No, I would stay here with Veronica. She took Polly's teddy bears and put them in front of her facing out of the window. It felt desperate, but also a complete contrast to who I had believed Veronica was. Jake's character assassination of her only adds to the growing list of his misdemeanours. I daren't even read Holly's file properly.

About three o'clock the phone rang, and Veronica moved fast to answer it. It was a wrong number. A cruel flash of hope or dread. I've barely known this woman days, but we have moved through awkward chat to soul bearing and now arrived at no need for words. I got up many times during the night to make tea.

Holly positioned herself under the kitchen table with a spare quilt wrapped around her. I don't know who she is or what life has thrown at her, but one thing is for sure; she is still in pain. Her desperation to get her story heard by the right people almost bursts out of her. I watched her sleep as I boiled water, selected tea bags and found some fresh milk. She is almost childlike. It's as if she was suspended in time and blocked by everything Jake did to her.

It was a long night of no news and now Bekah is standing in the lounge. Her long auburn curls are in a high ponytail and she is looking at her phone while Veronica looks at her for information. Eventually she speaks.

'Okay, there is no news as yet. We've had officers checking all known places Jake Clayton could have visited but there is no sign of him. We've had a trace on his registered mobile but it hasn't been used for a couple of days. We've got people out there.'

DC Sharples pulls up outside and Veronica turns her focus to him. She watches as he gets out of his car and when he is alone, she turns back to the room. Holly is the only person who slept all night, but now she is awake the innocence of stillness leaves her, and her ticking anxiety returns.

She goes back to sending messages. I look at the laptop for the millionth time and it is still ticking down. I take out my phone and check my emails. Two from work. I snort to myself as I realise how far behind me all that work drama is now. Clint and Co. haven't crossed my mind for an age, and I wonder if it was ever really as important as I thought it was. Yes, I have to earn money, but do I have to take it all on board?

I run through some emails from the bank about the loan I took out. It's been finalised already, and I quickly check my bank account. It's there, but it isn't enough. Even though Bekah Bradley told us we won't be paying a ransom, my mind tells me otherwise. It compels me to count up everything I am worth and put a pound sign in front of it. I couldn't stop the loan now even if I wanted to. Then the house will remortgage, and I will pay it off. I have the sudden urge to run again, just like the other day. To drive far, far away where none of this is happening.

But that's what Holly did. She went to live somewhere else and she is still there, collecting snippets of her former life and how she was wronged, all ready for someone to believe her. I check myself. Calm and collected on the outside but raging inside. A mixture of *why is this happening* and *I wish it would stop.*

I know, really, that life is messy. I watched a chaotic relationship blow itself out of the water, so I have form. I know things don't always go right. But three of us with the same story? Three of us, in this room, with a background of someone habitually lying to them? It's not a coincidence. I know my anger at Jake is simmering just below the surface. I know this is not directly his fault. Or is it? That someone else is responsible for this situation. Or are they? There must be someone else involved. He would never do this to Polly. But I can't help bunching all his actions together and being angry with him for this outcome. More than angry. Much more.

But he has form, too. Clearly. He has hurt these women for reasons I can't fathom. It seems to be about money, yet he had a decent job and never seemed short of cash. The horror that there might be other things I don't know about creeps up on me, but I push it down. It's not time for that now.

I check my messages. I am shocked as I open the app and see Flynn's face there, even though I know I messaged him. He's read it. My heart beats fast. He's read my message. But there is no response. I type a follow-up message and then delete it. I don't want to go to that particular place right now, although it is becoming increasingly clear that I can't avoid it.

Bekah is talking on the phone. She is waving at DC Sharples. She ends the call.

'Posh, get the laptop.'

He fetches the device from the car and plugs it in. She logs on and opens a file. It's CCTV footage showing the school. There are four cameras, one showing each entrance. She runs it on super-speed. Cars whiz by and people pass the school in a blur. But no one comes in or out. It runs for a while even at this speed, and then I see the blue and yellow of a police car park outside the school. She turns to Veronica.

'Okay, so Polly's teacher tells me she was in class at lunchtime and didn't leave until outdoor play at two o'clock. No one saw her after that.'

Veronica looks at the screen. 'Was her coat still there?'

Bekah shakes her head. 'No. Her coat and bag were gone.'

Veronica speaks clearly and slowly. 'What if she went off on her own? Tried to get home? And I wasn't here. I was chasing round after him. What if she's out there all alone? Or someone...'

Bekah sits down lightly. 'We will find her. We will.'

Veronica sneers. 'You're just waiting for her to turn up. It's okay, I understand. You've no idea where she is.'

'Not at the moment, but we do our best and will find her. However, as you can see, the footage isn't showing anything, which is puzzling. And there isn't another way out. That school is fenced all the way round.' She winds the footage back. 'And no cars parked until the kids leave for the day. And by then we were there.'

Veronica sighs. 'She can't have just disappeared. And she wouldn't go with strangers. She wouldn't. Whoever took her must have waited for her to get her bag and coat.' She looks up at Bekah. 'Maybe they made him go in for her?'

Bekah nods slowly. 'But there is no evidence. None at all.'

She turns the laptop around and we all watch the footage. She is right. All of this is vague, except for the laptop. None of it makes sense. Demands for cash, but no instructions to drop it off or where to transfer it to. Not yet. I look at the clock again. Maybe that will come when the time runs out. I hug myself. I feel cold and shivery and my stomach hurts.

At nine o'clock the plain clothes officers arrive. Bekah and

DC Sharples go outside, and they stand on Veronica's lawn talking. There is no hiding away like yesterday. No back door entries. Their faces are serious, and I wonder if it's bad news. Or no news. My phone rings and Bekah turns around. I hold it up and she nods. It's Paula.

'Hiya, mate. How's–'

I interrupt. 'It's not a good time, Paula.'

'Bloody hell. Not made up with Jakey yet, then.' I am silent. She laughs nervously. 'Is everything okay?'

'No. Look, you know when you saw Jake the other day, was he alone? Was anyone else at the house? Any cars outside?'

She pauses. 'No. No cars. He had the TV on. He looked a bit pale but...'

I feel acute impatience. 'This is really important. Was he acting... odd? Did he look worried?'

She groans. 'Oh my God, something's happened to him, hasn't it? All that stuff you told me. He hasn't... well... done something to himself?'

I sigh. Typically off track. 'No, not that. Look, what time was it? When did you call round?'

She is silent, thinking. Then she answers. 'It would have been about one. On my way into town to meet John.'

I feel a prickle down my spine. 'Were you in your car? Did you get out and knock on the door?'

'Yes. Course. How would I get there otherwise? How would I have asked him?'

'Thanks, love. Look, I'll call you when I can. Thanks, Paula.'

I end the call and press a button on my phone. I connect to a tiny security camera that Jake fitted to catch next-door's cat on our lawn. It looks outwards onto the street. There is no sound. It doesn't cover our doorway or look directly at anyone's property; its lens is street level. It's primed to catch the cat he hates. I run it backwards to the time frame someone took all Jake's things. I fast-forward through nothing. No removal van that would need to park directly in front of our garden. I'd see it even if it spanned the driveway.

I check the camera notifications. I remember when we first got it; all the annoying notifications every time anyone walked past our house.

I choose the time frame and run it. Not a single person or car passes our home in all that time. Leaves move on the ground and a bird lands on the lawn. But no car and no Paula. Either she is lying, or this camera is lying. I hurry over to Bekah. She turns from her messaging to look at me, her face serious. I turn my phone towards her.

'Okay. This.' I run the footage of nothing, and she frowns at me. 'It's the front of our house. There are three, probably more, times I know people would have been around. Paula, my friend, called the other day and gave me the time. Nothing.'

She studies it. 'Right. Play it again. Col.' She calls one of the plain clothes guys over. He stands and watches the footage. 'Col, this is the camera outside Jake Clayton's home. Kate says people were around at certain times and the footage says not. Can you have a look at it?'

He nods. 'Can you give me the dates and times? And the login.' He hands me a piece of paper and I write it down. He continues. 'So, the camera is twenty-four seven?'

'Yes. To catch a cat on our lawn.'

'And Mr Clayton has access to it too?'

'It was his idea. He hates animals.'

The landline rings. It is action stations in the room; everyone is moving to the laptops set up to monitor the slightest change. Bekah signals to Veronica. She picks up the phone, her face white and her hands shaking.

'Hello?'

A familiar voice comes through the speaker on the table. 'Mummy? It's me.'

Veronica's face crumples. 'Polly. Oh my God... are you...'

Bekah urges Veronica on through her tears with a nod and holds up the script they have prepared in front of her. She engages. 'Polly. Where are you, love?'

There is a TV in the background. The two officers are manipulating the sound and suddenly the TV becomes louder. Then Polly speaks.

'I'm at Daddy's. We went to the seaside and then...'

The line goes dead. She is gone.

Veronica drops the phone and grabs her car keys. Bekah Bradley catches her arm.

'No. Let us take care of this.'

She finally loses it. Veronica shakes herself free. 'I'll fucking kill him.'

But Bekah is gone with DC Sharples. Shouting into her radio and phone, then into her car and speeding off. I grab my car keys.

'Come on.'

Veronica and Holly run behind me. The plain clothes officers shout after us. 'You should stay here and...'

But we get in the car, and I screech out of Veronica's driveway and up the road towards Lynton Grove.

CHAPTER TWENTY-NINE

We arrive and the end of the road is cordoned off with police tape. I park up and Veronica flees, leaving the passenger side door open. Holly and I run behind her. Armed police have their weapons trained on my home, and Bekah Bradley stands behind the row of uniformed police by their cars at the other end.

An officer stops us. Veronica pushes against him but he catches her arm. I pull her back.

'Leave them to it. We don't know who's in there. We don't know who's behind this.'

She turns and sobs against me. I put my arms around her and hug her. I can only imagine how she must feel. My insides feel like jelly as a police officer with a loudspeaker moves forward. I feel Holly behind me, very close. The officer raises the loudspeaker.

'Come out with Polly. Come out with your hands above your head.'

The door opens and I see a figure. A familiar figure. Jake. He looks calm and collected. His hands are above his head and Polly stands in front of him. He lowers his hands and speaks. 'I think there's been...'

I see the armed police move their weapons and aim. I hold Veronica tight. The officer shouts loudly. 'Hands above your head. Polly, walk forwards.'

She looks scared to death. She starts to cry, and Veronica turns around. We watch as, in complete silence, Polly walks towards a female officer who beckons her. When she is in arm's reach, she snatches her up and rushes behind the line of officers. Veronica watches every movement and almost collapses when Polly is safe. But Holly's eyes are on Jake.

An officer signals. Two armed officers move towards him and the rest rush into my house. Boots trampling over my carpet. In my bedroom. Then suddenly we are moving. A female officer raises the tape, and we are ushered behind the police line where I can see Polly. Veronica runs to her and grabs her. She holds her like she will never let her go.

I turn and the armed police are pouring out of my house. The two officers guarding Jake lower their weapons. I watch as Bekah Bradley goes over to him. Suddenly he's pointing at me.

'This is down to her. All of it. I was just having my joint custody with my daughter.' He turns slightly to look at Veronica. 'My days, right?'

She nods in disbelief. 'Yes, but we didn't know where you were.'

He's crimson with rage. 'We? You mean her?' He's pointing at me again. Then at Holly. 'And that mad bitch...'

The armed police are leaving, and Bekah Bradley intervenes.

'Look, Mr Clayton, we had reason to believe your daughter had been abducted. We were–'

He is calm now. 'What? What were you doing? Looking for Polly. She was with me. I picked her up for the dentist's – you can check – then we went to Blackpool. On the train. Abducted?'

Holly pushes through. She is awkward and keeps her head

down. She doesn't want to look at him. 'This is what he does. This. Exactly this. Creates a situation then makes it look like you are mad. This is classic Jackson. Classic.'

He laughs. 'You've got to be kidding me. You three.' He looks at Bekah. 'Can you remove them from my property?'

I find my voice. 'Our property, Jake. I own half that house.'

He smiles at me. 'I want you to leave. You've caused all this. You and your overactive imagination. But you've gone too far this time and I'll be taking action.'

I feel tears rise. I am shaking. 'But the messages? Your stuff gone? And the ransom? How is that my fault?'

He stares at me. His expression is pure surprise and I take a sharp breath in. But I know that look. Then *I don't know what you are talking about* when his eyes are mocking. I've seen it before, I realise. He confirms.

'I have no idea what you are talking about. No idea at all. All I've been doing is caring for my daughter.' His voice breaks. 'You left me, Kate. You left. Not me. You.'

It's unbelievable. The officers who are left are all looking at me. Bekah says nothing, but another detective comes over. He stands in front of her.

'You've got to be fucking kidding me.' He leans in. 'He was in there eating fish fingers with his daughter. Table set and everything. This is all out of your budget, not mine. Some fucking domestic and we get the guns in.'

He walks away shaking his head. But she stares at Jake.

'Did you take Polly out of school yesterday? Early?'

'Yes. Like I said. For the dentist. I rang them and told them.'

'But the school reported her missing.'

He looks puzzled. 'That's impossible. I rang them. But you have to admit they are inefficient. Not my problem if they–'

She interrupts. 'Did you tell any of the teachers you were taking her?'

'No, it was break and…'

She steps up to him. 'A bit strange, isn't it? And there was no sign of you on the CCTV.'

He looks at me. 'Wow. You've really spun them one this time, haven't you?' He looks at Posh and Becks. Then he makes a whistling noise. 'CCTV? Bloody hell, Kate. You've been watching too many crime box sets. No sign of us? I don't see how that's my fault, either. I was obviously there. Then we went to the dentist. She's a liar. A serial liar.' Then he looks back at me. 'You left, Kate. I don't want you back. You can collect your things and my solicitor will be in touch. And now I'd like to finish my lunch with my daughter.'

Veronica holds Polly tight. She looks up at her. 'I want to stay with Mummy.'

He nods. 'Course, love. Course you do. You've had a shock. Come and give Daddy a kiss and I'll see you next week.' She wriggles free of Veronica's grip and runs to him. He hugs her and kisses her then lets her go. 'Be a good girl for Mummy.'

He looks at Holly, who is standing behind me, and then at me. He shakes his head and walks away. I turn to Bekah Bradley.

'Is that it? What about the ransom and the laptop? What about him tracking me?'

She blinks at me. 'Our investigation is over. Polly is safe. There was no abduction. If you've got a complaint, you will need to make it separately. As would Mr Clayton.'

I suddenly realise.

I feel the turn of the memory in my guts as Bekah Bradley's suggestion that Jake might have a case sinks in.

He blamed me. He made it look like all this was in my imagination. My confusion is trying to fight through the twisting turns of how he could have done this when Holly speaks.

'This is what he does. His MO. There will be an end goal. Oh yes. And whatever that end goal is will now be complete. I know. It's all in my file.' We stare at her. She is jittery and animated. Slightly slurring her words. She laughs. 'You think I'm a bit mad, don't you? A bit quirky? Probably wouldn't trust me? Wondering if maybe I'm on something?'

There is silence. We all know she is right. She laughs manically now.

'He made me like this. He fucked me up so badly up here.' She raises a finger to her temple. 'So badly that I didn't know what was true anymore. I couldn't trust anyone.' She turns to Bekah. 'And your lot. You did nothing. Because he was wearing a posh suit and I, by then, looked a bit mad. All he had to do was raise his eyebrows and those officers were off. Oh yes, *you know what Holly's like*. But believe me, he got me a lot of debt and a criminal record through his lies. I couldn't get a mortgage or carry on with my social work training after that. You've just seen him in action. He's done it twice. He'll do it again. You need to arrest him.' She turns and stomps down the road. She grabs her file out of the back of my car, the passenger side door still flung open.

I look at Veronica. 'Are you okay?'

She is still gripping Polly. 'I will be. I thought this was over.'

'I'm so sorry. I should never have involved you.'

She sighs. 'You didn't. Holly's right. This is what he does. Causes a big problem and then sets up someone else for the blame. This one is much more elaborate than the others. With me, he tried to get Polly. He badmouthed me to anyone who would listen, including social services. He even had my mum believing him I had changed, somehow.' She wipes a tear away. 'In the end, we went to family court. I divorced him. He made the mistake of writing it down and thinking I was too weak to challenge him. I was completely alone, but I found the strength somewhere.' She touches my arm. 'And you must too. This is only the start, Kate. But I'll be here if you need me.'

She gets into the back of Bekah's car. Bekah winds down her window.

'I wouldn't go back there now.' Her gaze strays to my home. 'I would let things calm down and get a solicitor.'

All the other officers have gone now, and she pulls away. Veronica stares at me through the window and mouths 'Thank you', but I wonder if I did the right things. I can't remember what made me do it, or why. What made me go to her. The mirror message, and the scrawl on the back of the agreement, yes, but I had already been there.

I stand alone on the grass verge outside my home. Our home. The place we cooked and laughed and made love. It was all a sham. An act. I thought it would be the place we brought up our children and grew old together.

We had always promised to be truthful with each other. We agreed that infidelity was a deal breaker for both of us, and if either of us wanted to break the relationship, we would talk to the other rather than act to hurt them. The past weeks tumble through my mind and I try to make sense of what has happened and how he can deny what he has done. There is evidence. There is proof.

But a sickly feeling invades as I remember that evidence is not always clear cut. That what someone says – or doesn't say – tells its own story.

I walk back to my car and open the laptop. The screen is blank. I push at the buttons and nothing happens. I wonder if the battery is dead. But I know really. I understand Jake has no further use for it. Just like me.

I sit down on the kerb and take out my phone. I consider trying to ring him. Asking him if we can talk. If I can get some of my things. He is right there, in our home, opposite. But I don't. I need some time to think. I need some time to work out what happened and what I need to do next.

I need to find a bed for the night, because right now I have nowhere to live.

CHAPTER THIRTY

I walk up the drive to Paula's house. It's usually the other way around. It's usually Paula who's been thrown out for not paying rent. Or Paula who has left the current love of her life over a single argument. I lost count of the number of times I've turned on the hallway light in the middle of the night and she's been standing there with some bin liners and a pull-along suitcase.

I haven't even got a change of clothes. I badly need a shower and to clean my teeth. It occurs to me she might not be in, but then I see movement behind the dimpled glass door panel.

'I'm coming. I'm coming.'

Her voice is muffled, and I watch as she disappears again, presumably to hunt for the keys. My phone beeps but I don't look at it. I need a break. I need to figure all this out. I hear Paula fiddling with the lock. She opens the door, still in her nightwear in the middle if the day. I look past her into the messy flat.

'Is it a good time?'

She looks closer at me, then gets a pair of glasses out of her dressing gown pocket. 'Jesus Christ on a bike. You look like shit. You'd better come in.'

I go through to the lounge and clear a space on the sofa. She detours to the kitchen, and I hear her fill the kettle and set it on to boil. Spooning out coffee into teacups and I am so thankful just for that simplicity. Then she reappears.

'So, what happened?'

I don't know what to say. The words stick in my throat. Last time I felt this upset I couldn't speak. I knew what I wanted to say but there seemed no point saying them. It took me almost a week to even start to form the right story, but then it was too late. I don't know if it is now.

Paula tilts her head to one side. 'Have you left him?'

I nod.

'For good?'

I nod again, this time harder. Somewhere inside me the words form. 'He... he...' I don't know what to call it.

'He didn't hit you, did he?'

She jumps up and comes to sit beside me. I've never warmed to this flat. Paula is fond of wall hangings and voiles. I've always thought that it is just a slightly more grown-up student flat, but it's exactly what I need right now and I'm starting to understand why she does in her perpetual state of drama.

'No. He...' What did he do? Trick me? Lie? More than that. Manipulate? He groomed me. Laid a clear path to whatever his goal is and then picked up the evidence behind him. I have no proof. None. I look at Paula. 'I'm completely helpless. He's duped me. He was tracking me right from the start.'

'Bloody hell. Not another Ian?'

'Worse. And now I can't go home. He said I left, and that he doesn't want me back.'

'You did bugger off. To... Hudd, was it?'

'I did, but I didn't leave. I didn't take anything. And I was always coming back. I never said I was leaving.'

She sets her expression. 'So go back, then.'

'There's just been a stand-off with armed police. I honestly can't go into details. I need a shower and some sleep. I'll tell you tomorrow. If I can stay?'

She looks shocked. 'Armed police? Oh my God! That little girl who was missing? Was that his daughter?' I nod. She hugs me close. She smells of booze and cigs and I am so glad of the familiarity. 'Bloody hell. Let me make some tea, now. You can never have too much tea. You need a big, big rest. And tomorrow we can talk about it all. But for now, tea.'

She is cheerful. I look around for evidence of her boyfriend but there is none. There are a few empty wine bottles scattered around and the ashtrays are semi-full. But only Paula's stuff is here. One brand of cigarettes. One empty coffee cup. No men's socks hung over the radiator, just hers.

My phone beeps. I grab it quickly and my heart leaps, still in the habit that it might be Jake. A message flashes across the screen telling me that my direct debit for the water rates has bounced. That can't be possible. I know I was paid last month – not sure about next month but I have savings. I log in to our current account and check the balance. It is five pounds fifty overdrawn.

My stomach churns as I fumble over the keys and finally find recent transactions. I vaguely remember a message, or was it an email, telling me the loan I applied for had been credited. The screen lights up with a list of activities and I stare at it. The loan has been credited; its balance added to the money already in the account. Then the full balance transferred to another account.

I grab my car keys and run. Out of the house and into the car. I speed into town and park right on the pavement outside the cashpoint. The bank is shut, but I can find everything I want here. I push in my card and select my accounts one by one. I chose printouts and collect the paper without looking at the balance for each one. I need a record. Solid proof to show people I haven't made this up. That I'm not mad.

Then I drive back to Paula's clutching the slips. I hammer on the door, and she flings it open.

'Kate – whatever it is I'll...'

I rush in and wave the slips in front of my face. 'This. I've got him. He's cleaned me out!'

I already know before I look. But I do look. I sit on Paula's sofa, and she puts a steaming cup of tea in front of me as I peer at the white slips. Each account is almost empty. The last account I look at is the one I opened for the cheque that I never cashed. The account I had used the pay the hotel bills. The account he has no access to.

But that is empty too.

I hand the slips to Paula. She reads them and shakes her head. 'I don't understand. If you're getting divorced, he'll have to explain this.'

She is talking about when someone stole from her and what she did, but I am reeling. I am somersaulting back to another time when I had nothing. Absolutely nothing. The night I left. I feel the same as I did then. Like I have been tricked out of what is rightfully mine. That someone who is much savvier than me has pulled a fast one. I feel stupid. I feel abused. But most of all I feel like I am going to do something I might regret.

I know where this is leading. I try to push down the fire but this time it burns too hard. I knew then who the object of my anger was, and I know now. Then, I had locked myself in the bathroom for hours and willed myself not to follow any urges that might make me do something rash. By the next day my anger had faded, and I was back into my stride. Back into the new life I was making for myself. Back to a job and a routine. I knew that was how I carried on. I had a purpose. I had a way to distract myself. But what do I have now?

Nothing. No money. No home. No job. And now I could be charged. With what though? I try to sort through everything that has happened, but it is too much. He told them I did everything.

That I had invented the whole scenario, assisted by Holly, because... of what? I look at the balance slips again. He's set up internet banking for those accounts. Four of them were joint accounts, but somehow he's got my passwords or pretended to be me.

Then there were the messages he said he sent to me at the party. And the CCTV footage. The laptop. And the camera outside our house. I can't remember now why I did all the things I did. I took the loans out to pay off the ransom for a kidnap he set up. I feel my stomach sink as I realise what this looks like. He's making it look like I set up the kidnap, got Veronica to get money together, and then took the money.

But I didn't take Veronica's money. I ring her. She answers in one.

'Has he got access to your bank account?'

I hear her take a deep breath. 'No. Oh no. He hasn't...'

'Yes. Every penny I borrowed and all our savings. Everything. Put a stop on all your accounts. All transactions. Tell them to freeze it. He could find a way. Is it the same account you had when–?'

She interrupts. 'Yes, it is. Yes. Look. I'll ring the bank. You ring the police.'

She ends the call. I look in my bag for DS Bradley's card. I find it and tap the number into my phone. It rings and she answers.

'Rebekah Bradley.'

I stumble over my words. 'DS Bradley. Bekah. It's Kate. Clayton. I just found out he's cleaned out all my accounts. He's taken everything.'

There is silence on the end of the line. A long silence that makes me think she has started to record the call. Eventually she speaks.

'That's interesting because I've just had a call from your husband claiming exactly the same thing. That you have taken all the money from your joint accounts.' More silence as I try to take in what she has said. When I don't speak, she does. 'Where are you staying, Kate?'

I grab the words from the bottom of my shocked numbness. 'At my friend's. Paula. 19A Foxglove Way. Bottom flat.'

She responds quietly. 'Okay, I'll be round in the morning. We need to talk.'

She ends the call. I didn't ask her what time, but I guess I have nowhere to go. My heart sinks. He's trying to frame me for taking the money.

I think back on all our discussions about saving. Our 'love fund'. How we planned for the future, and how he encouraged me to put all my bonuses from work into a savings account. It all sounded completely plausible, and he saved too. But of course he would when he knew that eventually he would get everything.

Even that night when he came back after the party, he mentioned my bonus. Right up to the last minute. My mind still fights it. I still can't believe that the whole of what we had together was a sham. And our demise was precision planned. But my rational mind knows it is true. I have seen Holly's evidence and heard Veronica's story.

I've seen the state he left them in. They both seem like nice women. But both of them seem afraid and subdued, and I have a suspicion that, like me, they are showing only the tip of the iceberg of hurt and there is a world of pain below. I know from how I feel now that I am not far from blowing. I am not far from becoming everything I have avoided and going all out for revenge.

I was never special to him. I was just another victim in a long line of women who he set up to knock down. And all for money. All for what he can get.

Paula fetches me some pyjamas. It's barely seven o'clock and we haven't eaten, not that I am hungry. But I have to keep my strength up. I know that this kind of remorse energy takes effort.

'Shall we order pizza? Or a kebab?'

She has a stack of takeaway menus and I marvel how different her life is to mine. Or how mine was.

'You choose. And you'll have to pay.'

She lowers the menus and looks at me. 'Bloody hell, mate, it's the least I can do. After everything you've done for me.'

She puts her hand over mine. I feel tears rise.

'Look, this will only be for a day or two. I don't want to get in yours and John's way.'

She takes her hand away quickly. She is suddenly tense.

'Kate, I don't know how to say this. But... this thing with John. It never happened. Well, the first bit did. But he dumped me. He never asked me to go back with him. I never saw him again.'

I stare at her. 'Why did you...?'

She stands up and flings her arms around. 'I saw you and him, Mr Fucking Perfect, and I was jealous. So I made something up. In reality, I was just here getting pissed. I'm in trouble, Kate. I know you don't need this now but I'm really in the shit. I've been signed off on the sick and work's made noises about finishing me.' She wipes her eyes. 'I've fucked up again.'

I feel my mouth curve into a smile. She watches me as I nod and smile at her.

'Okay, we've been here before with your fucked-upness. But we always sort it out. And for the first time, I've fucked up worse. And I don't think there's a way out.'

My phone buzzes and I read the message from Veronica.

> Nothing gone from mine. Here if you want to chat but seeing to Polly now.

Paula fetches two glasses and a bottle of wine as I log in to my internet banking. I feel sure he will have covered his tracks by setting up some random account to transfer the money to, but I want to be sure. I want to know everything. I tap on the transaction and see an unfamiliar account number, but a familiar name.

23867473

Catherine Mary Clayton

He's made it look like I've stolen my own money.

CHAPTER THIRTY-ONE

Bekah Bradley is due to arrive at 11am. Paula got up early and tidied up when I told her we were having a house guest. We didn't know the exact time, so she kept a constant teapot on the go just in case.

I didn't speak to her about pretending John was still on the scene. She has her reasons, and I don't have the bandwidth. I know she will bring it up again if she needs to. She mentioned going back into rehab, but her parents won't pay anymore. They've stopped her allowance as their business is not what it was and, as they tactfully informed her, she needs to behave like an adult now.

I've always seen Paula as a version of Jules in *St Elmo's fire*, with me as a more sensible Leslie. But I am not sure that is true these days. I am not sure I can be described as sensible after what I have done. As I sat there in Paula's flat wearing Paula's clothes and drinking Paula's tea, I realised that I have been fooling myself all along. I am not sensible. I am hiding from who I really am. And I am like her. Collette.

I've only been away from Jake a short while and I can feel the pull to him. He was my audience, the anchor that made me someone else entirely. I thought that was me. The true me. But all along I was still that unpredictable flash of light that reflected my mother's spirit. Right or wrong, I can no longer deny it. I structured myself stiffly to snuff out the flame, however, it was always there.

Now Paula is more adult than me. She continues to buzz around the flat, cleaning windowsills wearing yellow rubber gloves. All the wine bottles are in the recycling, and she has cleared away a week's worth of takeaways for one. She hoovers around me as I sit completely still, wracked with nerves. Finally, she sits beside me.

'You know, mate, you could stay here a bit if you want. I mean, if you've got somewhere else, fair enough. But...'

She looks hopeful, and I suddenly understand what has been missing from her life. She's lonely. Sitting in bars on her own. Pretending to have a boyfriend. Fictional lunches with workmates. All that time spent with her family trying to fit into a mould they had cast for her. But, as I know from experience, they are vacuous and focused on themselves, and it is easy to feel alone even in a room crowded with her close relations. I did, but I had no idea until now that she did, too. And this is her escape.

'Thank you. It would only be until I sort myself out.'

She smiles. She goes to clear some cupboards for me, and I wonder if Jake will let me have my clothes until I see Bekah get out of her car and feel the flame ignite again. She knocks and I jump up and let her in. She looks around and her expression is one of surprise.

'Not what you're used to.'

I nod. 'But my friend offered and I'm grateful.'

I sit on the sofa, and she sits on the chair opposite. Her red corkscrew hair drapes her shoulders and is framed by the light from the window, and it makes her look like some renaissance character. I glance at her left hand. No wedding rings. She looks very young, but the lines that sit under her eyes tell me she might be a little older than she appears. Or it might be the job. She fetches some papers out of her bag.

'It's where to start with this, really. The thing is, Kate, Jake is making noises about pressing charges. He says you have removed money from your joint bank accounts and transferred it. That is a civil matter. That would need to be dealt with by your respective solicitors in terms of a divorce settlement, if that is the way you choose to go.' She looks directly at me now. 'The more serious matter is around the alleged kidnap. That turned out to be, well, we all know what happened there. Mr Clayton is claiming that he has no knowledge of the events surrounding it and claims that you, jointly with Holly Brierly and Veronica Clayton, planned and carried out some kind of revenge plan.'

She stares at me. I can hardly believe what she is telling me. Yet I half expected it after yesterday.

I sigh. 'Right. Well, obviously that is not true. I absolutely did not plan anything. I honestly do not know how this happened.'

She taps her pen against the writing pad she pulled out of her bag. 'So I want to run something by you. I've compiled a list of what you told me from when you first noticed things were wrong. Your husband's job and the burner phone messages. When you ran, and when you returned. And everything that happened after that. The laptop. The CCTV. The camera footage from your home. It seems that this has been a carefully planned operation to elicit money.'

She hands me the list. She doesn't say who planned to elicit money. It's comprehensive and detailed. Her handwriting is neat and looped. She leans in to look with me.

'Is there anything missing? And specific parts of what happened that I haven't written down? Because I've spoken to Mr Clayton this morning. I told him what you said about his things being removed and–'

I feel my anger rise and escape. 'Not what I said. You saw they were gone.'

'And now they are back. The interesting thing is that he denied his belongings were ever removed from the house. He didn't seem to be aware that I had been round to see you. Or that one neighbour was off sick that day. He just told us he came home and found you had wrecked the house and tidied up before he picked Polly up.' She runs her pen along a line between me coming home and finding his things gone. 'So can you think carefully? What did you do before you rang this in? In detail.'

I am reeling. He's actually moved all his stuff back. 'He's moved everything back?'

She stares at me, unblinking. 'The items you told me were missing from the house when I first visited are now not missing. Yes.'

A warm wave washes over me. She doesn't believe him. She knows that stuff was gone. And she knows the rest of it doesn't add up. I suddenly realise that I couldn't have been in two places at once. I couldn't have been both in the places the map says I was, and she had seen the map in detail complete with dates, and moving Jake's stuff out of the house. I think hard. I was upset. I was relieved Jake was home but spoiling for a fight. I opened the door and sensed things were different. I looked for his shoes and the house felt empty. I stepped inside, picked up the letters and put them in my bag.

Time stands still. The letters. I grab my bag and she watches me. I reach deep into the tote and pull out the crumpled envelopes. Three letters. One from the bank. Another from the insurance company. And a plain white envelope. I go to open it, but she stops me.

'No. Let me.'

She pulls out some protective gloves and an evidence pouch from her bag. She holds the corner of the envelope and drags her pen under the top edge. She pulls the white paper out by the corner and opens it with the pen. In huge block capitals it reads:

NO POLICE

She drops it into the evidence pouch.

'We'll get that analysed.'

I snort. 'Well, I guess I missed out a very important part.'

I think I see a trace of a smile on her face. But it doesn't develop. She doesn't look like she smiles much. 'Yes. Otherwise…'

She leans back in the chair. I see Paula hovering in the kitchen doorway with a tray of tea. She brings it in and puts it in front of us. Bekah watches her and nods as she pours.

'Thank you. It's been a long day already. What I have to stress here is that whatever happens none of this is going to get either of you the money back.' She is choosing her words carefully. Making sure she doesn't say outright she believes me. 'As I said, it would be up to your solicitors to negotiate what happens next. I'd like to ask you about your IT skills. What level would you say you are?'

I baulk. 'Microsoft Office. I'm a designer so Adobe software and the like.'

She writes it down. 'So no programming or experience of recording equipment?'

'No. Unless you count logging into the garden camera, but you already know about that.'

She nods and writes. 'And, finally, the rings. You still have them?'

I stand and go to get my wedding rings from the bedside cabinet in Paula's spare room. I come back and drop them on the table in front of her.

'So you told us about a tracker attached to the laptop map, and you took the rings to the jewellers to sell, and the jeweller removed the bug. Which jeweller's would that be?'

'The pawnbrokers on the high street. Next to McDonald's.'

'And where is the bug now? Did you dispose of it?'

'No. I left it in the toilets at McDonald's, as I said. So, they…'

Fear jumps in my stomach. They. The unknown enemy that

only yesterday I had been terrified of. So terrified that I had committed to remortgaging my house to pay off. But it turns to anger as I remember there is no 'they'. There never was.

'Can you take me there? I'll drive.'

She stands and is out of the flat before I have grabbed my bag. She is on the pavement, breathing in the morning air, hands on hips. She clicks her key fob to unlock the car and I get in. We drive in silence to McDonald's and walk through to the toilets. A cleaner tries to stop us and tell us we need to buy food to use the facilities, but she flashes her badge at them, and they step aside. We reach the stall.

She takes out another evidence pouch and some more gloves. 'Show me.'

I feel along the top of the greasy ledge and it's still there. She plucks it from the dirt and holds it up to the light. Then she drops it into the bag and seals it. She pulls the gloves off and pops them in her jacket pocket. She holds the bag up in front of her.

'Right. Specialist equipment. You can't buy these on eBay. It's not top of the range but, believe me, these things are not easy to come by. Whoever did this would have to know where to find this sort of thing.'

She pulls down the seat and sits on it. 'Is there anything else at all you want to tell me?' I instantly wonder if she means about now or my past, but she qualifies it. 'Did you know Veronica before this? Had you met? Had you ever met Holly before?'

I lean on the sink behind me. I suddenly feel weak. 'I didn't even know about Holly. He never told me about her. Or Veronica. Well, I did know about her because he mentioned her once or twice.' I pause. It was more than once or twice. Much more. 'He would kind of compare us. What he told me about her, it just wasn't true.' She rolls her eyes. I get the feeling she already has a good picture of Jake in her head. 'And I only met Veronica when... well, when I went around. Obviously, I knew Polly. But

213

he kept us apart, me and Veronica. He told me she was horrible. Mad.'

'Yes, I'm starting to see a pattern here. So, I'm going to be collecting evidence to decide how we will proceed. Is there anything at all, anything, that you need to tell me?'

'I hardly understand it myself. I need to think. I need to work out what happened and how long it's been going on. That ring, my engagement ring, I never took it off from the day he gave it to me until I tried to sell it the other day.'

She writes it down, but even as I say it, I know I can never prove it was Jake and not me who put that bug in there.

We leave. Back in the car, she drives me to Paula's flat with the sound system blasting Adele songs. I wouldn't have thought she'd like Adele. She's more of an indie chick. We sit in silence. I wait for her to speak. She looks lost in thought, both hands on the steering wheel. Eventually, I speak.

'So what happens now?'

She looks me in the eye. 'I'll be in touch.'

The words are hard and factual, but her entire expression says *don't worry*. I know she has identified something important, and she doesn't fully believe Jake. But I am worried. I'm worried he has covered his tracks so well he has made it look like it really is me who has set this up. I'm worried I will be arrested and charged and go to prison for something I didn't do. Because I know it happens and I know I've read people's expressions, actions and intentions wrongly before, haven't I?

CHAPTER THIRTY-TWO

I am woken at eight o'clock by a loud knock on the door. Paula opens it and comes through to the bedroom.

'It's her again.'

I jump up and pull on Paula's dressing gown. Bekah Bradley. This can't be good. Why is she here again? My heart beats fast but I tell myself to hold my nerve. My fists are balled, and I am ready for whatever this is. She is waiting in the lounge, sitting by a pile of Paula's washing. I would have been appalled by this a couple of weeks ago, but now it almost makes me smile. But I don't. Bekah looks very serious, and I stand in front of her. She looks up from reading her messages on her phone.

'Kate. Okay?'

I shake my head. 'Not really.'

She grimaces. 'Yes, well, we're interviewing your husband at the moment, and he has agreed that you can go to your home and collect some belongings. Just clothes, shoes and make-up. He's apparently seen a solicitor and he's drawing up an inventory, but he wants you to go and take your things. As long as you are accompanied by us.' She glances through the window at her car where DC Sharples is sitting. 'Then I'd like you to come along to the station.'

I am shaking. I've been here before. On the brink of being questioned in a police station. That awful sinking feeling that I will have to try to commit a universe of feelings into a short police statement. I feel the impending doom that I will not be able to include everything. That I will forget something or say something wrong and somehow, I will be to blame.

'Are you arresting me?'

She sighs. 'No. We just want to ask you some questions and get a statement. I'd like to take that laptop in for analysis as well. The one with the map and the ransom.'

Paula appears, fully dressed. She reaches up to a high cupboard and fetches the laptop.

'I'll come with you.'

I shake my head. 'No. Honest, it's okay. I won't be too long. Right?'

I look at Bekah and she shrugs.

Ten minutes later I have pulled on my freshly washed clothes and tied my hair up in a high ponytail. It isn't until I am sitting in the back of her car that it registers that they have Jake in the police station. Bekah drives as DC Sharples checks his phone. I catch her eye.

'Have you arrested Jake?'

She shows no emotion. Her poker face is strong. 'No one's made a complaint, however, based on some evidence we've been able to question him.'

She catches my eye now, then looks away. She drives through town and in no time we are rounding the corner to Lynton Grove. Everything looks completely normal. Jake's car in the drive. No sign of the commotion of yesterday.

We get out and I grab my keys from my bag, but Bekah produces a key from her bag.

'He's changed the locks.'

I am shocked. Already? 'Is he allowed to do that?'

She pushed the key into the lock. 'Like I said the other day, you need to see a solicitor. Assuming you want a separation or a divorce. And I'd do that as soon as possible.' She pauses. 'I gave your husband the same advice, by the way.'

I glance at the agreement on my way in. The frame is dented and twisted and there is a chunk out of it, but he has rehung it.

The house is tidy and, as she told me, all Jake's things are back. I go to the bottom of the loft ladders and climb halfway up. All his equipment is back. It must have been some feat to both remove and return that lot. Someone must have seen him.

I step into the bathroom and breathe on the mirror out of habit. No messages, of course. It is polished to a high sheen and the rest of the bathroom is spotless.

I turn and stand outside our bedroom. It hits me all of a sudden. All those times we made love. Was he pretending? Did he ever care for me? He couldn't have. He must have planned all this. He must have plotted every second. For what? A couple of bonuses and some savings? He's tricked me into getting out a loan, but in the grand scheme of things it isn't that much, really. I'll still be entitled to half the equity in the house.

I have nothing else. I own nothing apart from half this house. My past made sure of that. Except... No. This can't be about the cheque. It can't be. I wrack my brains to think about when I first told him about Collette. Was it so early in our relationship? I remember telling him I don't see my brothers, but I can't remember at what point I mentioned the cheque and how I didn't want that money. I know I did tell him. I trusted him.

He supported me. He told me that whatever I decided was fine. He never pushed me. He never mentioned it. But he must have stored that information until the time was right. No wonder he went to such extremes. None of us expected either of our parents to be insured. They weren't the sort of people to pay something monthly, religiously. What I hadn't taken into account was that they were playing a game of chicken from day one, and both of them knew the odds.

I see Collette now, balancing on that cliff edge, mocking me. Her eyes laughing but her expression dangerous and taunting. And my father rolling in, almost unconscious from drink. They were waiting for it, poised in anticipation of the other one going just that little bit too far. The policy, it turned out, had been maintained for twenty years. It was a lot of money. But money I didn't want.

I look at our bed. The expensive wallpaper. The box on top of the wardrobe with my wedding dress in it. No wonder he didn't want an expensive wedding. It's hard to take in. My legs suddenly feel weak and my head spins. I was so serious. So committed. And all the while he had his eyes on my bank account. My God. I messaged Flynn. I fell for it. But it didn't work out exactly as planned for him, because he had underestimated how alone I really was. A feeling like melting butter runs through me, a soft dread of what will happen next.

I pull down my pink suitcase and pull my clothes out of the wardrobe. My sensible capsule wardrobe. I get some shoes and my make-up and a bottle of perfume he didn't buy me. I can't take everything, and I don't know what will happen to the rest of it. I stuff as much into the case as I can. And then I fetch some holdalls from the kitchen.

I fill them with the contents of the tallboy in the spare room. Some photographs and some documents. Bank statements and payslips. A selection of old phones and my fitness trackers. I feel under the duvet for my old laptop I watch films on. But it's gone.

I drag the bags downstairs and DC Sharples carries them out to the car. I wonder if they do this for everyone, or if they just feel sorry for me. I watch Bekah as she looks around the lounge and then the kitchen. I don't know what she's looking for, or if she's just thinking. She has a calm air about her, like nothing would faze her. Then we are leaving. Leaving my beautiful home that I thought was for life. I know in my heart I will not be coming back here. This is not where love is. This is not what I thought it was.

Fifteen minutes later we are at the reception desk of the police station. We wait for someone to open the side door and Bekah breaks the silence.

'I'll give you a lift back with all your stuff after this.'

'This being?'

She doesn't answer. She scans me in, and I stand in front of a camera and have a photo taken. The desk sergeant taps my name into a form, and we are in. She guides me along a grey corridor into an interview room. I know the script only too well. I know we need another person to conduct an interview.

But no one arrives. She sits down opposite me and gets a bottle of water out of her bag.

'So here we are.' She swigs the water. 'We brought Jake Clayton in for questioning. I'm not convinced that the accusations he is levelling at you are true, but he's going to make a complaint. And because, well, because we spent time on the supposed kidnap and then because I deployed the armed police, it will be investigated. You will be investigated. If what he says is true, then you will probably be charged with wasting police time.'

I gasp. My heart races and I am sweating. She goes on.

'We've covered quite a lot of ground so far. He told us you set all this up as some kind of revenge plan with his exes. That he knew nothing about it. That you left him last week.'

I can hardly speak. I gasp for air and stare at her. I must defend myself.

'But his job? He left it. And the CCTV? Surely–'

She interrupts. 'He showed us a trail of evidence that has your name all over it. Everything leads back to you. The computers are in your username. Everything. He can evidence his whereabouts at several critical times.'

She taps her tablet and holds up a photograph. I lean forward to see it. It's my lounge, covered in shredded paper. The agreement lying twisted on the floor. Debris everywhere.

'Do you recognise this?'

'Yeah. I lost it. I…'

'He says you're unbalanced. Verging on mentally ill. He says you attacked him. That you told him your marriage was over and left. Then he tidied it all up because his daughter was coming round.' She sips her water again. 'I have to think how this looks to a jury.'

I blink at her. 'But it didn't happen like that. I'd put up with months and months of strange behaviour from him. He didn't come home.' I realise I am crying. Big tears that I have saved up for a long, long time. 'I swear I did nothing wrong.'

She taps her perfectly manicured fingernail on the table. 'Did you break into Veronica Clayton's house? Did you smash a window?'

I stare at her. He would know I had been there. And Polly could have told him about the smashed window.

'Yes. Yes, but…'

'And did you go to his place of work and talk to his employers about personal issues?'

I am suddenly scared. I've been in this kind of trap before. Where it all starts out nice and friendly and then suddenly the questions get more serious. Where I am not sure if I am implicated or not, because everything seems melded together into one awful scenario that I have avoided thinking about.

'Do I need a solicitor?'

She shakes her head. 'No. No recording. No witnesses. Just you and me. I just need to know.'

I breathe in. 'Yes, I went looking for him. I went to find him to talk this out.' I wipe away more tears. 'I didn't know about any of this. I thought we were still… in love. I thought this was just a blip.'

She is punching something into her tablet. Then she holds it up in front of me. Jake is on the screen. He's sitting in an interview room very much like this one. I hear a male voice echoing. Mocking.

'So, you want to make a complaint about Mrs Clayton? That she has contrived a complex trail of evidence to get revenge on you?'

He stares at the man. I've never seen him look like that. Hard and cruel. My God. He spits out his words. 'She's dangerous. Looks like butter wouldn't melt. But she's not what she seems.'

The man sniggers. 'Whatever you say. But you will need more than that. We're not going to arrest someone because you think she is dangerous.'

'She wrecked our house. Completely flipped. Attacked me.' I gasp. Finally. Finally, I see him lie. Our whole marriage must have been built on fragile lies, just waiting to crumble. He goes on. 'She's crazy. You've seen the photographs. And she knew my daughter was due round. Then she led you lot on a wild fucking goose chase with that mad cow Holly. She's the same.'

The man scrapes his chair. 'Oh, so all your exes are the same. They're all mad, are they?'

There is laughter in the background. Male voices. Jake shifts uncomfortably in his seat.

'Oh no. No, mate, they aren't all the same. This one is very special. Very, very special. You see...' He pauses for effect. 'You know who her mum is, don't you?'

The laughter stops. 'No. Go on, surprise me.'

He looks up at the camera, and suddenly he is looking right at me.

'Collette Palmer. You know? Murdered her husband? Stabbed him through the eye.' He looks back at his audience. 'So you can see why I was worried, can't you? You don't know what she's capable of.'

CHAPTER THIRTY-THREE

I was cooking Ian's tea the day they came. The day the police knocked on the door. I'd stopped looking for her years ago, and I'd hidden the remnants of our relationship deep inside me. I even thought I was over it, whatever that is.

I opened the door, and I could tell from their expressions it was something serious. I expected it to be her they were here to tell me about. I expected it to be her falling over a cliff or from the top of a tall building. I expected them to tell me she was drunk or in a fight or in some other woman's bed.

'Cathy Palmer?'

I knew then it wasn't her that had been hurt. Or died. I knew then that she had sent them. Only Collette would use that name. Cathy. Wild, reckless Cathy. Running through the dark night in search of her lost love. A million miles away from Kate cooking Ian's tea in a striped apron.

'Kate. But yes, I was.'

I expected them to tell me whatever it was on the doorstep. I didn't want this inside the make-believe world I had built for myself. But they stepped forward. The tall police officer bent over.

'Can we come in, please?'

Ian had found his way downstairs and stood behind me. He placed a hand on each shoulder and spoke. 'Yes, officers, come in.'

Once again removing even the last spark of power I had over the situation. They trooped through the hallway and into the lounge. Everything decayed into slow motion as they sat down on the sofa, oversized and awkward. There was a long silence as everyone looked at each other. The smaller officer spoke.

'I'm very sorry to tell you that your father, Harry Palmer, has passed away.'

I remember thinking that he was reading from a script. Ian spoke next.

'She's not called Palmer now, by the way. It's Connor. Kate Connor.'

I started to laugh. A high-pitched hysteria rang around my head. Had they told her? Had they? I suddenly sobered. I know now this is what shock can do to you.

'Have you told her? My mum? Where is she?'

They exchanged a look that told me nothing because everyone looked wide-eyed when her name was mentioned. Eye rolls and nods. Yep. Collette. What's she like? The taller officer licked his lips and took his turn.

'Can you accompany us to the station, Miss… Mrs…'

Ian finished the sentence. 'Connor. Mrs Connor.'

I turned to him. 'Shut up. Just shut up. Not now, Ian. This isn't about you.'

I'd suffer for it later, of course. Not violence. The kind of suffering where someone who annoys you is allowed to go on longer than they should. Not the kind of suffering I am going through now. Not the emotional torture of betrayal. No.

He did shut up. And he wasn't allowed to come to the station. I sat alone in the back of the police car. Numb from the shock that my father was dead. I was a small child again, holding his hand. Dancing, him drunk on Christmas Day, swinging me around. Funny how all the good memories come rolling back.

Watching him walk away each time he left, and then coming back and kissing Collette when she forgave him and he returned. Him round at Grandma's, like a different person in front of his mum. All table manners and serious face. I found words from somewhere.

'What happened?'

The police officers looked at each other. 'Probably best to wait till we get to the station, love.'

I nodded. I thought I was going to identify him. To be officially informed, but when we got there, all three of my brothers were waiting in the cold reception area on the other side of a Perspex screen. The arrows on the floor told me I was going in as they were leaving. All eyes on me as I was shown through. I listened as I walked by.

'Right then, thank you for coming in and giving your statements. We'll be in touch if there's anything else. Give us a ring if you need anything.'

I turned to see them leave together as I arrived alone. But whose fault was that? I asked myself. Only Flynn looked back at me and smiled slightly. They were so young when he left. They never really knew Dad.

We turned into an interview room. Two men sat on one side of a table. One of them stood up to greet me.

'I'm Tom Parker. And this is Stan Brookes, our family liaison officer. We wanted to ask you some questions about your mother.'

I baulked. 'My mother. But isn't it my father who died?'

Confusion reigned as I wondered if I'd heard them correctly. Stan Brookes waved me to a chair and the uniformed officer who had shown me through left.

'I think you should sit down, Cathy.'

I sat and narrowed my eyes. 'It's Kate. Not Cathy. Kate.'

'Kate, sorry. Okay. Our officers have already told you about your father passing away.' He looks down at a file. 'So we think he was attacked between 11pm and 11.45pm last Friday. Unfortunately, he died from his injuries at the scene.'

I stared at them. Attacked? Died at the scene?

'Are you telling me he was murdered? Oh my God. Have you got the person who did it?'

Even as I spoke the words, I knew what was coming. I saw her eyes and her anger and her crashing through the house and destroying everything in her wake. I saw him shouting at her, calling her insane, demanding that she was committed. Then leaving and her dragging us to search for him. The screaming fights with other women. Her eyes always on him and, even when he wasn't there, the constant pining.

It all flashed before me in that split second Stan opened his mouth to speak.

'Look, this is difficult, but we have arrested your mother, Collette Palmer, on suspicion of murder. We wanted to ask you some questions about your relationship with both of them.'

I snorted. It didn't sink in. 'I haven't seen either of them years. They left.'

Tom leant in. 'Your brothers told us you were sixteen when you left.'

'I was sixteen when *she* left.' My voice is much more bitter than I imagined it would be when I finally spoke those words. I had underestimated how the sadness I harboured would look to other people when I finally spoke it. 'He walked out. She was only interested in finding him. Then she didn't come back one day. I knew we would be taken into care, and I would be responsible for my brothers.' I'd looked away, suddenly a moody teenager again. 'Not that I hadn't been already.'

Neither of them spoke.

'Are you asking me if I think she murdered Dad?' They just blinked at me. 'I don't know. I don't know who either of them are. That's the first time I've seen my brothers since then, out there. I have another life.'

I remember feeling the old anxiety pour through me, threatening to drown me.

Stan nodded. 'Yes, this is very difficult, and we want to give you all the support we can. Your mother has asked to see you.'

I reeled with the shock of it. After all the searching, she had decided that now she was in deep trouble she needed me. I almost laughed at the irony of the situation. But I didn't because I felt the anger bubble. The anger at her. The anger that she had finally got her ultimate revenge on the man who she lost everything for.

'No. I don't want to see her.'

Stan nodded. He shuffled some papers and arrived at the pages he needed. He looked them over. 'Okay. Sorry, just a few more things. I know you didn't see much of your mother for years, but we have a sample of fifteen police reports filed. There are more, but these are the reports we have pulled to try to get a picture. Did you witness any violence between your parents? Please tell us if you don't want to answer these questions, or if you wish to leave. You have no obligation.'

All I could hear was my father screaming at her. *Bitch. Mad. Insane.* And her crying and shouting back.

'I never saw her hit him, if that's what you mean.'

He shook his head. 'No, the reports are filed against your father.'

He slid a picture across the table. It was Collette's face and upper body. Her lip bloodied and her shoulders black with bruises. I blinked at the picture and a tear fell. I thought I knew everything. I thought they were as bad as each other. In fact, I thought she was worse, because hadn't everyone said Collette was mad? Crazy? And her jittery, anxious behaviour backed up this eyebrow-raising description.

'No, I didn't see any of this. I saw them argue and scream at each other.' I recalled the sunglasses and the thick make-up and the days she didn't want to get out of bed. A broken arm once, and that weekend we had to stay at Grandma's and she had a hospital band on when we got back. But she explained everything away with a wave of her hand.

It was too much for me to process. My feelings were conflicted. I was panicked and scared as my past fell apart in that interview room.

'How...?'

They looked at each other. 'Your father died of multiple stab wounds. One of his neighbours called the ambulance when he knocked on their front door. Sadly, he died at the scene before the paramedics arrived.'

'And did they see... anyone?'

He shook his head. 'No, but a woman answering Collette Palmer's description had been seen several times in the proceeding days.'

I was already thinking about the flash of silver in her handbag. The way she held that bag close to her, and the look in her eyes when she saw I had seen the cold metal. The faraway look when she got her little notebook out and began to write. Tapping the pen on her teeth as she plotted and planned to find out where he was. Who he was with.

The staring and blinking when Grandma arrived to tell her she was crazy and asked her what she had done this time. Not responding to her questions. But most of all a determination that she would get him back. That he was hers. That everything would be okay – whatever that was. Tom continued.

'We've interviewed your brothers. We understand they were taken into care after your mother left. And you...' He read his notes. 'Left. Were you reported missing?'

I faux laughed. 'You're kidding me. By who? No one actually gave a shit where I was. So, no. I just lived with a friend then got a flat.'

'And you never contacted your family?'

I shook my head. 'No. Well, I tried. I tried to find them through my grandma. Dad's mum. But she wouldn't tell me what happened. Then it was too late.'

They gripped their notes and stared at me. I wanted to ask them if my brothers asked about me. Asked how I was or where I was. Instead, they asked me the million-dollar question. A piece of information I would have sleepless nights over for years.

'One of Mrs Palmer's friends, someone who has known her all her life, told us that she carried a weapon. And that she had been known to threaten people. Those threats included your father. Would that be an accurate representation?'

I looked at the speckled table in the interview room. Yes, she had threatened him, but I never saw her harm anyone except herself, or use that knife. I panicked.

'She just had it in case one of the women she was following started something. There were arguments…'

Stan wrote down my words. 'So, she followed women?'

I swallowed hard. 'My dad would go off. I don't know for sure, but I think he had affairs. She would take us to their houses and try to find him. I think she was scared someone would…'

They were nodding. I knew it sounded bad. But it was the truth. All of a sudden it was over. Stan and Tom were standing, and Tom opened the door.

'Thank you for your co-operation. We'll be in touch if we need more information.'

I stood. My legs were shaky. They thought she'd killed my dad. They thought Collette was a murderer. I walked behind the two men to the reception area where I'd seen my brothers. I turned to them.

'Do you have any contact details for my brothers, please? I'd like to get in touch.'

They looked at each other. 'The best thing you could do is find a mutual relative. Or your solicitor. This might be a tricky time, Kate, with all this going on. We can't disclose any personal contact details.'

That was late February. When I got home, I thought about what I had said. How I had condemned her by my words. I'd confirmed she carried a knife. I felt terrible. I rang them and they told me to see my solicitor. I tried to put it a thousand different ways, but each time I ended up at the knife in her bag. Her confronting women she thought he was sleeping with. I didn't want to, but I started to admit to myself that she had done it.

By September she had been tried and convicted. She was sentenced to life imprisonment. She had pleaded not guilty, so there was a trial at Manchester Crown court. I wasn't called as a witness. I was going to go every day, but in the end, I was a coward. I only went a few times, and I sat at the back. I didn't go to see her, and I didn't go to see my brothers. I didn't even speak to them; I left before they stood up to go. I went to see whether there was anything of me there, in that detailed evidence. Anything that could predict the fire that was rising in me and the dreadful place it could end up. She didn't put up much of a fight. She barely said anything.

The relative peace of my everyday life drew me back to some kind of normality, but inside I was in turmoil. I read all I could about the trial. About her. The media had a heyday. And the centre of the evidence rested on someone telling the police about a knife and the notebook she always carried with her. I recognised everything they said about her. I'd seen the notebooks. Loads of them, all kept in an old brown suitcase.

While I waited for the trial to start, I thought more about her. In fact, I thought about little else. I turned over and over in my mind her erratic behaviour and my bitterness when she left, and wondered if she was really a murderer. I couldn't see it. The more I thought about it, the more I could see that she was scared. Scared of being alone. Scared of not being loved. And scared of him.

But, in a way, brave, because she never gave up. No matter how it was all turned around on her, she never stopped trying to find him. Trying to find answers.

Then, one night I woke at 3am. It was dark in the bedroom, and I went downstairs to get some water. I stood in mine and Ian's home looking out at the neatly manicured lawn. And I realised she wasn't trying to find answers, she was trying to make him pay for what he had done to her. She left her home and her children to make him accountable. To chase him. Maybe that's why she had the knife all along.

Everyone thought she was mad. Crazy. Insane. Affected. Jealous. So what did she have to lose, apart from me and my brothers who, if Grandma had anything to do with it, would have been taken from her, anyway?

CHAPTER THIRTY-FOUR

Bekah turns off the tablet. She clasps her hands in front of her.

'He's very convincing, and it looks like he's going to use everything he's got here. He's got most of the bases covered.'

I am still thinking about the recording. *You don't know what she's capable of.* I'd opened up to him. I'd told him everything. Everything. All about my childhood. All about the trial. All about the insurance money that I was entitled to but chose not to take. He'd nodded sympathetically. He'd agreed with everything. He only mentioned the cheque once when we were considering extending the house, but when I got upset, he apologised. I know now he tried to get it another way.

'I'm not my mother. I'm not Collette.'

'No. No you are not. But I am here to tell you that if you complain and this goes to trial, which it would because he will never admit to what he has done, the jury will hear all about it.'

I blink at her. 'Are you telling me not to make a complaint?'

She looks at the tablet and pauses.

'No, I just wanted to keep you in the loop about things.' She gets up and shuts the door. Then she sits and speaks in a low voice. 'Look, we both know what is going on here. He's set up some elaborate plan to get hold of your bank account. He has form. He did similar with other people. He has absolutely covered his tracks so that either you can't object because you are married and share money and property, or he set up accounts in your name. Or there is no proof either way. It's almost the perfect scam.'

She sips her water.

'But what he doesn't know is that I arrived too soon. That his instructions weren't followed. And he also doesn't know that you found the tracker. He could deny it and say you put it there, but it shows that he has underestimated what has happened.'

I think about my usual routine as I come in. Shoes off, coat hung up. Open letters. She's right. He'd been so sure I would go through my usual behaviour. He hadn't factored in how upset I was and how that would disrupt me.

'So, what will happen now?'

'We'll question him, give him a chance to make a complaint. Then we'll have to let him go. What he did, taking the money, it's not fraud because you have joint accounts and you are married. And the rest of it, although it is a complex set-up, could have been done by anyone; we have no evidence to suggest it was him. In fact, the evidence points at you.'

Of course it does. Like the evidence pointed at Collette. But I never really believed she did it. And I made it worse by telling the police about the knife.

'So, he'll get away with it.'

Her expression hardens. 'Maybe in court. But I… we need to make sure he doesn't make a complaint against you. The same goes – if you took the money, it isn't fraud. But he's trying to make it look like you've lost the plot and are harassing him. That you are in league with his exes. Put that all together and he's potentially got a case.'

I suddenly feel sick. How could this happen? She holds her hand up.

'I wanted to talk to you about this agreement. The one on your wall. I looked through Holly's file. It seems they had a similar agreement that he used to control her. And Veronica. Again, a similar set of rules that he completely ignored but expected her to stick to. I've started to build a case and this control aspect doesn't bode well for him. So when I go to question him, I'm going to mention it, along with the fact that I attended your property in response to an emergency call and will testify that his belongings had been moved. I then attended the property again, and they were returned.'

I smile. 'And that's what he's denied in his statement?'

'Yes. I think the words he used were, "Kate is deluded. You can check the camera showing the outside of our property".' She swigs her water again. 'I've got my guys working on that footage and the footage from the school. I'll be going to see his former employer to understand his capabilities.'

I lean forward. 'I don't know how to thank you, Bekah. I'm so scared.'

She suddenly becomes serious. 'Let's not count our chickens. My neck's on the line here because we got the guns out for nothing. An enormous hole in my budget. They could drop this at any time.' She brushes a long, spiral curl out of her way. 'And you know what this means, don't you? You will have no recourse, just like Holly.'

She doesn't say *and look what it did to her*. She doesn't need to. I know what happens to women with no recourse to justice. They hide away and plot and plan instead of getting on with life, like Holly. Or they put revenge above everything. Like Collette.

I think for a long moment. He has taken everything. I can't go back to Lynton Grove, even if I wanted to. I wouldn't be safe there. I'm left with a loan to pay off. But I can make him sell the house. I have a fraction of my belongings and no doubt he will dispose of the rest of them. I have no job. And I have no marriage. Most of all I have no trust.

I put everything on the line for him. For love. I allowed myself to be shaped by an agreement that set out to keep me in a false sense of security, while he planned to manipulate me into claiming the insurance money. Bekah speaks.

'So I need your agreement to tell him you testify his things were missing, and that you called an emergency number because you thought he had been kidnapped. It's unlikely he will bring up the note you didn't open, because how would he explain knowing about it? But I need to know you will back this up.'

I nod. 'I will. I just don't understand why he did this.'

She is silent. She seems lost in her thoughts for a moment.

'Some people thrive on it. Fraudsters and scammers. They get off on it. Some people think of it as a job. It's becoming more common these days, with internet banking. It's wrong, and it's cruel, but proving it's a crime is a different matter. He made you think something, Kate. You and Holly and Veronica. But how can we prove that? For all intents and purposes, he made it look like you were three bitter women out for revenge who set him up. And that's what he will go with. Or not, once I tell him I was at the scene.'

She stands and opens the door. I've been here before. On the day I was questioned about my father's death. Another day, another police interview room. As I walk down the corridor beside her, I feel a sense of an ending. I have to start again whether or not I want to.

Paula is waiting for me. She has brought my warm jacket. Bekah nods.

'I'll be in touch. I'll let you know how it goes and if you need to come in again.'

I turn to face her. 'Thank you. Thank you for believing me.'

And not him, I want to say, because I am not Collette.

Something niggles at me. Something Bekah said about Holly and Veronica. *He's got form.* I know Holly told me he met her through her parents. That he must have planned what he did. And Veronica. He must have known about her money before he met her, but it didn't go to plan when she had Polly. My God. Did he know about my insurance before he met me? Did he target me?

I stumble and almost fall. Paula rushes over.

'Are you okay, mate? You look very pale.'

'Yeah. Fine, considering. I need to let all this sink in. Can we go back to yours?'

She smiles and wraps my coat around me. I cannot count how many times I have done this to her. Wrapped my safety around her and taken her somewhere she can recover. She squeezes my hand in shared acknowledgement.

Bekah is gone and I am in Paula's car. She drives at breakneck speed, the way she does most things, back to her place. Her next-door neighbour opens the door.

'Was that the police earlier? I saw that woman on the telly.'

She sweeps past them like a security guard and pushes me inside. 'Oh, fuck off! None of your fucking business!' She slams the door and laughs.

'More tea, vicar?'

She takes her coat off and flings it on the chair. I resist the urge to hang it up. I am almost numb with shock. I try to capture the image of my brothers in my mind's eye. I am used to doing that. Making a mental collage of people I love but can never be in touch with.

My thoughts tumble and rest on Jake's words. *You don't know what she's capable of.* That exact phrase triggered something deep inside me. I don't like to think about the trial. The jury staring at her. My brothers sitting with their wives. Me, alone. As usual. And witness after witness describing Collette's life away from us.

Drunken nights on the town. Drunken days in bars. I tried

not to look at her. She never looked at me. She looked older and thinner and stared at the floor the whole time. Her hair was longer and straight and her strong arms, which I always remembered, skinny. Various men took the stand and went through the embarrassing details of how she used them to fund her search for Harry. *Harry, Harry, Harry. That's all she cared about.* The same story repeated over and over using different words.

Then one of his friends described a scene that made me sit up straight in my seat. I always entered the court later than my brothers and sat behind them. And left earlier. That day I saw them all shift in their seat as Joe Gallows told everyone how Collette would randomly turn up wherever Harry was. That more than once they had been at a friend's house and she would be outside, barely hiding behind a wall or bush. That she would follow him down the street shouting.

The defence lawyer had cross-examined and told Joe that although that behaviour was erratic, it didn't make Collette a murderer. He'd become agitated. He'd cowered dramatically, and he kept repeating it.

'You don't know what she's capable of. No, you don't know what she's capable of.'

I scan the court in my mind. Was he there? Was Jake there? Or is it a coincidence? I tell myself I am being melodramatic. That my mind is making more of this than what it can be. But that is how he has trained me. The long silences when I was brusque with him. The raised eyebrows and exit to his loft when I disagreed. This is what I do now. I keep the peace. I stick to the agreement to avoid a clinging or fawning. I make myself still and quiet so that I don't cause a fuss.

Paula returns with the tea. She places it on the table in front of me. I smile at her.

'Thank you. For this.'

She smiles back, and she knows I don't just mean the tea. The shock of today has made me weak and tired. I need more time to think about what has happened. Time to rest and calm down so I can think rationally. As I pick up my oversized teacup, my phone beeps. I automatically pick it up and see a Facebook message.

It's from Flynn.

Hi Kate. We need to talk.

CHAPTER THIRTY-FIVE

I hardly slept last night. It's like the past and the present have merged into one awful reality. I answered Flynn's message with a simple *Okay, let me know when*. No smiley and no kiss because I don't know what this talk will be about. I don't know if he will be angry about me asking for the money, or just angry in general.

In the time since I sent my message to him, he could have spoken to Michael and Patrick. They could have come up with a million reasons not to get in touch. Not to give me the money. Or they could have serious reservations, and who could blame them? In the early hours I scoured news channels and social media for any sign of the debacle at my home the other day. Anything about armed police.

I found reports about a missing child that had been found, but nothing mentioning my name. I am haunted by the feeling that Jake targeted me. I want to know more. I want to find out if he was in court that day. I don't remember signing in. It was a while ago and I have no idea if they keep records.

Now I am making tea. Paula has gone above and beyond in her catering, and I fetch her a tea tray in bed. I knock on the door, and she makes a 'come in' noise. For a moment I am back at the beginning of our friendship when we found so much comfort in each other. I open the door and she props herself up.

'Here we are. Some tea.' It's all I can manage, and she stares at me.

'Sit down, Kate. We need to talk.' I climb onto the bed and lay down beside her. She turns over and rests her head on her elbow. 'I'm sorry I lied to you about John. I was trying to... I don't know. Be like everyone else. But that isn't me.'

'I'm sorry too for judging you. But it's only because I care. And you know my issues with booze.'

She screws up her face. 'That's what I wanted to talk to you about. Don't hate me, but you've been a bit of a control freak. I mean, it's up to me if I want to pass out on my own bathroom floor.' She laughs.

I know it's a joke, but it's too reminiscent of Collette. I stare at her. That's who she reminds me of. All these years I haven't been able to see it. She looks nothing like her, yet she is very similar. Her chain-smoking and her don't-give-a-fuck attitude. Her commitment to absolutely nothing except her current obsession. It could be booze. It could be a man. Or it could be a coat she wants. But never anything serious or lasting.

Of course, that is why I want to look after her. That is why I took her to rehab and collected her every time.

'Yes, you're right. I thought I had the upper hand. Nice house, nice car, love, all that. But it turns out Jake is a con man. I never had anything.'

I feel the sobs erupt. Like so many times before, we hug in silence and one or the other of us cries it out. It's me this time. When it subsides, I pull away. She speaks.

'Do you remember that day about a year ago when you gave me that big lecture in the pizza place about being independent like you? Not taking money from my parents?' I nod. I did say that. She goes on. 'You told me you were completely independent, but I couldn't see it. You kept harping on about that agreement and how it let you and him be yourselves. But it didn't seem like that. You were watching him. Looking at your phone a lot.' She touches my arm. 'You can say it as much as you like. You can keep saying it, but as far as I'm concerned independence is a verb. And you were saying it but not doing it. I don't think you ever have, Kate. But there's no time like now.'

I look around her bedroom, strewn with clothes and shoes. Every room in this flat has Paula's hallmark uniqueness. It is the opposite of my minimalist home whose only stamp of me were those curtains I insisted on. It was empty, like me. Paula is right. I need to fill myself up with something. I don't know what yet, but something. I don't say anything. I don't agree or argue or even comment. I just nod my acknowledgement. Despite Paula and I being so different, we fill a gap in each other that I am beginning to see much more clearly.

My phone beeps in my dressing gown pocket. It's Flynn.

Meet me at one o'clock in Piccadilly Gardens. We can take it from there.

I turn the phone screen to face Paula.

'I'm meeting my brother. This isn't over yet, Paula. Jake might have taken all my money and all my pride, but he can't stop me doing this.'

I hurry into my room and pull-on jeans and a T-shirt. I brush my hair and apply some light make-up. My stomach churns yet I feel slightly excited. Even if he hates me and tells me never to contact him again, I will have seen him. Spoken to him. I won't die without seeing at least one family member. The thought shocks me, but there is no time. I grab my keys, bag and phone and run up the road for the tram as I'm too nervous to drive.

I watch the suburbs turn to the city and I feel the anxiety build. I will be early. He will see me before I see him. I want to give him the chance to not turn up. To change his mind. To remember the past and what I did and decide it's not a good idea after all.

The tram whizzes along and soon I am getting off. I walk along the Manchester pavements and suddenly remember a time when we came to the city as a family. They were taking us to see Father Christmas, but we never got there. Instead, we spent the afternoon in a faux Alpine mulled wine shed hastily assembled in Piccadilly Gardens to make a fast buck out of Christmas shopping. We were sent to play on the frosty grass while they, initially, embraced under the mistletoe. However, it soon disintegrated into an argument, and Dad stormed off. Mum dragged us home. She was sick on the bus. Back then I thought she was ill, but now I know she was just blind drunk.

I instinctively know why Flynn chose this meeting place. A shared memory between us, because that was the first time Dad ever hit Flynn. He was crying to see Santa, and Dad lashed out hard and knocked him off his feet. I picked him up and dusted the grass from his coat. I stroked his red face, finger marks swelling on his cheek.

I sit in a prominent position so he can make his choice. I haven't been here more than a second when I see him stride across the bridge and along the shopfronts. He is grinning. I relax a little. As he nears, he hurries. I stand up and wonder whether to hold out my hand for a handshake, but he grabs me and hugs me. Then he holds me away from him by my shoulders. He is a good six inches taller than me, and I look up into his familiar features.

'Flynn. I...'

He shakes his head. 'No, let's not talk about all that. I came to ask you something. I talked to everyone else, and we wanted to know if we could all meet up. If you want to, of course.'

I can't believe it. 'Well, yes, but I need to tell you–'

He interrupts again. 'I meant to get in touch when all that happened. When we saw you. But it all hit me harder than I thought and then with the trial.' He looks away, 'I might as well tell you. I don't think she did it.' I stare at him. His words are thick with tears. 'I believe they put two and two together and got six.'

I sigh. 'I told them about the knife. Well, they asked and I confirmed. I didn't realise what had happened. It was probably my fault.'

'It was not. It wasn't your fault. You weren't even there at the time. You were long gone. Whatever happened wasn't your fault. None of what happened was.' He wipes away a tear. 'I've had a lot of therapy and it took me a long time to realise that. We were all children.'

I see myself in my mind's eye the day I left. Not even fully grown, but a makeshift adult all my life. I can't remember ever being a child.

'But I don't think she did it. Sure, she'd been around him, but the CCTV was broken that night. All the rest of that area was okay, but that camera was out. It could have been anyone. So don't hate her.'

I blink at him. 'So how did they know she was there?'

'They looked at the surrounding streets. They couldn't see her, but someone said they thought they saw her. The case was mainly based on DNA evidence. She'd been in that flat all right. She was on that camera other nights. Just her DNA and his DNA and an old story about a knife.'

We sit in silence then I speak. 'Have you seen her?'

He shakes his head. 'No. Have you?'

I snort. 'No. She asked to see me, but I couldn't. I looked for her, and you, for a long time, but no one would tell me where you were.'

My voice breaks and he puts a sturdy arm around me. My little brother protecting me now. Comforting me. We have come full circle.

'Well, I'm here now. And so are Michael and Pat. Let's leave it at that and set a date for a meet up.'

'Thank you so much. You don't know how much this means. Message me with the details and I'll be there.'

We stand and hug. He walks away, looking back to wave at me. I watch him disappear around the corner then sit back on the bench. No cameras. No cameras. It all comes down to cameras again.

I dial Holly's number. She answers quickly.

'Hello? Kate? Are you okay?'

She sounds hyper-anxious. I feel bad asking her this question, but I have to.

'I am, but I need to ask you something.'

She laughs. 'Oh. Okay, shoot.'

I take a breath. 'Did you know Jake before you became a couple? How did you first meet?'

She is silent for a moment.

'We met in a bar I went to a lot with friends, but we had met before. I was working in Dubai. I know, you can't believe it now, but I had a high-ticket job. He said he met me at a party, and I vaguely remembered him. And someone told me he'd been asking who I was. We joked that he'd tracked me halfway across...' Then she is silent. 'No. No, he couldn't have.' Her voice is shaking. 'We joked about it. Did he...?'

I listen to her sobs. Even now she hadn't realised the full extent of his deception.

'I don't know for sure, but it's looking like he selected us.' I can't even begin to tell her how he selected me because the horrific fragments of information are still forming in my mind. 'Holly, I'm going to go back to DS Bradley with this. She is looking at your file, so she might call you. Let's meet up soon and call me if you need anything.'

She sounds calmer. 'I will. Anything, Kate. Just ask if you need anything.'

CHAPTER THIRTY-SIX

I am back at the police station. I tap my fingernails on the reception desk and the receptionist summons Bekah Bradley. I can feel the words that I need to say to her pushing against me, revving up my anger. It's a bittersweet mixture of desperation and helplessness at being conned by someone you thought you were in love with, and the building excitement at realising that you are discovering the truth.

I should have written down what I wanted to say. That's my usual MO, but this is not a usual situation. No, this is a shot in the dark from someone who is used to sitting in the darkness. Someone who has acquired the torch of experience. So, I'm just going to tell her.

I wait. The receptionist looks up from time to time and smiles. Five then ten minutes pass. Then she appears on the other side of the door with DC Sharples. I wave and smile. I have nothing to lose here. She will either take this on board or she won't, but I know I am right.

In the same way that Holly compiled a case, I am building the evidence. Like Bekah said, he's covered his tracks. However, there are still things that can be uncovered. Holly's fire rose too quickly, and she burned out. But if Collette gave me anything it's tenacity. I've spent most of my life pushing that fire down. Practising the calmness that is water instead of oil.

I glimpse myself in the Perspex partition. I look confident and collected, yet inside everything is swirling around and threatening to sink if I don't get it out soon. I wait while Bekah opens the door and comes around the reception desk.

'Kate, what can I do for you?'

She has a 'this had better be good' tone about her and I smile.

'I need to speak to you about Jake.' She looks at DC Sharples and nods. I continue. 'It's not about what happened the other day. It's about my mum.'

A frown forms on her brow and she pauses. 'Oh. About the money?'

'Yes. That. And something else.'

She takes a key ring and opens a door to a side room. I follow her and it is like the triage room at my local A&E, right down to the smell of disinfectant. She moves a cup from the table to the windowsill and sits. DC Sharples takes the seat beside her. I sit opposite them. They stare at me.

'I met with my brother. He texted me about the money. We talked a little about Collette.' I feel her name on my lips, unusual and sweet after all this time. 'About how Dad died. He told me a CCTV camera that was usually on was out that night.'

I see Bekah's eyes narrow almost indescribably. Her lips are pursed. 'Go on.'

'So, I got in touch with Holly, asked her if she knew Jake before she started seeing him. She said she met him at a party when she worked in Dubai. He knew she was loaded. And Veronica. I couldn't work out why he would even bother with me until I thought about the insurance money. So someone needs to find out if he was working for Union Insurance around the time my dad died.' Her lips curl a little into a smile. I continue. 'And would the CCTV for that area still be on the file for my mum's case? Not just that street. The streets around it, too.'

She leans back into her chair. 'This might all come to nothing, you know.'

'I know. But it might not. You told me the other day he had covered his tracks, and it could be that he had back then because no one knew him. But if he's on the CCTV now, he's connected.'

She turns to DC Sharples. 'Would you? It's Collette Palmer and Harry Palmer.'

He leaves. She straightens up and leans over.

'What are you expecting from this? I don't want you to get your hopes up.'

I smile at her. 'Nothing. I'm expecting nothing. I could be wrong, but my brother told me he didn't think Collette killed Dad. And neither do I. I didn't know he'd hit her until the other day, but believe me, there were plenty of other times she could have done it before then. Plenty.'

She logs on to the workstation next to her. She taps in a password and then her eyes flit across the screen. The noise of a mouse scroll wheel is loud in the silent room. Finally, it stops, and she speaks.

'I'm applying for a warrant to run a background check and some other checks. That should tell us where he worked. Let's see what Posh comes up with.' She looks me in the eye. 'I don't need a warrant for looking at past case CCTV, but if we find anything, you need to keep quiet about it, right? Not a word.'

Her usually pale skin is flushed red.

'Would that mean you could arrest him?'

She shakes her head. 'It would mean he'd be under suspicion of murder. We would have to go over the evidence again with his DNA.' She checks the screen. She is seething. 'This is how they work. Ducking and diving. Lying. Scamming. I thought this one was an opportunist who just got cockier, but now…'

I suddenly feel scared. My God, if he had killed Dad I had

been living with a murderer for years. He could have killed me. She continues.

'He's been clever, for sure. But even if he knew your parents were insured, and he had his eye on you, how would he know about your past? Someone would have had to tell him.'

I slump. The people I have gone into detail with about my past I could count on one hand. Paula. A therapist I saw for a couple of months. And Ian. I scour my memory for anyone else I might have poured my soul out to, but there is no one. Ian has worked at the same job for years. No chance of him working at an insurance company or in software.

Then I see it. Clear as day. Jake didn't talk about his job a lot but told me he had worked for Jenkins Stuart for years. His boss confirmed it when I went to see him. He worked on client accounts. He wrote bespoke software and IT solutions. I vaguely remember Ian saying his company, Lansdown Engineering, had a new system and that he'd struggled to use it. That he sat for weeks with the software people fine tuning it.

But Jake also worked on maintenance contracts. Audits and upgrades. He could easily have offered to work for the insurance company, chosen a big policy and then hunted down the beneficiaries. I will never know the full details of how he chose my parents' policy, or how he heard about my life story and designed a way to get that cash. I straighten.

'Do you need a warrant to ask Jake's last employer for their client list?'

She shakes her head. 'No. Unless they don't co-operate, and we already requested it once.'

My gaze moves to her mobile phone.

'He worked at client offices. We need to know if he worked at Union Insurance and Lansdowne Engineering.'

She smiles. 'I'm already in enough shit. I guess this won't make too much difference.'

I pass my phone across the table with Jenkins Stuart's number visible.

'It's Dave Lord you want. He's worried about Jake. He left there a couple of months ago, suddenly.' I try out her limits. 'He'll think you're worried about him, too. You could mention you've spoken to me. He won't know what it's about.'

She snorts and nods. Then she dials. She maintains eye contact as she speaks.

'Yes, hello there. This is DS Bradley from GM Police. I wonder if I could speak to Dave Lord?'

Her voice is bright and crisp and my heart beats though my chest.

'Hello, Mr Lord.' A pause. 'No, nothing to worry about. I'm calling about a Mr Jake Clayton. I believe he worked for you and left suddenly. I'm trying to trace his whereabouts, and I wondered if you had a list of all the clients he worked with. I think we already requested it, but your staff haven't...' Another pause. 'No, no, I completely understand. GDPR. But yes, just the company names would be fine.' She listens. 'Yes, I did speak to Mrs Clayton. I'm sure everything is fine. It's just routine. It's just in case anyone remembers anything he said.'

She is good. And I have a feeling she has done this before.

'Actually, could you send it to my private email so I can see it on my phone? Yes. BBradley3535 at gmail.com.' Another pause. 'Of course I will keep you informed, and you can ring me on this number anytime. Thank you so much.'

She sighs. She's a pro. Her own email address and her own mobile number.

'I don't like doing it, but he gave that info of his own free will.' She swipes a screen on her phone and leaves it face up on the table on her Gmail screen. DC Sharples returns. She moves her phone to the side.

'Any luck?'

He nods. 'Yep. It's all been digitised so it's still there. I sent it through.'

She taps on the keyboard and turns the screen around. I was shown the footage back then to see if I recognised anyone, but I didn't. There were people about – Dad was living in a shared house on a terraced row in Ancoats. The houses were built on a grid of eight streets beside a mill. The end of each street turned onto a major artery road into the city, so there were speed cameras and, because of the high crime in the neighbourhood, observation cameras covered a lot of the area. The camera that pointed down Dad's street was broken the evening he was killed, but the police appealed for any of the people on the other cameras to come forward.

There was only one way into the street, and one way out. The houses were back-to-back too; there was no back exit – the alley gates were locked and visible. The other end of the street was a solid mill wall as the houses were built right up to it. My mum wasn't on that footage, I was sure of that, but other people were. It was closing time at the local pubs and people were up and down the main road and that street.

The prosecution in Dad's case suggested that she might have hidden in a crowd of people who turned the corner. They didn't offer a route out of the street, but the jury must have believed it.

It is on the screen now and I see the familiar street angles in six cameras. There is 24-hour footage on each side and I see the CCTV has been tagged with those people who came forward. Bekah looks at me.

'Just the pre-footage for now, a couple of hours before. Four times faster. Posh, can you cover?'

He looks excited. 'Yep. We've gone on surveillance out on King Street on the Mallory case, have we?' She nods. He punches some details into his phone. Then she grabs his arm.

'No, scratch that. Book it to this case.' He raises his eyebrows.

She snorts. 'I know, I know, but I feel like we have to do it. Even if it's to close it off. You in?'

He nods and changes his booking. She presses play, and the frozen figures move on the screen in front of us. I watch as they move super-fast to their destinations. Couples and groups of people walking along the main road from pub to pub. A normal night in a normal area. Cars whizzing by and the odd ambulance on its way into the city.

Bekah slows the footage at each single figure that turns into Dad's row and zooms in just before they become invisible. Last time we did this we were looking for a middle-aged blonde woman. This time it's my husband. I know his walk. His gait. All the things about him you can't change. The slight droop of his shoulder and the way he shoves his hands in his pockets.

We sit for more than an hour staring at the monitor and suddenly my heart skips a beat. I look up at the time. Ten twenty-one. Familiarity pricks me and I point at the screen. She winds it back until the exact point the figure appears and then zooms in and progresses the frames slowly. I lean in. I see him. I see his shoes and the slight turn in of his toes as he walks. It's February and the scarf across his face is not out of place. My heart beats faster as I watch. The curl of a stray lock of hair across his forehead that I have touched so many times.

Bekah looks at me. 'Is that him? Can you make an ID?'

I feel the fire in my throat.

DC Sharples holds his hand up. 'Okay, the warrant is available for the background check.'

Bekah checks her phone. She reads an email as the figure flickers on the screen. She throws her phone down. 'No Union Insurance on the Jenkins Stuart client list. But Lansdowne Engineering is.'

DC Sharples speaks. 'Oh, and we've got the insurance company records. No sign of Mr Clayton at their end. And it says here the insurance money is still sitting in the account unclaimed.'

I shrug. 'I never took mine. It didn't seem right.'

We turn back to the screen. She moves the figure on frame by frame. I am mesmerised, and he turns the corner to Dad's house. My whole life flashes through my mind. Things I intentionally buried resurrect themselves against the backdrop of this. I take a breath in and nod.

'Yes, that's him. That's Jake. I'll testify in court.'

The room is quiet, and the CCTV footage still tracks a quiet Saturday night in Ancoats as Flynn rounds the corner to our father's house.

CHAPTER THIRTY-SEVEN

Two weeks later, Paula and I are sitting in a Pizza Express in the city. Jake was arrested and bailed. He had no alibi for the night my father died. Bekah Bradley interviewed Ian, and he told her that Jake had worked on the new software system with him and brought up the subject of money and partners. They had in-depth conversations about my 'inheritance', as Ian called it, and Ian confided in him I wouldn't take the money.

Bekah isn't sure what will happen or if there will be enough evidence to convict him. What I do know is that my mother's conviction for murder is unsafe. I went to see a solicitor, and he told me that there could be an appeal.

It's the first time I have been out socially since all this happened and I am nervous. Flynn text me last week and asked if I would come along to meet him, Patrick and Michael and their wives. I wasn't sure and I couldn't tell anyone why. I can't even confide in Paula because this is something just for me to turn around in my mind. Something to consider and mull over.

I came to the conclusion that Jake will get what he deserves. And I will let go now and let it unfold. No doubt he has already lined up his next victim. Bekah told me it's like an addiction and each time it gets riskier. She told me that he would have seen me as a challenge. Something to control into claiming that insurance and, with it, any savings. A dangerous game to play, but she doesn't think he will stop unless he is formally charged with murder and jailed.

I watch now as my brothers file in. Big men now, all broad shoulders and stubble. Their wives follow. Women I feel like I know through social media now come to life, their curiosity piqued as they spot me. I get up out of my seat and walk towards them. In a moment we are huddled together, holding each other, their strong arms around me like my arms were around them all those years ago.

I step backwards. 'I'm sorry. Sorry for leaving you. I...'

Patrick laughs. 'Bloody hell, Cathy, I would have too if I'd been old enough. No one blames you.'

Michael laughs too. 'No one except Grandma. But she blames everyone.'

I nod and smile, but I am thinking she didn't blame everyone, did she? She didn't blame the person who, at the bottom of all this, was responsible. She didn't blame her son.

Flynn stands at the back, letting it all go on in front of him. His wife holds his hand and smiles at the scene. I catch his eye and nod. His face asks me a question, but I turn back into the crowd and introduce Paula.

Soon we are surrounded by pizza and garlic bread, and this is clearly not the environment for questions and recriminations. I drink some fizzy water and laugh as Paula downs a large glass of wine. My brothers tell me about their kids and how they can't wait to meet Aunty Cathy. No one mentions Collette or the time that has passed between her leaving and now.

The dessert is served, and Flynn goes outside and lights a cigarette. I follow him and stand beside him in the cool afternoon air. I touch his hand.

'I know.'

He glances at me. 'What? What do you know?'

I don't look at him. 'I know it was you. I saw you on the CCTV.'

He visibly slumps. 'But I thought...'

'Yes. My husband. I need to tell you that little story someday. But I wanted to let you know it will go to the grave with me.'

He is quiet for a moment.

'I didn't think they'd find her and blame her. I thought they wouldn't find out. I was careful.'

I nod. 'They are able to enhance footage these days, but they would never know it was you. Unless they knew you like I do.'

I see a tear trickle down his cheek. 'Would she have seen it? The footage?'

My God. My God! Of course she would. She would have recognised her own son. The woman who I thought had abandoned us. She saw him and said nothing. She took life. For us.

'I don't know.' I squeeze his hand. 'I was there all those years ago. I saw what happened. That's all I'm saying.'

We sit in silence for a while. Then he speaks. 'She was seeing him again. She was going round there.'

'I know. The police told me.'

He shakes his head. 'He was using her. He was still using her. She was getting dressed up and going round there. But at times he had other women there. And... I saw her crying. I'd been searching for her and eventually I found her. In some scruffy backstreet boozer asking around for him. I was asking for her and she was asking for him.' I nod. The same as me, then. He continues. 'I followed her and saw her come out of his house crying and I just... something just came over me and I saw red...'

I squeeze his hand again. I don't want to know what happened. I don't know if it will change anything if I hear the details.

'No, Flynn, no. I don't want to know the details. I'm not

saying it's right, what you did. But... but... you need to forget it now. Like it never happened. Need to put it behind you. All this. You've... we've carried it all for so long now. All of us. And now we need to put it away. It's done and it can't be undone. None of it. But we can change what happens next.'

He nods and scratches his head. 'So what happens now?'

I turn around and see the scene inside the pizza parlour. Paula is entertaining everyone with her stories, and everyone orders more drinks. It seems like only Flynn and I are weighed down by the past, but I know that is not true. None of us took the insurance money. None of us wanted the dirty cash that would not recompense us for our lost childhood.

And her. I know her better now. I know why she was cast in the villain's role. Collette shone just that little bit too bright, and she didn't know how to handle that light. I look at Paula, head back and laughing. A little bit crazy. *She's mad, her.* And suddenly everyone believes it. My grandma was chief accuser in the court of Collette's sanity with my dad the ringleader, rounding up his sad captains and side-affairs to torture her into deeper madness.

Eventually she believed the hype. She acted out her sideshow with us in tow. She never gave up trying to prove that she was right about him. She kept a notebook. She must have written everything down. Committed it to memory then went about trying to prove it. And in the end those private thoughts made the difference. Those things we think about people in the dead of night when no one is listening. Hers were laid out in a courtroom in a trial that she knew she had to lose.

'Nothing. We just carry on. We try to be a family. I have a lot of time to make up for and if everyone's happy I'd like to make this a regular thing.'

He puts his arms around me. He doesn't need words; I feel the strength of his love envelop me. I hug him back, and then we let each other go. He manages a smile.

'Of course. It's been brilliant. And you haven't changed a bit.'

But I have changed. I've changed into someone who was so traumatised she allowed a bad person to take advantage of her. I am still reeling. I am ashamed that Jake and I slept together, and I never even knew that he faked every second of our relationship for money.

And other things have changed. I will never again be tied to another person or thing. As Paula says, independence is a verb. I need to find my own space in this world now and come to terms with the huge reshuffle that just happened in every aspect of my life. There is one thing I need to say to Flynn.

'I have! I'm practically an old woman!' I push his arm gently and he laughs.

'She wasn't Irish, was she?'

Finally, I can share a psychic space with someone who is thinking the same thoughts as me. Running the same memories through their mind and coming up with the same conclusions. I know he is in the kitchen, a little boy with cold feet on terracotta tiles, dancing a jig with our half-drunken mother. She swung us round, and we howled with laughter. Her four-leaf clover apron and matching oven gloves seemed, along with her red hair, conclusive evidence that she was definitely a Galway girl.

But I know better than anyone that just because the evidence is right in front of you doesn't mean you know what is going on. I'm still trying to work out how Jake pulled off the money stunt. Bekah Bradley reckons he was just about to trigger the kidnap when I drove away into the distance. He had to change his plan, but he was soon back on track. He had trained me in certain habits on purpose. The texts at the junction. Picking the mail up before I took my shoes off. It's called habit chaining. What he hadn't factored in was panic. And that was his downfall.

According to her, he is still denying everything, even the things they can prove. His 'no comment' stance isn't deterring Bekah, who is determined to get some kind of conviction. I am pretty sure she will never let this one go.

'No. According to a friend of Mum's...' I mimic the policeman who interviewed me, 'she was born in Bolton.' I hear Collette's voice echoing thorough me and I smell her cigarette burning down to the filter. *We are who we want to be. You make your own life.* I turn and face him head on. 'Would you want her back in your life if she got out? Because it looks like she will.'

He stares. A ten-mile stare just like her. Then he answers.

'I don't know. The kids... what about you?'

I've thought about it. I have nowhere to bring her to live with me. I could rent a house, but I don't even know her. I have no money and I'm not even sure I still have a job. I rang in to confirm I needed compassionate leave and Sonia Platt, the HR director, rang me up and asked for a meeting.

I don't even know if I have forgiven her. My heart wants to, but my head tells me that no one changes that much. I worry I am embarking on a mission to free her that will be met with desertion. Abandonment. The same kind of hurt I felt time and time again. That I would throw myself into the fire, and for what?

But I must. I've come this far and uncovered so much. Only weeks ago, I would have steered away from this. The risk would have been too great for my lifestyle. Now I realise I wasn't really living. I was surviving with a con man. Living is taking chances and really feeling emotions. Letting them flow and jump and dip while we try to make sense of this chaos.

'Yes, I think I will. I'll take a chance. I can walk away if it doesn't work out.'

He nods. 'Okay. I will if you will. And I expect they will too.'

It's getting dark now. Some twinkling lights illuminate the canopy we are sitting under, and we both look up. I turn to see my younger brothers having a drinking competition with Paula. Their wives sit either side of her and everyone is all smiles.

I look back at Flynn.

'It's over.'

I feel tears rise but he shakes his head.

'I'll never get over it. But I'll give it a try.' He looks into the restaurant. 'Come on, we should go back in.'

I squeeze his hand one more time, and we leave our secret behind in the dark skies as we step back into the bright lights.

CHAPTER THIRTY-EIGHT

I am sitting in a greasy spoon café with Holly, Paula and Veronica. I am sipping tea and telling them what happened at my solicitor's appointment.

'So I can't get any of the money back until I file for divorce and even then, I might not. I've invited him to offer to buy me out of the house. He has no choice but to give me half the equity. Thank God the remortgage didn't go through.' I realise what I said too late. 'Sorry, V, I didn't mean…'

She waves it away. 'Believe me, I'd rather be in debt and see the back of him.'

I smile. 'And they haven't charged him over my dad yet. He's helping them with their enquiries. But there's no rush. They'll be collecting all the evidence. They've had the CCTV camera footage from Polly's school with a specialist and he says they've been tampered with. He's looking at our lawn cam now. Same over the scam. Bekah's seeing what she can do.' I take a breath. 'I owe Clint an apology as well.'

Paula's mouth drops open. 'Clint? You're kidding me?'

I didn't lose my job. I took some sickness leave and cited stress. It was true. I realised I had been stressed for most of my life. Resner Platt rolled on without me and Pam was promoted to manager. She felt so guilty telling me that I didn't find out until I went in to let them know I would be coming back.

I'd felt sick as the lift climbed to the executive floor. I knew that once I told them I was no longer on sick leave they could give me notice. But as I walked into Andy Preece's office I knew that was not going to happen. It was all smiles and handshakes and *are you feeling better* gushing.

Andy is the Company Chair, and he had his sidekick Brian Lownes there. His secretary offered me tea and took notes. Clint had been to a rehab clinic and was now back in post. Apparently, he was a changed man and desperately sorry for what he had put me through. Someone had shown him the footage of the meeting where he had made fun of me, and recordings of him at the party. Andy shook his head.

'We should have looked after you better, Kate, but I hope we can put all that in the past. I'd like to offer you your own department. It's about time.'

I'd blinked at him. 'Thank you. But I have to admit to something. I accused Clint of breaking into my office to set me up. It wasn't him, it was my husband. Soon to be ex. I can't apologise enough.'

They smiled and told me it didn't affect the job offer, and I would have the opportunity to talk to Clint with a witness present to make me feel more comfortable.

I explain this and Paula snorts.

'So, he broke in for what?'

I take a deep breath. 'I kept my bank cards in my desk. I know, I know. He'd been in and out several times apparently. In and out with a copy he made of my entry cards. All on the dates money went missing. But Bekah is looking after it now.'

And she is. She has made a lot of progress. Holly intervenes.

'I gave her everything she asked for. Let's hope she can do something with it.'

I have my doubts. If anyone can, Bekah can, but she admitted it would be tricky. But now I am onto the main event. I called them here today for support.

'So I didn't tell anyone until it was certain, but the court of appeal are going to hear Collette's case. My solicitor tells me the chances are high as the case against her was so flimsy. With me and my brother's testimony and the additional evidence, the Crown Prosecution Service said it could go ahead.'

Paula grips my hand. 'I'm so fucking pleased. And let's hope that bastard gets life.'

He won't, but I don't tell them that. He is one of those people who live on the edge of danger just for the hell of it. When he is in danger of tipping over, he will fight tooth and nail to survive. But the silver lining is that I will never have to see him again. My solicitor will handle everything.

'Yeah, fingers crossed. But the big news is I'm going to see her.'

They stare at me. Veronica speaks for them.

'Your mother?'

She is aghast. But I smile at her.

'Yes. I'm going to tell her about the appeal. And the new evidence. Keep her in the loop.'

They look at each other. Paula is spokeswoman now.

'Mate, are you sure it's a good idea? You want me to come with?'

I shake my head. 'No. Flynn's coming.'

I've spoken to Flynn several times over the past months. I've met him and taken him over to the house we all lived in. We've spoken about memories we had all hidden but have now come flooding back. Worse things than we want to tell ourselves. Things that are hard to think about someone you are supposed to love; denied and pushed down until you wonder if they really happened.

He told me what happened that night. He told me he'd gone

round there to tell him to leave Collette alone. To stop hurting her. He told me Harry attacked him. His own dad. Harry said it was none of his business and they were both adults. He asked him if he hadn't got the message – they left; he wasn't wanted.

Flynn had cried. He told me Harry hit him first and there was a tussle in the tiny flat. Then suddenly there was a knife in Harry's hand, swooping and slashing at the air that smelt of whisky. Flynn saw red. And the next thing he knew it was done.

He almost ran. We all have it in us. To run away from it all and let it take care of itself. But he didn't. He said he went home and cried and cried and waited for the police to come. They never did. They didn't find his DNA, and no one saw him. He swears that every time someone knocks on the door, he fears the worst.

I made a final decision. I considered asking him to tell the truth and face the consequences. But I decided not to. I decided to leave it to him and his conscience. I know what he suffered as a child. And I believe him that he was defending himself. The whole thing is a mixed-up mess of people treating each other badly, but if we can draw the line here and we have a chance of making things even a tiny bit better, I'm game.

Paula grins. She looks at the others and they pull approving faces. I stumble over my words.

'I just wanted your support. You've been so fantastic. And neither of you two,' I point at Veronica and Holly, 'neither of you needed to have anything to do with me. You could have told me to get lost.'

Veronica fake frowns. 'Especially after you broke my window and stalked me.'

We laugh even though it isn't funny. Because what else can we do? I turn to Paula.

'And you. You put up with me through all that judgemental shit. And now you are letting me sleep in your spare room.'

She laughs loudly. 'As long as you like, mate. As long as you don't hide my booze.'

The ancient bell on the café door pings and Flynn has arrived. He stands by the door and Paula shouts at him.

'We won't bite, you know.'

I stand. 'I have to go now. Wish me luck.'

Their faces tell me I won't need luck. I nod at Flynn, and we leave. We drive in silence to the prison. The radio plays cheery songs but I feel the nerves creep up. Flynn's knuckles are white on the steering wheel as we hurtle down the motorway. As we slow to a stop in the car park of the prison, I look at him.

'You don't have to do this. I can go from here.'

He still grips the steering wheel. 'I don't know how I'll feel. You know, after she…'

'Left us.'

'Yes. And the rest. Him. What he did to us.'

I sigh. 'She couldn't have stopped it. Look what he did to her. I'm not saying she was without fault. Not at all. She could have done a lot of things differently as a mother. But I guess she knew that, and I think that's why she left. So we'd have a better life. Because everyone told her how bad she was. And no one told her how loved she was.'

He sniffs. 'I did. I remember. But she still left.'

I blink into the brightly lit prison grounds. We can do this another time. I put my hand on his arm.

'Come on, let's leave. You're not ready.'

He lets go of the wheel. 'No, no, you go in. I'll wait for you.' He hands me my pass. 'I'll be here when you get out.'

I suddenly feel very heavy, like I can't move, but I drag myself out of the car and I'm walking across the car park into the visitor area. I silently pass through their airport-style security gate and then I am in a waiting area.

A calmness washes over me. I suddenly realise that I have nothing to fear. I am like Collette, but she wasn't who I thought she was. There was no danger at the end of this long road. But I'd not held myself down for nothing. All of us. Me, Collette, Michael, Flynn, Patrick. We all had that fire. I see it in my brothers' laughter and in the way they kiss their wives in public. Unlike me, they have channelled it into something positive. Not a job where you can be replaced the next week. Not pointless hate and fury, except Flynn's terrible episode. They have channelled it into love.

That's what I have to remember now. I know what I have to say. I know it won't be easy. And then I am walking towards her. She is sitting at a white Formica table in a grey tracksuit and trainers. I am momentarily shocked at how much she has aged and then I factor in the ciggies and the booze and this place. Her hair is still red, but lighter, and long, piled high on her head.

She doesn't stand. She sits. Hands out on the table. Palms down, watching me. I stand in front of her. There are guards walking around and the tables are close together. I don't want anyone else to hear what I have to say to her. It must be my word against hers.

She smiles slightly and I feel a prick of anger. No, no, that's the past. I pull out the chair and sit.

'Mum.'

Her lips tremble. 'Cathy.'

I don't correct her. Instead, I watch the guard pass, and I lean forward.

'Now listen very carefully. I know about Flynn.' She goes to speak but I shake my head. 'Only you and I know. And you will not mention it to him or anyone. Understand?'

She nods. 'I saw him. I saw him watching. I knew it was him. I couldn't admit it. I just couldn't because then Harry would have won. But I couldn't let Flynn…'

I stare at her. 'It's over. He's dead. Harry. And we're alive. And if all goes well, you'll get an appeal heard and get out of here. But if you hurt Flynn, even by accident, by telling him you know, I'll…'

She nods fast and hard. 'I won't, I promise. I know my promises don't mean much to you, Cathy, but I'm older now. I've had a lot of time to think.'

I pause and wait for her to say sorry. I swear she is going to say it, but she doesn't. There were never any apologies then, just sweeping everything under the carpet only for it all to burst out in an argument much, much later. I wonder if she knows how to say sorry. I realise I am slipping into the past and pull myself back. She freezes and pales, and I wonder if this is more of the games she used to play, but when I follow her gaze I see Flynn standing in the doorway.

I catch her eye and raise my eyebrows. She nods and the smile is there. The lie-show she put on most of her life is alive and kicking. But I don't mind. It's part of her. This is the start of a new journey now. One that won't be easy, but what in life is, really?

Flynn sits down and takes her hand. He raises it to his check. He smiles at her, and his features are soft.

'Hello, Mum. We've got a lot of catching up to do.'

THE END

ACKNOWLEDGEMENTS

I want to start my acknowledgements for this book by thanking you, the person who read it. I've been writing for a while, and the success of *The Replacement* blew me away. I am grateful for every single person who reads my work, so thank you.

This was the first book I wrote after lockdown. The thought of someone simply not taking the turning for their home and just driving away was compelling as a premise. But after the trauma of a pandemic and the uncertainty of publishing in its wake, I wasn't sure if it was possible to write it. The first time I went out for lunch after lockdown was with my friend, Sarah Cassidy, who this book is dedicated to. Sarah is a talented playwright and screen writer, and I met her a while ago at a screenwriting workshop. We went on writing retreats together and I trust her implicitly.

I ran the idea by her that day and she listened to me go on about the seed of a plot and half-formed ideas. When I told her about the premise she stopped dead in the street in Manchester city centre, stared at me, and told me to do it. Definitely do it. It would resonate. Write it. It isn't the first time Sarah has encouraged me. At the end of a Scripts North workshop we were asked who had inspired us in the session. Sarah chose me, told everyone she loved my storytelling voice, and as someone who has not been 'chosen' a lot in life, it meant a lot. I was ready to give up, but Sarah's words gave me confidence to continue. In an arena where competition is strong, lifting each other up is important. If it wasn't for Sarah's words that day, this book would never have been created.

I would like thank my lovely agent Judith Murray for all her wise counsel. Also, everyone who read the draft and gave me input. I am so grateful. And to Betsy Reavley and Fred Freeman at Bloodhound Books who are so responsive and brilliant to work with and have made the whole publishing process so exciting and straightforward. Thank you for loving this book and the opportunity to work with you. To Abbie Rutherford, my brilliant editor, and to Vicky Joss and Katia Allen for their marketing genius.

Big thanks to all my writing colleagues – too many to list here but you know who you are – for your support. Especially Anstey Harris for her endless support and Phaedra Patrick for her lunch availability and listening ear.

Thanks to Lindsay Bowes for her enduring friendship and for listening to my rambling plots, more lately over long distance WhatsApp. Thanks to Sue Lees for the hilarious discussions in Costa Coffee and all my school friends, especially Karen Schofield, Janet Starkey, Julia Dawn Bowers and Karen Fitzpatrick for the lunches and the book launch support. And Debby Harley for making me laugh until I cry, and for being so strong.

London Writing Salon provided space for me to just write with other writers online with no pressure. It was exactly what I needed to keep going and stay productive and thank goodness it's still going strong. Thank you Matt and Parul for what turned out a writing-life changer.

Thanks to my children Michelle, Victoria and Toby for their patience and to my grandchildren Evan, Leah, Lincoln and Phi for just being themselves. And to my brothers for their observations and being proud of me. You all keep me going.

But the biggest thanks goes to my partner Eric. You help me more than you know and make this whole thing a lot easier that I ever imagined it could be. Thanks, love.

ALSO BY JACQUELINE WARD

The Replacement

The Jan Pearce Series

Random Acts of Unkindness

Playlist for a Paper Angel

What I Left Behind

A NOTE FROM THE PUBLISHER

Thank you for reading this book. If you enjoyed it please do consider leaving a review on Amazon to help others find it too.

We hate typos. All of our books have been rigorously edited and proofread, but sometimes mistakes do slip through. If you have spotted a typo, please do let us know and we can get it amended within hours.

info@bloodhoundbooks.com